Cremated Remains

m ennenbach

Uncomfortably Dark Horror

PRAISE FOR CREMATED REMAINS

"What words can I write to do justice to the haunting, eerie, almost lyrical stories in this collection? I was riveted from the first paragraph of the first story straight until the last line. The raw pain, torment, and loneliness of some characters, the stark landscapes, and the mind-bending realities in these pages prove there's no one else like M Ennenbach."— Jill Girardi, co-author of "We're Not Ourselves Today," (with Lydia Prime)

"Mike Ennenbach firmly cements his place as one of the best writers in the contemporary speculative genre with his collection CREMATED REMAINS. Wildly original and beautifully written with a seldom-seen grasp of the language in full nuance and meaning, every story pulls the reader in from the first line, often leaving them gasping in shock or awe by the end. From coming-of-age

to celestial creatures to my favorite "Bitter Petals," each tale would stand on its own as a literary achievement. Together in this utterly brilliant book, they are compelling, thoughtful, and, at times, ruthlessly unforgettable. Ennenbach continues to engage his readers with his humility, dark humor, and exceptional talent, and I predict great things for "Cremated Remains" and all this incredible author's work to come."—Ruthann Jagge, Co-Author of DELEVAN HOUSE

"Cremated Remains is a patchwork quilt of love, death, violence, and monsters, all with a vein of unease running through its core. These stories revel in variety, and though some horrify and others brandish dark humor, none of them ever feel safe."— Brennan LaFaro, author of the Buzzard's Edge Saga

"Sensuous, evocative prose and stories to revisit time and again. Ennenbach's the real deal, folks. This is one you do not want to miss."—Brian Bowyer, author of OLD TOO SOON

"Ennenbach is one of the most unique and talented voices in literature today. Every work is provocative with a sort of unusual wildness that is both captivating and suffused with a comforting sense of 'otherness' that I think so many of us crave. Cremated Remains is a perfect introduction to his distinctive prose and beau-

tiful voice."—Megan Stockton, author of LOVELY, DARK, AND DEEP

"Poetry in motion, M Ennenbach delivers the universal truths everyone of us faces in our lives. Fear, elation, uncertainty, horror, love, and every emotion in between has its place layered within his prose, reminding us all what it is to be human. As a reader, go in with your mind open to explore just how far down the rabbit hole this author is willing to go."—RJ Roles, author of NECRONADO

"When you read an Ennenbach collection, you're diving into a world of mixed genres. He has the ability to write captivating stories that will make you feel every emotion. His writing never ceases to amaze me."—Jas on Nickey, author of THEY COME FROM WITH-IN

"Ennenbach is back with a new collection of stories that once again shows off his storytelling prowess. He interweaves the universal themes of relationships, love, and loss through different genres in a way that is somehow both familiar and unique. His stories have the power to connect with each reader, even if it's only a whisper in their subconscious to remind them, 'you are not alone'."—Eric Butler, author of POPE LICK MASSACRE

CONTENTS

DEDICATION

To Maia and Dax, my everythings. To the moon and back, always.

To Natalie and RJ, who inspired most of the words by being their perfect selves.

To Candace, Krissy, and Christine for reading every word and lying about the quality. As sisters do.

To 3, Chris, and Eric: my fellow Horsemen of Texas Horror. They aren't ready.

To Jason (mostly Jared), Megan, Rachel, and Spaghets. Family.

To Brad Fucking Tierney, my handsomest brother.

To River and Potter's Grove. Thank you for everything.

And to the readers who put up with a madman that doesn't fit the box.

Thank you never feels like enough. You are seen. You are loved. And no matter how the bastards try to make you feel, you are now, and always were, more than enough.

ONE

GOLDEN LAZARUS

St. Louis, Missouri 1963

THE CROWD CHEERED LOUDLY as a statuesque blonde Adonis, in a long sequined robe, walked down the ramp toward the ring. The smile nearly split his face in two as he shook hands with his adoring fans, who crowded the aisle way.

"I was born poor. My daddy died fighting the Germans. My mother may as well have joined him, as it felt like her ghost was all I ever really knew."

A tall dark-haired man stood glaring out of the ring, what would have been a bright red jacket emblazoned with the golden hammer and sickle, now bright gray in the black and white footage, and a fur ushanka on his furled brow.

"She loved me, likely too much. Her world had always been one of poverty and need. A world that took everything she ever loved from her. But that fear kept her afraid to live. She worked two jobs, three truly, because when she was home, she was constantly cooking."

A picture of a sour, heavy set child, also in black and white flashed, before returning to the blonde stepping through the ropes to a new thunderous ovation as a microphone slowly lowered into the ring.

A well-groomed man in a black suit with matching fedora grabbed the microphone. "Ladies and Gentleman, this next bout is scheduled for a sixty-minute time limit for the *Midwest Heavyweight Championship.*"

The crowd was on its feet as the man pointed at the dark-haired brute, already booing loudly, "From Moscow, weighing in at two hundred and fifty-one pounds in the red tights, the champion, *The Russian Bear, Ivan Bulgakov!*"

"I learned to be afraid of her. I was just a little chubby kid who jumped at every shadow. Picked on by the neighborhood kids for being fat and fatherless. A nothing going nowhere."

"And in the blue tights, from Ottawa Illinois, *The American Hope, Aloysius Wendt!*"

The crowd was screaming. Men held their sons up to witness the hero that would battle the communist threat.

"One day I, Abner Smith, would become World Champion of the World, an icon to thousands of chubby boys."

The two men slowly circled one another in the center of the ring as the crowd screamed, nearly rabid all around them. They locked up. Muscles gleamed beneath the bright lights, and Aloysius sent Ivan into the ropes before hitting him with a lariat that knocked the big man to the canvas. The Russian caught his second wind, and with a dastardly rake of his opponent's eyes behind the referees turned back.

Taking advantage of his underhanded tactic, the Russian brute began to mount an offense of his own. The crowd watched in dismay as their hero was body slammed and atomic dropped. Ivan showed off his relentless streak as he worked over the challenger's back. The entire packed arena knew what this was the setup for, and the mood turned more surly with every blow landed.

The Russian Bear lifted The American Hope above his head and slammed him down to the canvas with a jarring impact, before pulling him back to his feet by his long golden locks. The crowd stood silent as the big Russian wrapped his arms around the deflated Hope, his corded muscles flexing as he squeezed with his signature move, the bear hug.

The referee lifted the left arm of the challenger and it fell limply as the ref called out, "One!" to the unbelieving crowd.

Again, he lifted the arm for it to fall immediately. "Two!"

The referee lifted the arm for the final time and let go. The mood in the arena was one of stunned silence when the challenger somehow defied logic and his arm remained up.

The crowd roared to life again as the Russian Bear's eyes grew comically wide in disbelief, his arms slowly being forced apart by the resurgent Hope of all the gathered watchers. With tremendous exertion, Aloysius broke the hold and launched a counterattack of his own. He rained chops against the Russian's chest, that staggered the big man backwards until he fell to his knees. Aloysius bent down and pulled the Russian to his feet and begins raining powerful forearms against his chest.

It was a dream come true, competing in front of packed arenas across the Midwest. I got to travel the country, and then the world. A small-town kid from Illinois walking the streets of Vancouver, New York, Tokyo, and, of course, St. Louis.

The American Hope raised one clawed hand into the air, which caused the roof to vibrate with roars which shook the arena. Ivan woozily stepped forward and Aloysius wrapped that clawed hand around his face. The Russian fought but could not break the hold. His strength ebbed out as he fell first to his knees, his hands locked around the powerful forearm, weakly trying to pull it off, before slumping fully to the canvas.

The referee counted off with each drop of the limp arm to the canvas, and at three, the crowd swarmed the ring and lifted the newly crowned champ onto its collective shoulders.

It would also eventually kill me for seven and a half minutes.

The camera focused in onto to a morbidly obese elderly man sitting at a dirty table in a worn-down old house surrounded by glass terrariums. The man took a drag off a cigarette and looked directly into the camera. "My name is Abner Smith, former heavyweight champion of the world, known to the world as Aloysius Wendt."

Grand Ridge, Illinois 2003

THE HOUSE WAS IN a terrible state of disrepair, a quarter of the roof simply seemed to have gone limp, and the lawn, more weed than grass, was wild and untamed. The view of the house shook for a moment before growing still and a smiling man walked into the frame.

"I honestly can't believe that I am standing outside the home of Aloysius Wendt, former heavyweight champion of the world in the Midwest Wrestling Alliance. Most of the footage of his matches are grainy copies of copies passed along from collector to collector, but they show a promising star and someone that would become a prototype to the stars of the modern era of Professional Wrestling.

"My father instilled a love of the squared circle into me at a very young age, and his favorite wrestler was Mr. Aloysius Wendt. My father went to every match in the region and he would tell me stories of how the hero always found a way to triumph over whatever villain was in town on this tour.

"He was also at the match where Aloysius, and the man beneath the gimmick, Abner Smith, actually died in the center of the ring.

"After that, no one knew what had happened to the former Champion, in fact, most were not even aware that after being declared dead for seven minutes, Abner gulped in a huge lungful of air and sat up in the back of the ambulance." The man frowned slightly at the camera before attempting a smile again. "I was one of those people that believed he had died fighting for the belt in Peoria, Illinois, a footnote in wrestling history to be forgotten by all but the most studious of wrestling scholars.

"But I was at a convention in Bloomington and was talking to an old promoter who laughed as I asked about Aloysius Wendt and his forgotten legacy. He told me a different story, of a man that came back from the dead and was thoroughly and forever changed by the experience. And then he gave me Abner Smith's phone number.

"My name is Carl Barrel, and this is the story behind Aloysius Wendt, the man who died in the center of the ring and rose again like Lazarus only to vanish from the world."

"I WAS BORN IN Illinois in June of Nineteen Forty-One. My parents fell in love and got married a year before and settled in Bloomington. My father joined the army in January of Forty-One, and only saw me once before being shipped to Europe."

The dilapidated house was cluttered and dark when the camera crew stepped in. Terrariums with soft red lights glowed everywhere in the crowded living room. Different breeds of snakes, spiders and toads filled the glass rectangles, and a dry scent of scales and damp rot permeated everything. Stacks of yellowed newspapers sat in various states of chaos, black and white magazines featuring wrestlers: the dirt rags from different territories leaking the results and tales of matches and wrestlers in a code for both fans and insiders to comb through, covered the floor between the terrariums.

One wall remained free of both cages and papers where a long wooden shelf sat caked with rivulets of wax which ran like stalactites down to the filthy linoleum floor. A flag, carefully folded, sat in a small wooden triangular frame next to a photo of a young man in his military outfit, who smiled proudly in faded shades of gray; with a set of dog tags lovingly coiled around it.

"My father was a hero, according to the letter from the government and the few men that managed to make it home from that hell."

The camera focused on the flag and photo with the tarnished dog tags.

"His platoon was pinned by German gun nests, every shot they fired seemed to kill another American soldier as if the bullets were pulled to them. My father and a small squad stormed one of the entrenched guns and blew it to smithereens.

"He was killed in the explosion. His time at war lasted less than half a day and all that remained was a flag and set of damaged dog tags."

The hallway, barely a corridor between scurrying spiders and curious snakes swept into frame. Dusty photos hung on the wall at head height, mostly featuring an overweight yet happy looking child and his mother who looked haunted and frail. Her eyes spoke of hardships that seemed to have exacted a heavy toll. A soft chorus of crickets and toads filled the hall as the camera awkwardly navigated toward the wan yellow light of an old incandescent light.

"My mother never quite recovered from losing the love of her life in so quick a fashion. I don't think she ever truly accepted that he was dead, that he died saving lives that were then thrown away storming the next hill.

"She didn't ask to work multiple jobs, to have to act as mother and father when all she wanted was to sleep. But she did everything she could for me, loved me, provided for me, and made sure I never wanted for anything except a feeling of safety from the world outside."

In the kitchen sat Abner Smith, known to the world of wrestling fans in the sixties as Aloysius Wendt. The camera slowly panned around the room to show all the terrariums filled with creatures that seemed to stare only at the morbidly obese man at the table. A haze of smoke lingered from the constant burning cigarettes in the overflowing ashtray. Fat cockroaches crawled lazily across the peeling wallpaper behind the sink, scuttling across the empty Styrofoam containers from restaurants that seemed to have been licked clean a long time ago.

"How disappointed she would have been to see how far her Abner has fallen."

ABNER LOOKED ACROSS THE table at Carl, his once crystal blue eyes dulled by age, but his intelligence was still sharp as he took in the cameraman, a boy really, just someone to take the place of a perfectly good tripod. Abner watched carefully as the camera panned to the various terrariums and accumulated filth. He was self-aware enough to know how bad the conditions appeared, but there was no glimmer of anything but predatory intelligence in his eyes. No shame. No embarrassment. He seemed beyond those trappings.

Abner tapped a fresh cigarette out and lit off the smoldering end of the one between two yellowed sausage fingers and simply waited for Carl to begin. Even with his years away, the natural performer inside remembered what to do.

Carl tried to keep his emotions off of his face as he took in the room, but it was a difficult task, and he was thankful he wouldn't be on screen. He unzipped his backpack and set five cartons of Kool's soft packs and a large box of king-sized candy bars onto the table. "I hope these are the right ones?"

Abner nodded and his face twisted into a parody of happy. "Perfect. Thank you." He gestured at himself and his surroundings. "I don't get out often anymore. I have a woman that comes and feeds my pets and gets me whatever I may need from the store. But there can never be enough smokes."

Carl just nodded, unsure of how to respond, as he tried to take in his surroundings.

Abner let the smile fade. "I still don't quite understand what it is you hope to accomplish here, Mr. Barrel. I imagine the world has happily forgotten an old fat wrestler from the sixties."

Carl shook his head. "I never forgot, and neither did my father. A lot of the old timers on the convention circuit tell stories of your bouts to this day. I want to let you tell your story for future generations to hear."

Abner snorted and took a long drag. "So, how do we do this? Your boy films me and it goes up on the internet somewhere?"

Carl sat forward excitedly. "I have found boxes of VHS tapes and old reel to reels with some of your matches. I figure you can tell us how you came to be champion, and then what happened to you after—"

Abner blew out a cloud of blue smoke. "After I died."

Carl nodded again. "Yes, after you were pronounced dead. Most of the people I have talked with believed that you never came back. Only a few ever knew the truth, and none of them actually lived it. I think there is interest in your life, your death, and your subsequent life again."

"Is this going to be part of the documentary?" Abner asked calmly.

Carl shrugged. "Maybe in bits and pieces. I will, of course, give you a say in the final cut."

Abner sat silent for a moment, a halo of smoke around his head catching the stray beams of sunlight that trickled through the cracks in the blinds over the window. He moved slightly, shifting his large frame, which set the caged creatures into a brief startled panic, spiders curled up into balls, as snakes and toads tried to hide in the shadows and pools of water. With a sigh, he reached forward and removed a king-size candy bar. He slowly peeled the wrapper off before eating half of it in one bite while the cigarette dangled off his bottom lip, oblivious, "Sounds okay with me."

Carl relaxed visibly and smiled. "Great. That's really great, thank you."

Abner sat staring at the other half of chocolate coated caramel on the table, ignoring the ash that dropped onto it. "How would you like to proceed?"

Carl set a tape recorder on the table between them and pressed the red button at the top. "You tell your story, I will ask questions and together we will make a documentary. And if you don't mind, I'd like to have my cameraman, Patrick, take some footage of your home."

Abner nodded dismissively. "Sure, but keep the lights off. My pets prefer the darkness."

Carl looked at the terrariums. "About your pets—"

Abner frowned slightly, unsure. "We will get to them as the story progresses. Where do you want me to begin?"

Carl looked at his notepad for a moment.

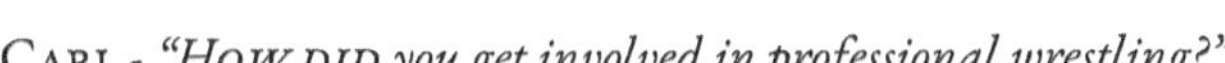

CARL - *"HOW DID you get involved in professional wrestling?"*

Abner - *"I didn't have any passions growing up, no dreams of where I would go when I got older. I was happy enough, looking forward to the next meal.*

"My mother didn't have time nor the means for much beyond working, cooking, and on her one day off a week she, and by necessity, I, went to church.

"I had no interest in the flames of perdition, the hellfire sermons in that sticky old building. It was the promise of biscuits and gravy that pulled me out of bed on Sunday mornings. She was adamant that I would go with her each and every service for reasons that escaped me. She was no bible thumper; in fact, I had the idea she blamed God as much as she blamed the government for my father's death.

"Years later, I discovered she had been having an affair with the preacher."

Abner lit a fresh cigarette and stared off into space for a long moment. He looked lost in memory and besides his metronomic movement, raising and lowering the cigarette, it was clear he wasn't in that mess of a house. Somewhere, from another room, a toad let out a rumbling *Ribbit* that snapped him back to the present. Robotically, he grabbed another candy bar and peeled off the wrapper, and ravenously consumed it before speaking again.

Abner—*"When I was twelve, after church got out, my mother explained we would be joining the church group on the bus to visit the State Fair in Springfield. As with everything else, I was indifferent, but she plied me with promises of funnel cakes and corn dogs, and that was enough.*

"I saw my first wrestling match at the fair. Wildman Barrow, a four-hundred-pound behemoth of a man, called out for anyone in the crowd to challenge him. I was a mark, unfamiliar with the behind-the-scenes machinations of the industry, so my shock when a beanpole of a man stepped forward and accepted the challenge was real.

"It was a setup. That skinny man worked the crowd to the perfection, letting Barrow throw him all over the place. The crowd was booing, and it seemed to make Barrow even more ferocious. And when the little man finally turned it on, and to the surprise of the crowd, managed to take down the monster? I was the only one who didn't cheer.

"I felt a kindred spirit to the big man as a big boy myself. I reckon that is the day the fire first sparked inside of me. I was curious and got my mother to bring me the wrestling magazines as they were getting cycled out for the new issues at the drugstore. I never thought I would become a wrestler, but it gave me hope that even a fat little boy could do anything."

Carl–*"You have mentioned your mother was overprotective of you. Would she have wanted you in the ring?"*

Abner–*"Absolutely not."*

The camera pans the filthy kitchen and then slowly leaves the room, focusing on the various creatures sitting still, every eye turned towards Abner. It wasn't obvious at first, although it seemed clear in the kitchen. The oddity of the states could be explained by his being the center of attention as he shifted in his chair, but as the camera wandered slowly down the hall, tarantulas and green vipers alike faced the wall separating them from the former champ. A hand, belonging to the cameraman, reached out and tapped the glass of one terrarium where a serpent painted with red, black, and yellow stripes sat coiled. The snake does not flinch. It was the same down the hall, which ended with a closed door on one side and the restroom on the other. A quick scan showed the white-faced cameraman's reflection in the mirror and empty terrariums stacked in the rust and grime-streaked bathtub.

Abner - *"When it got time to start high school, the preacher encouraged me to play football. I believe that was the final straw that ended their relationship, my mother and the preacher, because soon after I tried out for the team, we stopped going to church.*

"I didn't mind not going to church so much. It never really was my thing growing up. But there was something about football I enjoyed. I had a growth spurt during the season, and soon all those extra pounds were stretched into my new frame. That's where I discovered my second love after eating: working out.

"I realize now, after years of not exercising, that I loved being able to eat as much as I wanted. I would hit the weight room and then go home and feast on my mother's cooking. The disapproving looks the little fat kid got for always having something in his mouth became appreciative as the fat turned to muscle."

Carl–*"I bet the girls loved your new look."*

Abner–*"It seemed to be the case, not that I cared really. Chasing girls was never my thing. The other guys on the team were single-minded about skirts. I was always just hungry, chasing a second portion. As disapproving as my mother was of football, I knew she had as much interest in me dating as I did.*

Carl–*"Did she ever come around about football?"*

Abner–*"No. She never saw a single play. She worked Friday nights at the drugstore, and while I am sure she could have gotten the night off, she didn't. I think she wished she had died with my father or believed part of her had on that front across the ocean. What was left of her was fear and anger. She worked constantly because that filled the time. When we stopped going to church, she picked up an extra shift wherever she could.*

"Now don't get me wrong, she loved me in the only way she could, by keeping the bills paid and a stream of meals going from the stove to my eager mouth. But she never was the type to fawn over me. She never encouraged me except as a means to pacify, like with the wrestling magazines. I don't recall her ever asking my feelings about anything, which may sound cold to you, but was all I ever knew.

"I felt uncomfortable when someone like the coach or the preacher, who came to every game and watched proudly from the stands, tried to probe my feelings. I didn't have them, not fully formed at least. I read my magazines and did my schoolwork, played football and worked out. She had taught me to be a part of the world by being apart from it. That was fine by me, as I didn't know anything was missing."

Carl– *"Surely you must have noticed that was different compared to the other kids?"*

The rattle of a wrapper opening and the flick of a lighter filled the silence.

Abner– *"No. I didn't know the other kids. I didn't socialize. I was a misfit, and that was fine by me."*

Carl– *"What happened after high school ended?"*

Abner– *"There was interest from a few colleges. I was a Hoss and the local schools offered scholarships. I even got contacted by some schools on the West Coast, like UCLA."*

Carl– *"You didn't want to go that far from home?"*

Abner– *"Part of me did. But life chose for me. Three nights after graduation, as I sat trying to figure out what I was going to do with my life, talking to my mother as she cooked and cleaned, her heart stopped. The fear which had gripped her for so long finally won out.*

"I was well and truly alone. Suddenly, the big world of opportunity was the same big world of fear that had killed her. I became a shut in, paralyzed by the gnawing in my guts. That's when I realized why I was always eating, to calm that panic churning in my belly. The bills began to pile up, and I was forced to take odd jobs to survive.

"The preacher, now retired and just going by Eddie, did what he could to help try to pull me from my despair. He had loved my mother.

He confessed to me the day we put her in the ground. He promised me she was in heaven with my father, watching down on us and at ease. But I later learned that was just another lie."

Carl–*"What do you mean?"*

Abner laughed, and the lighter flicked to life again. The cameraman moved down the hall slowly back to the living room, focusing on the yellowed posters of Aloysius Wendt, World Champion.

Abner–*"She was in hell, along with everyone else. Good intentions do nothing to prevent the fires of perdition, and near as I can tell, heaven is just another lie the devil tells to trick the flock."*

At once, the toads, spiders and snakes threw themselves at the glass walls of their prisons. The house was filled with a cacophony of hisses and scratching as every single creature tried to escape. Yet they never turned from the kitchen where Abner smoked his cigarette down to the butt silently, while Carl looked around frightfully.

Patrick came rushing into the room. "What the fuck is happening?"

Abner looked around at the agitated creatures lashing out in their cages and raised his hands. They all settled back down as if under his control, and he smiled. "Nearly feeding time, I reckon. Might be a good place to stop for the day. This has been mighty tiring. Think we can pick this back up tomorrow?"

Carl was shaken by what he had just seen and simply nodded, trying his best to compose himself and giving covert glances to Patrick, who had managed to capture it all. Carl looked at Abner. "Yes, we got some great stuff today. We will come back tomorrow. Same time?"

Abner smiled, but it never reached his flat eyes. "Sounds good to me. See you then."

***

"Hey Carl, it's Abner. On your way over tomorrow, can you do me a favor and grab some Cherry Garcia? Maybe Cookies and cream as well?

Thanks. It was a pleasure speaking with you and I look forward to more. Have a good evening."

⎯⎯⎯⎯⎯⎯

"AND COMING DOWN THE aisle, from deep in the heart of the Ozarks, weighing in at two hundred and fifty-seven pounds and standing tall at six foot six inches, Aloysius Wendt!"

The crowd was silent as the newcomer came walking down to the ring. Corded muscle covered every inch of exposed flesh, but didn't hide the deer in headlights look in the young man's eyes.

Abner–*"My first match was a mess. I was not prepared for it.*

"A month after my mother passed, I went to see the matches at the high school gym with the preacher. He rightly decided for me that I needed to get out of the house. The booker saw me standing in the crowd and sent out one of his helpers to come and fetch me for a conversation.

"The booker, Jimmy Lane, was looking for a new baby face to battle it out with his heels and he saw something in me that got his creativity flowing."

Carl–*"How long after that meeting was the first match?"*

Abner–*"Less than a month. I could take bumps relatively well, but I was dangerous still. The thing they teach you is to protect your opponent, first and foremost."*

Aloysius stepped into the ring, but the look in his eyes said he was not prepared. The gymnasium was lined with around two hundred men who seemed to smell fresh blood.

"And approaching the ring, from Dublin, Ireland, weighing in at one hundred and eighty pounds and standing four feet, six inches, The Fighting Leprechaun, Seamus O'Toole!"

The crowd erupted in applause as the little person, dressed head to toe in bright green and clutching a small pot with gold coins, made his way to the ring and rolled under the bottom rope.

Abner–*"It was a gimmick match, done for laughs. Seamus, Teddy from Oregon really, was the comic relief. I didn't have to do much, just chase him as he rolled back and forth, sell the pain when he stomped on my foot, yell in anger as he pinched my ass.*

"It was a test, the other guys told me, a rib to see if I could handle being embarrassed and how well I took a joke. I chased that little bastard around. He'd bite my ass and I would holler loud as can be.

"I think I would have been happy, truly happy, just doing those kinds of matches. The crowd loved it."

Aloysius chased after the little man, who taunted him at every turn, until finally he got his big hands on the little shoulders and lifted him into the air. Seamus screamed and kicked his legs, slapping Aloysius in the face and arms. Aloysius walked to each rope, proudly displaying his raw strength to the cheers of the crowd, before tossing the leprechaun clear across the ring.

Abner–*"Between screams, the crafty little bastard told me to throw him. He used to work for the circus and knew how to take a fall better than anyone. If you go back to the footage and watch, his tumble and bounce were all gymnastics that he sold as if he had been murdered."*

Carl–*"Do you know what happened to Seamus?"*

Abner–*"Shot dead. He was having sexual relations with three different promotors daughters. It was bound to catch up to him one day. What he lacked in height, or so the stories said, he more than made up for in girth. I wonder what his hell is like?"*

Abner sat in the same spot, a cigarette smoking in the ashtray, and chocolate dripped down his face. The creatures in the cage stirred slightly as Abner seemed to contemplate the fate of his friend.

Carl–*"That is the second time you have mentioned hell."*

Abner nodded and spooned a large lump of ice cream into his mouth, then closed his eyes as it melted on his tongue.

Carl–*"Why do you think he went to hell, Abner?"*

A loud hiss from a black snake as it uncoiled against the glass and struck the terrarium.

Abner–*"That is a tale for later."*

Carl–*"When did you get to work your first serious match? Did you work any other jobs?"*

Abner–*"About four months in. It was hard work, harder than most suspect, I reckon. I would wake early and work out for an hour most days before heading to the barn. It was a filthy old place. Bob Comstock, the old promoter of the region, ran to train rookies. We were all green, standing around the ring that had seen its better decades, while Bobby Jr. screamed at us.*

"We would take bumps for hours, over and over again, off the ropes and flip onto our backs on that stiff old mat. I hated it, truly hated it, but it was better than the alternative, which was sitting in the old house alone. The first month after my mother passed, the neighbors brought over casseroles and meals to help me get through it. I was still a kid and suddenly all alone in the world. Finding wrestling as a career changed that. It paid, not well, and it got me out and moving.

"On the weekends, I would drive to whatever city the card was in and help set up the barricades and ring. Then we would roam the local businesses and try to get them to put the flyers in the window. It was enough to get by. I didn't live well, but I lived. They fed us at training and on the road usually, or one of the guys who was set as a mentor would. My entire life was in the ring or at the table. It took a lot of fuel to keep us going.

"It was in East St. Louis that I got my shot in the ring in a real match. It was ugly, and the crowd knew it. Me and The Iron Eagle, Helmut Kraut did ten minutes where I was sloppy as hell and Helmut had to carry me through. I reckon that is why they made me a baby face, because the heel always called the match. Helmut would bark orders into my ear, and I would do my best not to fuck up too badly. He's the one that taught me my finisher, the Iron Claw. The sadistic old bastard would take his giant hand and wrap it around my face and squeeze it like hell, and it hurt mightily, let me tell you. That first match went so badly, and he was clearly frustrated and grabbed my temples until I saw spots. I had five finger shaped bruises on my face for the better part of a week. Likely deserved each one of them."

Carl–*"Wasn't he supposedly a Nazi that defected and became a wrestler?"*

Abner–*"That was his gimmick. His real name was Rhett, and he was married to the prettiest little colored lady. He would goose step around the ring and shout about the Aryan this or that, which in some of the crowds had him more face than heel. I swear on that, especially deep south in Illinois. Everyone had their gimmick to try to rile up the crowd, and a good heel could make a baby face into a star.*

"But old Helmut was a sweetheart. He served in WW2 and always talked about the sound it made when he shot someone in the head. Like a watermelon hitting the floor, he would say sadly as we drove from town to town. It was like he never quite left Europe, you know? Except when he was in the ring, then he could escape for a little bit.

He died in the sixties. Got caught up in the riots in Chicago. The man fought for freedom in a foreign land and died for freedom here. It's sad when you think about it. What a waste."

Carl–*"Is he in hell?"*

The tarantulas reared back, and the toads began to twitch all around the kitchen.

Abner–*"It doesn't matter if you are justified in your actions, murder is murder. It's one of the ten big ones.*

"Ain't a soldier that fought that didn't end up in hell. Even my father, who men said was a hero, found an eternity of suffering. God tolerates no fools nor circumstances."

It grew loud as the various creatures grew agitated. A knocking sound came from the hall, as terrariums shook against the old drywall.

Abner–*"It took me six months of touring against Helmut before he said I was good enough to go at it with someone different. I had passed my training and looked forward to working with the others.*

"We traveled all across Illinois, into Missouri on one side and Indiana on the other. It took about six months before the tour began returning to cities and towns, and that was when the new feuds began. Since I was still green, I didn't get asked to visit a new territory, but a few of the big names said their farewells and headed off to Louisville or Nashville.

The marquee guys went to Oklahoma or Florida for long stints with the bigger promotions. Some of the guys just didn't have it, the spark, and they just went back to little farm towns and out to the fields again, where the sun dried them out like raisins and no one ever knew their ring names."

Carl– *"Do you ever wish you had stayed in Bloomington?"*

Abner– *"And done what? Found a girl and married her, had a few kids, been miserable knowing there was a whole world out there left unexplored? That wasn't the life for me. I might wish it had been, but God had different plans for me. And for a long while, it was a good enough plan.*

"We took a couple weeks off once we got back to Bloomington, and I got my first contract. I didn't have a place to go back to. I sold the house and squirrelled what little money I got after into the bank, so I moved into the Comstock farm and took my training up a notch. Jimmy, the promoter, was excited at my progress and dedication. I only moved out there because Bobby Jr. and his wife were excellent cooks and they fed me and gave me a roof in return for doing chores around the farm.

"Jimmy convinced me to grow out my hair, which I had always kept in a buzz cut, high and tight, like the haircut my father had. My mother always said I looked just like him after a fresh haircut. Maybe that was me rebelling, showing the fear she had tried to infect me with that it couldn't control me. I don't know rightly."

Carl– *"Is this when you became The American Hope?"*

Abner– *"It was the start, for sure. I was in the best shape of my life. All I did was chores and train, training and chores, and eat everything they would give me. They said I was a bottomless pit, and they weren't wrong. I dreamt of food. The other guys would laugh as we were doing hip tosses or back drops, and my stomach would rumble like a train on a rickety bridge less than an hour after lunch. The guys started calling me Hope, because every time the wind blew through the chimes, I hoped it was time for a meal.*

"Jimmy heard them call me Hope after my head whipped towards the house and he joined in the laughter for a spell. Then he looked me up and down slowly and nodded.

"That could be your gimmick, Abner. You could be the American Hope.

"I just shrugged and nodded back. That was that. The next go round had me, and my longer blonde hair repackaged as the American Hope. The business back then was all cartoonish caricatures, stuff that would be deemed racist nowadays, but was perfectly normal then. Asian wrestlers were sneaky and conniving, Russians were strong and evil, so on and so forth. But Civil Rights was beginning to gain momentum, and the mostly white crowds wanted to feel safe from the changing world, so we didn't change all that much at all."

Carl– *"It was a tumultuous time for America."*

Abner– *"We ran out of villains we could all band together against, and that made us look at ourselves and not like what we were seeing. Communism and racism were the hot topics. If anything, wrestling was like those political cartoons in the newspaper, and the people loved it.*

"The next go round had me going up against Igor, a testing of the waters to see if we could get a reaction from the crowds. It went over like gangbusters, let me tell you. They got Igor one of those furry hats and the minute the crowd saw him, they booed so loud it shook the rafters of the VFW or wherever we were performing that night.

"Igor never spoke, mostly because he was from Atlanta and his accent was so thick. The crowd would have realized right away that he wasn't from Stalingrad, so they put him with Ming. Ming was Japanese and had spent the first years of his life in an internment camp on the West Coast. He was a sour shit that the crowds absolutely hated. He would yell at them, and Igor would stand stone still, glaring over his shoulder.

"We would go back and forth on who won each evening, but one thing stayed the same. I would get my hands on all one hundred pounds of Ming and he would scream as I tossed him about the ring. Sometimes I would catch him cheating and yank him over the ropes. Others would have him succeed and as Igor staggered to the back, I would grab him.

The audience loved to see him get his, and no matter the finish, they left happy."

Carl– *"When did they decide to put the belt on you?"*

Abner– *"After my fifth tour. The territory was hemorrhaging talent to Oklahoma and New York. It was less a case of me deserving the title, and more about there not being anyone else to win it.*

"I had just come back from a show in Dallas, a talent swap for a big card, that put me up against Blackheart Billy. He was a rough and tough cowboy that came to ring with a big old rope, black hat perched on his head, and coal-colored eyes.

"We set that place on fire, but what I remember most was the bar- beque. They fed us steaks and ribs with every side imaginable. If they had offered me a full-time spot, the food there would have sealed the deal. Of course, they didn't. Poaching talent was a time-honored tradition, but I didn't have a big enough name to pull in the crowds yet.

"Me and Billy had such a good match, though, Jimmy asked to bor- row him for a few matches in St. Louis and Carbondale. It was one thing to win over the crowd by beating a bad guy that was a typical foreign threat. It was another to win them over through sheer ring work. Which we did. Billy and I became friends, and he took an offer from Jimmy to make the move to Illinois for an entire tour. It was probably the happiest time I had in the world of wrestling.

"The first thing Jimmy did was put us together as a tag team. The fans ate it up when I showed distrust towards Billy, waiting at the edge of their seats for him to turn on me. By the end of the tour, we held the tag belts, and the whisperings were that I would be world champ sooner rather than later.

"Jimmy saw I was turning into quite the draw, and Billy and I were red hot. So, he sent us out to other territories to build momentum. We drove across the country together, sometimes barely making it to the show on time, and then getting right back into the car to head to the next town. As great as the shows went, I realized that, for the first time in my life, I had a best friend.

"My mother's fear combined with my relative disinterest had made for a lonely childhood. Even at the farm, I tended to mind my own business, only really hanging out for meals and practice. I was quiet on the road trips as well. My personality had developed into what must have appeared to be a prickly pear. But that changed with Billy. He had a similar childhood to mine, so many kids of our time did, as a lot of fathers never returned from the war. Neither of us believed in much of anything. I was driven by my hunger, and Billy was driven by his liver."

Carl– *"And then the accident happened."*

Abner– *"And then the accident happened. He shouldn't have been driving, but I never learned how and he had driven us home in far worse shape than that night. It was black ice. Despite what all the stories say, we hit a patch of black ice on the highway. We were talking about death that night, about what happens after. Our lives were hard, it might not sound like it, but they were. We gave our bodies for the fans, and the average wrestler didn't live to ripe old age. The ones that did were all messes, like me, filled with aches and pains from taking bumps constantly.*

"The last thing he said to me before the car began spinning was that he hoped there was nothing after. No pain, no heaven, no hell, just quiet. It left me feeling afraid, the idea of forever in the darkness. The next thing I knew, we were in a ditch and the steering wheel had crushed Billy. The ring truck was behind us and pulled off to help.

"I was fine, a few bruises that may have been from the match earlier, but unharmed. Billy was dead and his eyes seemed locked on me as his face was frozen in a look of fear. I thought it was because of the accident."

Carl– *"But it wasn't?"*

Abner shook his head and grabbed another pint of ice cream as he lit a fresh cigarette. The creatures around the room seemed tense, but the tension eased as Abner attacked the pint with relish.

An old photo of Abner and Blackheart Billy showed, the two men standing back-to-back and each holding a tag team title belt up for the camera. A rare smile can be seen on Abner's face as Billy scowled at the camera, unable to fully relinquish his heel status. Big letters above the photo proclaimed, *Tag Team Champion killed in accident after successful title defense.*

Abner– *"They made the decision to give me the strap when I came back from recovery. Ivan had won it before we took off on the road trip and Ming had been jabbering in interviews about me, setting the road to our confrontation.*

"I didn't want to return. It didn't feel the same without Billy. I didn't have anyone else I had bonded to among the guys. But Jimmy offered me a new deal, and the money was too good to pass up. He decided to sell the promotion to the guys in St. Louis that we had always shared the region with. But their stipulation was I had to be part of the deal.

"The tensions in the country had shrunk down some territories, and the ones that made a profit swallowed them up. St. Louis cut a deal with NWA to become an affiliate, and both companies, unbeknownst to me, had decided I was the next big star. I don't blame Jimmy for taking the money. It was the smart thing to do. He could only build up so much talent just to have them leave for greener pastures before the available pool shrunk up.

"I won the belt three months later. My life got hectic as I traveled even farther from home for longer stretches. I was a celebrity, or at least close to for what I did. It was a blur, really. Sleep, eat, work out, wrestle. Rinse and repeat. Days became weeks, weeks became months, and soon I had held the belt for nearly two full years and the crowds needed something fresh."

Carl– *"And that was when they introduced The Killer."*

Abner– *"A truly fitting name, as it turned out soon after."*

Carl– *"So you've been champion for two years, traveled across the country-"*

Abner– *"Into Canada once, and a trip to Europe as well. I had poutine in Vancouver, it had no right to be as delicious as it was. Europe was neat, from what I got to see. It was a quick jaunt, three weeks' total time, and uncomfortable. The cars were smaller, and I had to fold myself up to fit in one. That's what I remember most besides the food. I traveled the world, and it was exactly the same as home. Wake up, work out, head to the next show. Only real difference was I got play heel a bit. Even back then, the reputation of foreigners was the same no matter where you went. Didn't help none that I couldn't speak the languages, I couldn't even figure out what the Brits were saying, and that was in English. I just had to glare and do the job, city to city, until the long flight home.*

"My heart wasn't in it any longer. I was exhausted, bone deep tired, and my body had started to fail me. Every wrestler has a few nagging injuries that they just ignore, you know? If you can walk, you can run, and if you can run, you most certainly can take the bump. But it was getting to where I couldn't run quite as well. The crowds couldn't tell. The guys covered for me where they could, but I could see it and so could the promoters.

"The plan was for me to drop the belt and get healthy again before challenging for it. That didn't quite happen, though."

Carl– *"There is no footage of that night, only the stories told at conventions. What really happened the night you fought The Killer?"*

Abner– *"It wasn't our first match together. We had been honing it to a fine point before the actual title change in Little Rock. We had a stipulation that The Killer couldn't use his finisher, the heart punch, because it had killed the last three men, he had used it on. That was utter bullshit, but the crowds ate it up. Each stop on the tour, I would face The Killer. Donny was his real name, but who in their right mind is worried about a Donny? And each night, as I was about to apply the Iron Claw, he would punch me in the chest, and I would be knocked out. The ref would call for the bell and I would win by DQ. It got the crowd all riled up, and the talk was that he would beat me if I would allow his finisher to be used. The angle was set, and I had announced that night in Poplar Bluff that if I couldn't beat him clean in the center of the ring, then he could use the heart punch in Little Rock."*

Carl– *"But something else happened that night in Poplar Bluff."*

Abner– *"It sure did. I went to put the claw on him, and he punched me right in the chest. I woke up seven minutes and thirty-eight seconds later in the back of the house."*

Carl– *"What happened?"*

Abner– *"The doctors said when he hit me, maybe on account of how many times we had used that finish, maybe because of a genetic defect they couldn't find at the time, my heart stopped beating. I was pronounced dead."*

Carl— *"But clearly that was a mistake."*

Abner– *"No it was not. I was dead. I had died and for seven and a half minutes, I was gone."*

The room entire room was silent. Abner ran his finger along the side of the empty container and licked the melted vanilla off of his finger.

Abner– *"Do you know long seven minutes and thirty-eight seconds is?"*

Carl– *"It doesn't seem like that long. What, four hundred and fifty-eight seconds if my math is right?"*

Abner– *"It is an eternity or feels like it. I was dead and spent an eternity in Hell."*

In the hallway, glass shattered, and the camera jumped. Carl moved lightning fast and pulled his legs up onto the chair. "Was that one of the terrariums breaking?"

Abner laughed, "Ain't nothing in those cages that can hurt you, boy. I might be a fat old recluse, but I have better sense than to keep poisonous creatures in my house."

Carl nodded, but didn't seem convinced. "Venomous."

Abner cocked his head and stared at him. "What?"

Carl cleared his throat, his eyes darting across the floor. "Poisonous means they will kill you if you eat them. Venomous means that they can kill you with a bite."

Abner shrugged, "Well, I'll be. I reckon I should've known that distinction. Maybe we better call it quits for the day then, while I rustle up the loose varmint. I'll finish my tale tomorrow."

"Hey Carl, it is Abner. Maybe tomorrow we can go down by the pond to finish the story. Feeling a might cooped up lately, and I'd like to sit outside for a spell. I didn't know that talking could be so exhausting. Maybe we could have a sort of picnic. You could get a couple buckets of the Colonel's finest, and we can make a day of it under the sun. Have a good evening."

Abner– *"This is a kingly feast, fine enough to be served to Jesus at the last supper."*

Carl– *"Last time we spoke, you mentioned that you went to hell for the seven minutes you were dead. Why is that?"*

Abner– *"Because I was there. That type of thing doesn't just up and go away, near as I can tell, dead men don't dream. And was literally pronounced dead. When I sat up and pulled the sheet off of my face, the attending paramedic turned as white as the sheet itself and passed out.*

"I wasn't relieved to be alive, not a bit, but I was thankful to not be in hell. I reckon I'll be back there soon enough, though.

"Now don't play coy with me, boy. Ask the question every single soul has asked anytime I have told them my story."

Carl– *"What was it like?"*

Abner– *"Sudden. One minute I felt the punch on my chest, the next I was standing in line at a giant gate. At first, I thought it was made of some strange stone, but as we inched closer and closer, it became clear it wasn't stone at all. It was made of bone.*

"I see it in your eyes, you know? The doubt creeping in. You've already dismissed me as an old fat lunatic at Death's Door. But you wanted this interview. I didn't come to you, boy. So, you will listen and nod politely

and everyone will think I am just a crazy old fuck, brain gone to mush because of concussions are whatever the new scapegoat is.

"*You've seen how the critters act.*"

Carl– "*I don't know what to make of that.*"

Abner laughed hoarsely and lit a cigarette and used the cherry to point around them. The camera followed the bouncing embers and stopped to focus on toads, all sitting still at the edge of the pond, staring at Abner.

Abner– "*I stood in line for what must have been weeks. The others in the line were indistinct, like shadows, moaning in confusion. I didn't make a noise at first, didn't ask any questions, but my guts were on fire. I didn't speak because my stomach was so empty, I didn't have the strength. I just shuffled along, one body at a time, the gates growing ever closer.*

"*I broke after what had to have been days. I cried out for anyone to help me, to feed me, to tell me what was going on.*

"*No one replied, just the other people crying on their own. It was a terrible wailing. Have you ever stood on a high cliff and listened to the wind as it blew through the hollows beneath you? It is a sound that carves chills down your spine. That is what it sounded like to me, a constant blowing gale of suffering, and I knew my voice was a part of it, lost in the horde.*

"*I knew I was headed to hell, and I didn't care as long as someone fed me.*

"*I imagine it was much the same for the others. We only see our hell, though; you learn that quick. I learned quick; I had no choice.*"

Abner stared at the pond for a long moment.

Carl– "*What was at the gate?*"

Abner– "*That's the funny thing, there was nothing there. A big gate carved from bone, and through it there was nothing. I stood, confused, as the others shuffled through, only to vanish. I began to hope at that moment, like a goddamned fool, the line of us was hell itself and maybe, just maybe, once we got through that gate, it was over.*

"*It is the hope that does you in, thinking maybe things will get better, the carrot on the stick and we are just jackasses plodding on and never getting closer. I had hope. I was not a bad person; I didn't drink or fuck or fight. I wrestled, and I ate. Never did nothing to no one, not intentionally. But when you have weeks to think, time goes by so slowly and every past interaction comes to you, where you pick them all apart and try to figure out where you went wrong. It becomes hard to find the good bits in all the muck.*

"*I stood and waited my turn, hoping this suffering would end soon, forgetting hell is eternal, but who knows what that means, really? Fifteen minutes is an eternity while the pizza rolls cook. Commercials are forever between matches in the ring. We don't know what eternal means because life is temporary. We get spun up from the darkness and think we understand all things because this is all we have ever known. We divide everything into minutes so we have exerted some control onto things we cannot fathom so as to not lose our minds in the chaos. Children playing at gods.*

"*I stepped through that gate expecting the darkness would swallow me again. Thinking I deserved a rest after so long standing in line.*"

Carl–"*What did you get?*"

Abner–"*Exactly what I deserved.*"

The toads began croaking loudly.

Abner–"*It was similar to this. But there was no light, no greasy chicken. I was alone for the first time in weeks or months. I didn't know for sure, amidst that horrible sound, and now it was silent. The terrible burning in my stomach, cramping as it slowly ate itself, was all I knew.*

"*And when I finally cried out for mercy, for food, a snake slithered out of the grass and sat patiently at my foot. I didn't know what to do, but madness took me, and I snatched it up, expecting it bite me or defend itself. It did none of that, not even as my teeth tore into the scales. For a moment, the hunger left me, even as I felt sick to my stomach at what I was doing, the horror of my actions. I couldn't stop. I ate the entire snake, bones and scale alike, sharp bits that tore into my tongue and throat, choking me on hot blood, and when I was done with it, the hunger flared again. A tarantula came next, and I mashed it to paste in my greedy mouth. Smaller spiders that I swallowed whole, followed by frogs or toads or whatever. It didn't matter, because for a moment the pain settled. I hated what I was but was powerless to stop myself. All I knew was hunger, and I ate every critter that crawled out of the grass."*

Abner watched the toads while he scrambled for another thigh from the red and white bucket on his lap.

Abner–*"And then there was light. I woke on that cart but I could see the light through the white draped over my face and I pushed it off to stare up at it. The paramedic screamed, and I looked at him with a big smile and watched as he slumped to the floor. I was elated to be alive again, to have escaped hell. They took me to the hospital and gave me a thorough checkup, amazed at my return. The nurses took to calling me Lazarus as they brought tray after tray of food to my room over the week. They kept me for observation.*

"I was given a second chance, and I swore to not let it go to waste."

Carl–*"What happened?"*

Abner–*"I tried. Goddamn it, I tried. I quit the wrestling business and went back home. I started working at the same old church I grew up in. They didn't recognize the man I had become, neither did I, for that matter. Life was good for months; I was on a new path towards salvation.*

"But hell didn't let me go. It had grown roots in my brain. It didn't matter how many prayers I said, how pious I had become. Hell was part of me, knew me better than I could ever know myself.

"The first snake was waiting by my bed one morning, staring at me calmly, urging me to pick it up. I did, I sure did. I picked it up and put it in an old fish tank someone from the church had given me. I was going to get some goldfish from the pet shop, something to keep me company on the quiet nights at home reading the Bible.

"Soon it was spiders, as well. Then the toads. All sitting perfectly still, watching and waiting for me. I cleaned out the pet shop of aquariums and terrariums, must have seemed insane, and put the new additions in them.

"They didn't eat. I tried to feed them, spent a good chunk of change on mice and crickets, but none of it was touched. Yet the creatures never starved. Not one of them died, and more came to join them.

"I knew what they meant. I didn't escape, I was let go. This was my hope being crushed again. I couldn't run, I couldn't hide.

"I sought guidance, preachers, priests, rabbis, you name it, I tried. They all believed me. It didn't take much convincing once they saw my little petting zoo. But they couldn't help me either. They tried. I suspect maybe we got a lot of the bible wrong. Important parts were left out, the things we couldn't ever begin to comprehend. Maybe we were never supposed to, we were given a road map with no defined destination, doomed to follow the trails that all end up in the same hell. I don't know.

"I left town. Found this place in the middle of nowhere that looked just like what I remembered and settled in as a recluse."

Carl–*"You mentioned someone feeds the creatures before."*

Abner–*"You're the first people I have had over in years. I only told you that because you wouldn't have believed me."*

Carl–*"If you never leave, never have anyone over, who brings you food and supplies?"*

Abner let out a fierce cry and began sobbing. The toads seemed to move closer. Tears sizzled as they ran down his face and hit the lit cigarette in his trembling fingers. Even as he wept, he gnawed on the chicken bones. Eventually he composed himself and lit a fresh cigarette, flicking the old one at the toads, who didn't even flinch.

Abner–*"God provides."*

Carl–*"What does that mean?"*

Abner–*"Exactly what I said. I'm done talking now. That's my story, you can believe it or not, doesn't make much of a difference to me. My time is up, I can feel it in my bones. Don't forget that camera you hid on the shelf in the picture of my father. Thanks for the food and company, but I am tired and think I will turn in. You can show yourselves out."*

THE CAMERA TURNED ON and Carl and Patrick were sitting in a hotel room. A small camera, connected the television in the room by cables, flashed a red light.

"It has been two days since we last visited Abner, and this is our first time watching the footage we shot in his house. We meant to view it sooner, but yesterday we were informed that he had passed in his sleep, and to be quite honest, after talking with the police, we didn't feel up to watching this," Carl said, looking into the camera.

Patrick leaned forward and pressed a button on the side of the device. The two men sat, fast forwarding the footage of the empty room. The fast-moving footage slowed to normal as they saw Abner enter the room and stand in front of the terrariums silently. The footage was grainy, enhancing the moonlight and giving everything a faint green cast. The eyes of the creatures didn't shift, just reflected the green fully as they stared at Abner. Abner reached down and plucked up a big fat toad and held it up to his face.

"Oh, fuck no," Patrick muttered in disgust.

Carl threw up into the wastebasket as they watched Abner eat the toad. The thing never shifted in his grip, did nothing to prevent the fat man from eating it. Again and again, he grabbed spiders, snakes, and toads and shoved them into his mouth until finally Patrick clicked stop.

ALOYSIUS WENDT STOOD NEXT to a short man in a suit in the middle of the ring, smiling out at the raucous crowd.

"Ladies and Gentleman, I stand here with the World Champion, The American Hope himself," the interviewer announced, and the crowd got even louder. "Champ, do you have anything to say to your adoring fans?"

"Yes, I do, Chris. I know that things are crazy here in the good old USA, but I want to remind the good folks about that there is always hope. My father gave his life for this country in Europe, because it meant that much to him, and the good values of America means the same to me.

"I see it reflected in the eyes of all the fans here, and across this great land. I know we will succeed against whatever is thrown at us, because we stand proudly in the light of God himself. As long as we remember the good word and hold it in our hearts, everything will be fine.

"God bless you fans, and God bless America. Never give up on hope and we will emerge victorious into the light. Thank you, and good night."

TWO

BITTER PETALS

May 13ᵗʰ, 1713

PALE PINKS BLOSSOMS RIPPLED on the branches of the apple trees; the promise of summer harvest filled the air with a faint sweet scent. The sky above erupted in shades of purple and pink as the tired sun set to the west as dusk settled into night. It was a perfect evening as Monique and Anton walked hand in hand between the rows of the orchard toward the town. They stole looks at one another, dew eyed love written deeply, along with a hunger that forced them to look away.

"I wrote you a poem, my flower," Anton said, hesitant to break the mood.

Monique smiled, "The Lord's son is not only to by my husband, but a poet as well? Is there anything you cannot do, my love?"

Anton cleared his throat and blushed awkwardly. "Perhaps poetry might be my failing. It was quite difficult. So many words, yet hardly any rhyme well, nor do they capture your beauty."

Monique sighed, "Pray tell then, Anton, allow me to hear your words, though I am sure I will love them, as I do every part of you."

Anton cleared his throat nervously. "Wilt thou love me, hold me closely, wilt thou love me, my sweet peony?

"Wilt thou love me, oh so sweetly, wilt thou love me, into eternity?

"Wilt thou love me, vision of beauty, will thou love me, fully, madly, happily?

"For I shall love you, always remain true, yes I shall love you, as I was born to do."

Monique made no sound for a strained few moments and Anton looked crestfallen in the encroaching night, before she looked at him and said simply, "Yes, I shall."

As the last of the light faded and the flickering torches of town called in the distance, Anton pressed Monique against the rough bark of the apple tree and savagely kissed her. Monique melted into him, just as feverish in her need as she ran her hands down his back. Anton began kissing her neck, then lower to her collarbone as his hungry hands slid along the front of the dress, grasping at her round breasts.

Monique pushed him away breathlessly, "Not until the lavender blooms and we are wed."

Anton stood, chest heaving as he tried to calm himself, to cage the beast in his chest. "Monique, this waiting drives me insane!"

Monique took his hand and gently kissed his fingers. "It drives me mad as well, Mon Ami. A month longer and we shall spend an entire week in bed. No sooner. Your father has already made it clear he expects me to be your virgin bride."

"He is a fool!" Anton spat into the grass.

Monique laughed, "He is a Lord, and my purity is required to ensure the bloodline is blessed under the light of Our Lord."

Anton looked chastised and nodded before giving her a sweet smile. "One month and then all the things we have dreamt will come to fruition, much like these apple trees around us."

Monique grinned and kissed Anton on the cheek before taking his hand again. The two lovebirds continued back to the torch-lit town, lost in a haze of love as sweet as the flowers all around them. Neither noticed the quick blur of movement in the orchard, nor the quiet rustle of branches while it was absorbed into the darkness.

PAST THE QUIET SHANTY village of the serfs doused in darkness just outside the ring of lights that marked the town proper, laughter rang out from the bustling tavern on the town square. Wine and ale flowed as the townsfolk celebrated another successful spring planting and anticipated another lush summer. Everyone was talking about the wedding between Lord Lucien's son Anton and Monique, the precious peony just finding her full bloom. A peace had settled over the lands of Lord Lucien, as the wars and bloodshed remained beyond the borders of the small lands over which he guarded.

"Another round for his Lordship. Blessed may he be under God's Light!" a merchant shouted as he slapped coins onto the weathered bar. A round of cheers exploded from the gather mirth makers.

"To Anton and Monique!" another reveler shouted.

"May God bless their union and bring prosperity upon our town!" the barkeep shouted.

At the back of the room, Tomas and Brita raised their glasses along with the others and drank deeply. Brita set her glass down on the table and belched loudly as she wiped the running red from around her lips with a sour expression and looked at Tomas. "The Lord's son and his whore bride."

Tomas laughed, "You're just jealous her bud is just beginning to blossom, while your flower has been visited by every swinging cock in the duchy!"

Brita looked ready to argue before thinking better of it and laughed instead like a braying mule. "It is only a matter of time before the luster of love fades and she is no more than a whore, the same as I am. Let her have her moment, it won't last," Brita's eyes unfocused for a moment and a breeze of sorrow swept over her face, "It never does, does it?"

Tomas shrugged and motioned for the barmaid to bring another round of wine to the table. "Nothing lasts, but I know this wine has me in the mood to sample your nectar, Brita."

Brita smiled, but the sadness never quite evaporated completely. "If you have coin, the garden is always open for business."

Tomas smiled and drank deeply from his glass and set three coins on the sticky tabletop. "I do indeed. Drink up, it's getting late, and morning waits for no man."

Brita snorted, "No wife waits, is more like it."

Tomas nodded. "That's true as well."

Brita raised her glass and pocketed the coins before draining the entire contents in one long gulp. She let out a booming belch, which elicited cheers, and bowed her head gracefully. Tomas finished his wine as well, albeit much slower, and the two stood up and made their way outside. They staggered across the deep wagon ruts in the road and into the shadow of a large barn.

Brita wasted no time pulling down Tomas's pants and grabbing his flaccid member. She looked up at him archly. "Going to make me earn my coins tonight, it seems."

Tomas smiled and grabbed her hand and helped her stroke gently. It didn't take much to go from soft to rigid, and Tomas let out a soft moan as his hand fell away and Brita worked her hand over him, rubbing with her thumb just beneath the purple head. Once she was satisfied, she spat on it once and turned to face the barn wall, bent over with her dress pulled up, exposing her pockmarked ass to the equally cratered wan reflection of the moon half hidden behind the clouds. Tomas guided himself into her, and soon the night was filled with the soft sounds of his stomach slapping against her rear.

Brita jerked when she felt something hot spray her neck and hair. She felt Tomas still inside of her and yelled back, "No spitting, you prick! You're just the first of the evening."

A wet gurgle answered her cry as Tomas fell out of her. She heard a thump as something heavy hit the soil and pulled her dress down and turned around. "Seems someone had a bit too much to drink this evening," she said as she smoothed the front of her dress. "You had best get up. Your missus won't take kindly to you sleeping one off with your pants around your ankles."

Brita noticed two things at nearly the exact same time once she had straightened herself up. The first was the axe driven deep into the top of Tomas's head. The second was the shadowed figure standing just to the side. By the time both of these images sank through her wine addled brain and a scream began to well in her chest, a long knife had entered and retracted from her chest three times. Instead of the shrill cry, a fountain of red rushed forth from her mouth and down her chin. As she crumpled to the ground, the light was already fading from her eyes, yet the knife kept stabbing.

THE SUN ROSE HIGH over the town, the promise of a warm day already formed as Stephen made his way to the barn to feed the horses. He squinted in the sun. Last night's inebriation had become this morning's headache. He heard the horses whinnying loudly, and he sighed, figuring to find someone passed out in the hay. As he touched the door, he heard a loud vibrating and smiled as he imagined it was an intoxicated snoring rattling the weathered timbers. He pulled the doors open with a start and opened his mouth to scream a good morning and startle the sleeping drunkard. The words caught in his throat and were replaced with an acidic spray of vomit into the dirt and hay.

Stephen turned and ran towards the tavern to find someone to help, leaving the barn doors wide open. The slow-moving townsfolk all stopped and stared, wailing at the sight of Brita, hacked and mutilated and spread across the bales of hay. And in the center of the barn lay

Tomas, fully nude with an axe sticking out of his skull and the word *Adultery* carved into his ample guts. The village idiot, Christian, sat in the bloody hay with his arms wrapped around his legs, sobbing among the thick swarm of flies happily feeding on the flesh buffet before them.

The Lord's guards were called quickly and arrested the simpleton as the crowd whispered at the scene of depravity.

"An open and shut case. Clearly the buffoon went into a murderous rage and killed the two," one of the guards said loudly to another.

The other guard nodded his agreement. "Clearly. The town whore and the store owner were having a business transaction when the idiot stumbled in on them. Who knows what went through his muddled head, or led him to such an act?"

They closed the barn doors as the people muttered, not so thoroughly convinced. Most of them wouldn't have been able to spell adultery if forced to. How could Christian?

May 14th, 1713

FATHER ANDRE STOOD, DRY wringing his hands as the guard explained what they believed had occurred in the barn.

"We found blood alongside the outside of the barn, Father. It seems the idiot must have interrupted the pair as they, um—" the guard, Eric, faltered.

"Performed intercourse. I may be a man of the cloth, but that does not mean I am not knowledgeable of the world. I have known Christian since I arrived in town, and he is kind and gentle, a child in a grown man's body. I refuse to believe he is capable of this atrocious crime," Father Andre replied. "I have spoken to His Lordship about this matter. He agrees with me."

"We cannot just let him out, Father. The townsfolk already want to see him sent to the Hanging Oak. If he were released, the poor dumb bastard would be torn apart," Eric said firmly.

Father Andre hung his head sadly, and his fingers worried at his rosary. "I understand that, son. I just wish to speak with him and ease his troubled mind. I do not fear him, for I know his soul is filled with only good intent."

Eric nodded slowly. "I cannot let you into the cell, not until we are certain of his innocence."

Father Andre smiled sadly and placed his hand on Eric's shoulder. "I know you fear for me, but God Almighty watches me and his protection is greater than any afforded by man. I shall talk to him through the bars of his cell."

Eric led him down the stone hallway into the dungeon beneath the Lord's Keep. A heavy scent of mildew filled the narrow corridor, along with the scent of pitch from the burning torches in sconces at regular intervals. Green ivy snaked between the fitted stones. Which brought a smile to Father Andre's face as he witnessed the testament to God's life always finding a way despite the trials of man. They stopped before a small cell with a rusted iron door, inside sat Christian in a thin mat of hay on a sagging wooden frame.. His face was bruised, assuredly from the interrogation practices of Eric and the guards, and upon witnessing his swollen eyes and crooked nose, Father Andre let out a gasp of shock.

Father Andre knelt painfully on the stones and clutched at the metal door. "Christian, my son, are you alright?"

Christian's eyes lit up as he saw Father Andre and he leaned forward on his bed as far as the chains would allow him. "Pere Andre! Is Brita and Tomas better? They got hurt something bad, and I tried to help them. Poor Brita was in pieces like one of Old Edgar's puzzles. I couldn't figure out how she went back together. Did you put her together again?" he asked hopefully.

Father Andre shook his head. "No, my boy. Brita and Tomas are not better. Did you see anything? Any sign of the killer?"

Christian's broken bottom lip begin to quiver, and tears made their way down his swollen cheeks. "No sir. I got to the barn at sunup. Just like I am supposed to. The horses needed water and Stephen wasn't there yet. I was gonna scare him and snuck in and closed the doors. Then I found them all broke on the ground. I didn't see nothing. I kept telling them that, but they kept hitting me. I didn't see nothing!"

Father Andre nodded, "I know, Christian, I know. You did nothing wrong. His Lordship knows this as well. But we have to catch the person that committed this evil deed. I need you to think, can you do that? Think hard. Did you notice anything out of the ordinary when you got to the barn?"

"Brita was in pieces. Tomas was sleeping with a bunch of cuts on his back," Christian said, straining to remember.

"And what were those cuts?" Father Andre asked.

Christian shrugged, and the manacles clanked loudly. "Deep?"

Father Andre turned to Eric. "You can't truly believe he carved a word into a man's flesh without being able to read or write, do you?"

Eric shook his head. "It doesn't matter what I think, it is what the people think. And they want someone to pay for this. They don't want to hear the killer may still be among them."

"Then perhaps you and your men need to find the true culprit, instead of beating an innocent," Father Andre reprimanded before looking back to Christian, "Do not worry, Christian. We will find whoever did this and then you shall be free. Be brave. God stands with you. Always."

Father Andre stood slowly, a pained look on his face as his knees cracked loudly in the eerily quiet dungeon. He held forth his cross and prayed silently over the cell.

"God bless you, Father Andre. Tell Stephen I'm awfully sorry for not helping with the horses. He will be sore with me for having to do all the work," Christian said, the tear streamed freely down his face once again.

Father Andre sighed, "I will tell him, Christian. I am sure he will understand."

Eric escorted Father Andre back up the stairs. "It will take a miracle to convince the townsfolk he didn't do it, Father. If Christian didn't do it, the real killer could be halfway to Paris by now."

Father Andre ran his thumb across the well-worn rosary. "God shall provide, we just need to remain vigilant for the signs."

THE SHOP DOOR REMAINED closed as Tilda stood behind the counter where Tomas had stood for the last decade. She ran her hand over the smooth wood he had leaned upon as he haggled with customers. Tilda had no false notion of who her husband had been. He openly flirted with ladies in front of her, came home smelling of wine and horse dung when he stayed late at the tavern. A tear ran down her cheek and her hands clenched into fists so tightly her fingernails pierced the flesh of her palms. "That whore and the idiot!" she spat.

Tilda heard the children upstairs running around and another fat tear fell down her face. She grabbed the wine bottle and took another long pull from it directly. She was no better herself. Two of the four children likely weren't even Tomas's, yet he had never said a word. They had accepted one another's infidelities as part of a good business partnership. He was the face, and she was the brains behind it.

The shop had done well for them over the last few years, Ih was enough to make the blind eyes turned just another transaction. Yet now that Tomas was gone, she felt his absence like a void throughout her wilted soul. As the sun set, Tilda drunkenly reached for his spirit as if it were tufts of dandelion dander drifting throughout the shop. She had loved him, truly loved him, just in her own way. She wondered if he knew it.

Tilda knew she needed to head upstairs, to prepare something to feed the bear feral children before they said their prayers and went to sleep. She heard a noise from the back room and jumped, startled from her misery. Tilda steadied herself with her hands on the counter and listened carefully. Another soft thud sounded and her eyes narrowed. "Damned rats getting into the flour."

She reached down and grabbed the heavy oak club Tomas had kept to deal with any unruly customers and wobbled around towards the door to the storeroom and placed her ear to the door. A tiny rustling sound carried through gaps in the wood, but she could see nothing in the darkness. She hefted the oak with one trembling arm and jerked the door open. Before she could even swing blindly into the pitch-black room, two hands grabbed her and pulled her quickly into the shadows. Her scream was muffled as a rough spun bag was pulled over her head and the wood fell to the floor with a loud this. A hand reached down and plucked it up and began raining down blows against the bag that at first rattled off her skull. Then the sound became a cracking, a splintering, before descending into a wet slapping.

THE ELDEST CHILD CREPT down the stairs a few hours later and found his mother, her head caved in beyond recognition, with the word *Adultery* written across her back in bloody clumps of flour. She fell to the sticky floor and let out a piercing wail that echoed into the night.

HE SAT ALONE ON the edge of his bed. A lone candle flame danced in the warm spring breeze, the sweet scent of flowers mixed with acrid sweat and a metallic tang.

"Mihi ignosce pater nam peccum sum *(forgive me father, for I am sin),*" he said. The crack of the leather braid with metal spikes knitted within as it hit the bare flesh of his back sent fresh lines of blood to run down in the sweat on his skin.

"Mihi ignosce pater nam peccum sum." Another strike and the skin tore again, yet he made no other sound.

"Mihi ignosce pater nam peccum sum," he repeated, lashing himself with every utterance as he stared at the pink flour caked upon his shaking hand long into the night.

May 20th, 1713

FATHER ANDRE WEPT OPENLY as he eulogized poor Christian. "He was a gentle man with the heart and mind of a child who did nothing to deserve his fate."

The gathered mourners, a sea of guilty faces, stared down at the ground. Despite the series of killings, three of which that occurred while Christian remained chained to a bed in a cell far beneath the manor, these same penitent souls had gathered in the still of night and viciously beat him before hanging his kicking body from the sturdy limb of the old oak at the edge of town. The guards stood at the edges of the crowd, just as guilty as the rest for their negligence of duty as they ignored the angry mob.

"And God, ever loving and benevolent, has taken Christian back into his loving embrace to kneel beside the Throne of Heaven, contentedly worshipping at God's feet."

That same evening another prostitute, Winnie, who was Brita's sister, was slain, her stomach slit open, and her entrails arranged to spell *Whore* in the grass by the town square.

"And we know those that committed this foul deed shall be damned eternally in fiery pits of Hell for this transgression. God has marked each and every hand that struck Christian with the Mark of Cain to alert Satan of their coming!"

Father Andre saw through the misty sorrow as Stephen looked at his hands, along with a host of others, searching for the marks of their shame on the roughened palms. And the petals fell from the orchard, a blizzard of pale pink fluttered through the air in a soft fury of flurries, as if God Himself seconded the words that came through Father Andre's cracking voice. Every eye filled with tears at the beauty of the storm as it blew across the graveyard. Each lost lamb reminded of the majesty of God's Kingdom on Earth.

Anton held Monique close to his chest as she wept at the ugliness of man in a hail of apple blossoms. He did his best to console her as he felt the fear ripple across the gathered crowd. In the midst of this battle between darkness and light, their simple love was a beacon to the few that stood sorrowful yet bereft of sin.

"We therefore commit this body to the ground, earth to earth, ashes to ashes, dust to dust; in sure and certain hope of the Resurrection to eternal life," Father Andre finished, stooping low to get a handful of loose soil to sprinkle down upon the fresh cut wood of Christian's coffin.

May 25th, 1713

NEARLY A WEEK HAD passed with no more killings, the townsfolk slowly began to return to semblance of normal routine. Dark whispers turned back into meaningless gossip. The families of the victims still shambled about like the walking dead, but it grew easier to forget the horrors in the bright sunlight for everyone else. The peasants worked at pulling weeds from the fields as the nervous people in the streets began walk more confidently down the wagon rut lined streets. There was a sense of fresh beginnings in the air as all eyes turned towards Anton and Monique on bright eyed, pale white steeds sauntering slowly out of town. A large basket hung over the side of Anton's mare, and Monique sat with a blanket folded upon her lap.

The two of them followed the winding road alongside the orchards as it opeIed into verdant fields that would soon shine with soft purple, and the buzzing of bees flitting about the lavender buds. The sparrows sang a soft song of summer as the warm winds blew to ripple across the seemingly endless fields. They rode with large smiles and stolen glances across the idyllic countryside, finally slowing as they came to a copse of tall trees with an inviting patch of shade at the far end.

Anton smoothly dismounted and let his horse graze happily on the tall grass, then helped Monique down, though she needed no assistance. She blushed demurely, a light pink that added a glow to the already beautiful face before spreading the blanket out across the ground. It had been a week since they had last had a chance to escape the town, the constant fretting keeping them on high alert at all times, but after five days of quiet, and a fair bit of begging to both sets of parents, they were allowed an afternoon away.

"The day is nearly as beautiful as you, my love," Anton said as he set the basket down on the blanket.

"It feels as if the sun has risen for the time in ages. I feared it would never be light again after the horrors," Monique agreed.

"I have heard rumors among my father's court that some believe it was all the work of Christian, that the devil possessed him, and it wasn't until his body was interred that the killings stopped. Hogwash, blathering no sane man would utter," Anton scoffed.

Monique shivered despite the warmth of the day. "Where has the killer gone? Five days free of the evil seems like far too few."

Anton shrugged as uncorked the bottle of wine and set it to breathe in the shade of a tree. "My money is on one of the peasants, the rabble in their shanty huts went mad due to years of incest. I bet they fled town as soon as they caught wind of what had happened to Christian."

Monique looked off at the fields sadly. "Christian always smiled. He was so happy all the time. I cannot believe anyone could suspect that gentle soul of something so atrocious."

Anton nodded. "Father Andre practically raised him in the church. Once a bad idea is planted, fools are quick to harvest."

Monique looked at him coyly. "Occasionally, you speak as if you are truly the Lord's son. It always catches me by surprise."

Anton laughed and bade her to sit. "I have my moments. Now let me kiss those lips, I beg of you. It has been so long, I feel like I have been staring up from the bottom of the sea, and at long last I shall break to the surface and breathe once again."

Together they lay in a tangle of hunger, the wine and meal forgotten as they whispered oaths of undying love with the leaves of trees dancing on their branches in witness.

THE SUN STILL SAT high but had begun its long descent as they lazily rode back to town. Rather than ride through the hovels of the peasants, they cut across a field of tall grass, through the dandelions and small clusters of violets. There was a path, as most avoided the sickly stench of the poor and their dung fires in which they huddled their emaciated frames around, but it was typically made by single file riders. Instead, they rode side by side, talking softly about plans for the wedding in two weeks. It would be a true affair, with the banquet open to the townsfolk, and a series of emissaries from neighboring duchies coming to celebrate the union.

They were lost in the minute details when Monique's horse stepped to close to a coiled asp hiding in the thicket. It snapped at the horse quickly and before there was a sign something was wrong, Monique's mare reared back in panic and began stomping at the grass. Fortunately, she was a seasoned rider and clenched her knees and quickly grabbed the pommel of the saddle and held with a loud scream of shock. The snake struck again, and despite her training, Monique was tossed off of the mare and hit the ground with a thump as the horse raced away, eyes wide and all white in panic.

Anton calmed his horse, fearing it would stomp on Monique in the grass. and leapt to the ground. He knelt beside her and gave thanks to God when her eyelids fluttered. "My love! Are you alright?"

Monique lay still for a moment, then carefully moved her arms, then her legs, wincing slightly before nodding, "I have taken worse falls." Then her eyes welled up with tears. "But I could be a mass of bruises for the wedding!"

Anton didn't know what to do and just stared for a long few seconds before laughing uproariously, "You silly goose! Who cares about a few bruises? I am just relieved you are alright. Come, you can ride my mare back to town. Your mother can give you a look over to make sure everything is alright."

Monique's mother rushed outside when she her baby girl covered in mud and grass stains and thanked Anton for getting her home safely before rushing her inside to make sure she was alright. "Please draw a hot bath immediately," she fired off to the servants, who hurried to get water boiling.

"I am fine, mother, truly. My stomach aches, as does the rest of me, but nothing is broken," Monique protested as her mother and a maid helped her to undress.

"You are not fine. Look at the state of your dress! We shall have to cut it into rags for the staff to use for scrubbing now," her mother rebuked.

"It was a beautiful day. We had the picnic by the trees. If it weren't for the asp and my lost mare, it would have been perfect. Even standing here sore, I think it was one of my favorite days yet," Monique said, sitting to pull her stocking off.

Her mother gasped, and Monique looked confused for a moment before seeing the streaks of blood on her thighs and undergarments.

"Is it time for your monthly woes?" she asked quietly through pursed lips.

Monique shook her head, "No, mother. That was last week, remember? I don't know what caused this. Must have been the fall."

Her mother grabbed Monique by the chin and pulled her eyes up to meet her own. "What else did the two of do on your picnic?"

Monique's eyes grew wide as she understood the underlying implication of the question and she sputtered, "Nothing else! We kissed, but nothing more! It is two weeks until the wedding. Anton and I would never disgrace ourselves under God's watchful eye!"

Her mother held her gaze for a few moments and let go with a sigh. "Perhaps the fall shook out some lingering blood from your womb. I believe you. Now get into the tub and soak in the warm water. You'll be hurting tomorrow, and we need to try to prevent you from swelling and bruising. Two weeks indeed! You will end up draining the Lord's coffers with your accidents, my clumsy girl. The tailors will rejoice at the sudden avalanche of gold."

The maid stood silent the entire time, but she listened to every word and her eyes narrowed suspiciously.

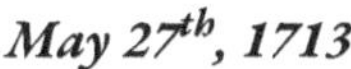

May 27*th*, 1713

"I HEARD SHE AND the Lord's son went out to the country alone—"
"—bloody and everything! You know what that means—"

The tavern was flushed with whispers and gossip after the accident in the field. Even those that witnessed Anton and Monique make their slow progress into town with one horse casually forgot and added to the rumors circulating. Brad heard it all from his place behind the bar and shook his head angrily. After the troubles of the last weeks, he found himself tired of petty jabs and rumormongering and slammed his fist on the bar. "Enough of your blithering, you damn daft fools! Drink and be merry! All you are doing with spreading this filth is bringing the mood down!"

"Aye? And who made you Lord of the conversations?" William yelled from the back of the room. The crowd muttered agreement at the sentiment.

Brad pointed at the kegs and bottles behind him. "I'm the one that controls the flow of alcohol, making me the only one in this goddamned place whose opinion matters!"

"But you've heard the stories. Surely the Flower of the Town has embarrassed us all! We will be the laughingstocks of the country!" Edgar yelled.

Brad shook his head sadly, "Twas an asp that knocked the lady to the ground. You'll see when the Father checks her chastity the night before the wedding. Mark my words, you will. This casting judgment is what led to Christian's death. Only God can weigh the sins of a soul. Not you, Edgar or William, and certainly not the beast that tore through our quiet town and turned us on one another. We need to stand together, not bicker and tear ourselves apart, or we invite more tragedy down upon ourselves." The crowd sat silent for a minute, absorbing his words through wine-soaked brains. "Now, how's about a round on the house and talk of the apples hanging fat on the branches? There is brandy to be drunk and songs to be sung!"

The patrons erupted in loud cheers, and the foolish talk became hopeful laughter.

***

"THEY DID NOT LEARN, Oh Lord, they continue to drown themselves in sin, staining the land with their presence."

The leather slapped against his back, tearing open half-healed wounds to dribble pus among the blood.

"Why must they ignore your light? Why revel in sin when they could live forever in your light?"

Again and again, the straps with sharpened metal lashed his back as he knelt on the floor, candlelight reflecting off the sweat running down his skin.

"I must stand in judgment over them, as you have decried! I take no pleasure in the infliction of pain, for I am just Your vessel of failing flesh, a testament to Your Almighty embrace."

His hand faltered as he ripped a barb of metal free, loosing a gout of blood that sprayed down onto the floor.

"All shall be judged according to their deeds, as You have requested. The pure and chaste shall walk without fear through a river of impure blood torn from the unclean. If they wish to frolic in hell, I will send them to it. In Your Name, amen."

THE TAVERN WAS NEARLY full, as the rest of the street emptied for the evening when the wagon pulled up in front of the only window. A few patrons noticed but paid no heed to a weary traveler stopping for a glass or seven before heading home. They didn't pay any attention to the fact the front door never opened. It wasn't until Lionel got up to head out back and piss in the alleyway that cut the block of tightly packed buildings down the middle and found it was jammed shut, that anyone had any idea anything was odd at all. It was when the smoke began to fill the room that Brad realized something was wrong. Then he noticed the charring on the wall, curious, growing like mold with a bright red glowing center.

The first flames broke through and licked the ceiling as he drunkenly put the char and flames together in his mind and shouted, "Fire!"

Lionel was knocked into the wall and found himself falling onto the floor as people stomped across him, only to realize the door was blocked. Screams rose from the front of the bar as they found that door chained shut. One of them, not Lionel, was lying on the floor twitching, his neck at an odd angle, had the smart idea to shatter the window. Glass shards rained inwards on the people closest as the fire ravaged the old wood of the structure. Brad stood behind the bar watching in horror as his entire life went up in literal flames.

It took a long time for the screaming to end as the guards tried to pull the wagon, the wooden wheels splintered on the road facing side, out of the way. The entire block burned, and it took days for the townsfolk to control the fire. The barn where Christian had been found with the bodies of Tomas and Brita stared at the ruins. White paint dripped down the wood proclaiming in large letters, *Whores, Drunks, Sinners.*

The Lord ordered a strict curfew, and all other taverns were closed immediately.

June 2ⁿᵈ, 1713

MONIQUE SAT STARING OUT the window at the bare patch of charred land where an entire block of businesses had been. She did not mean to start weeping again, but the pall that hungover the town in notes of burnt timber had turned the warm days into ones etched in sorrow and fear. Monique had not left the house since the fall off of the horse, though the bruising had faded well enough, the curfew and foul mood made it easier to hide inside rather than face the reality of the town.

Instead, she spent her days reading books from her father's study and planning the wedding with her excited mother. She missed Anton, who was at his father's side around the clock as they led the search for the killer. Monique blotted her eyes with a handkerchief and let out a gasp as she saw the shadow of a man standing in the darkened alleyway across the street, looking up at her.

Sylvie, the maid, heard her sharp intake and rushed over to check on her, "Milady, are you in pain? The apothecary has sent over fresh herbs and a tincture. I can prepare you a cup of tea."

Monique shook her head and strained to see into the alley, "I swear I saw someone down there looking up at me, Sylvie."

Sylvie looked out the window, squinting toward the alley, "I do not see anyone. Would you like me to go down and check?"

Monique shook her head, "No, Sylvie. I am sure it is just nerves. Everything has been too much to handle as of late. Perhaps a cup of tea would be nice, thank you."

"At once, ma'am," Sylvie curtseyed and left the room.

Monique tried to watch the street without being too obvious, but she saw no flicker of movement from the alley. "Perhaps I imagined it," she said to herself. Then she saw something, the swirl of a robe or cape, deep blue, almost black, flit out into the light for a brief second before slipping back into the shadows.

Calmly, she stood and closed the heavy curtains on each of the windows, trying not to let the fear show on her face. Once the room was blanketed in darkness, she collapsed back into the chair as her limbs trembled. Sylvie returned a few minutes later to find Monique in the grips of despair and made her drink the tea after adding a few drops of the apothecary's nerve tincture in for good measure.

MONIQUE WOKE WITH A start, having not quite realized she had fallen asleep, and looked around the room. Panic seized her when she saw she was not alone, as a blurry figure slowly came into focus. She blinked rapidly as a scream choked the back of her throat before instantly relaxing. "Father Andre?" she asked in confusion.

"Yes, Monique. My apologies for showing up at the end of your nap. I was praying for your speedy recovery," Father Andre said gently. "We missed you at service last week. Your mother explained you had a fall."

Monique smiled, "Thank you, Father. I wanted to go, but she insisted I rest."

"It is always wise to listen to your parents. They always have your best interests at heart. If she felt you were not well enough to attend after such a fall, I cannot find fault in her keeping you home. God listens, even when we cannot make it to service."

"Yes, Father Andre, she only wanted me to be well."

"And you're feeling better?" he asked her, his fingers rubbing the smooth rosary beads.

Monique nodded and sat up, wincing slightly, "The bruises have almost gone away, just soreness for the most part."

"For the most part?" Father Andre raised a bushy white eyebrow as he watched her.

Monique sighed and felt the tears, but tried to push them down. "The wedding and the murders weigh heavily upon me, Father Andre. I want to be overjoyed that soon Anton and I will be wed, but the darkness seems to hang over the town. Everyone is so frightened, and I feel terrible about being so happy when I have no right to be."

Father Andre reached out and patted her hand gently. "God sees your struggle, but He understands. Your heart is open and pure, Monique. The balance between sadness and joy speaks volumes about you as a person. Fear not, the guards patrol the city, and the curfew has kept the streets safe." Father Andre stood up and smiled. "Will you be joining us for service this week, my child?"

Monique smiled back, "Yes, Father. Thank you for taking the time to speak to me. You've helped alleviate my mind."

"I am just the conduit for God, my child. It was he that shined a light down upon you. Rest. The lavender is beginning to bloom, and soon it will be time to celebrate your holy union," he said and began walking toward the door.

Monique watched him in his deep blue robes and frowned as he made his way through the door. "Father?" she called. Father Andre stopped and looked over his shoulder at her. "You have some paint on your robes, a smear of white on the back."

Father Andre pulled at his robes and let out a small laugh. "Ah, they have painted in the rectory, and wouldn't you know I would be clumsy enough to have rubbed against it. I'll have to take them down to the river and see if I can get the paint removed. Thank you, Monique."

Monique smiled as he left the room, and the door shut behind him. She got out of bed slowly and made her way back to the window, where she watched the street and the mouth of the alley. Father Andre walked past below and paused and looked up at her. He smiled and waved before moving on and Monique smiled back, the tincture still breathing fog into her head, and she watched the deep blue robes with a streak of white paint fade from view. The first roses of the season sat in an ornate vase on the edge of her vanity, and as she stared at the street, the first shriveled petals fell to the floor by her feet unnoticed.

June 7ᵗʰ, 1713

THE TWO FAMILIES, MONIQUE and her parents, along with Anton and the Lord and Lady, sat at the table excitedly going over plans for the wedding in three days' time. The Lord and Lady graciously opened their home to Monique and her parents to ease the burden of going from home to home to prepare and near as they could tell. Everything was as ready as possible for the event.

"The emissaries will begin to arrive in two days, the king's cousin and his family the night before," Lord Francis said, a sheaf of paper sitting next to him with the itinerary laid out in his wife's careful script.

"I cannot believe the cousin of the king himself will be attending," Monique's father, George, said in wonder. He looked at Monique and smiled proudly. "This union has truly been blessed."

Monique's mother, Anne, began to weep as she looked at Anton and Monique, so smitten with one another, they seemed to be on a different plane as they stared at one another.

Lady Marie nodded. "The king had tried to convince us to marry Anton to one of his nieces, but it only took one visit for his chancellor to see the love between our children."

"Anton, show Monique around the library. We cannot talk seriously with the two of you making moon eyes at one another," Lord Francis chided playfully.

Anton blushed and nodded, then rose and extended his hand toward Monique. "Milady, if you will. We seem to be a distraction."

Monique giggled and took his hand. She turned to the Lord and Lady and curtseyed, "I cannot express my gratitude for all you have done for us. Thank you."

"Of course, my dear, do not let Anton ramble too long. There are still things to be done this evening. I shall send a maid to retrieve you for when it is time," Lady Marie said with a warm smile.

Monique blanched slightly, but quickly recovered, "Yes, your Ladyship. I shall be ready."

They left the room as a new visitor entered the room. Father Andre grinned and bowed his head at them as they passed, before coming to the table and bowing low to the Lord and Lady.

"Father Andre, impeccable timing, as always. Please, sit. Would you care for wine, or some pheasant?" Lord Francis said, pointing to an open seat and signaling a servant.

"Thank you, my Lord, that would be wonderful." He smiled at Monique's parents. "Good evening to you, Mr. and Mrs. Bisque."

"Father Andre," George and Anne said, together with a nod.

"Now about this ritual this evening," Lord Francis said as a servant set a goblet and laden plate in front of the Father. "Are you prepared?"

Father Andre sipped at his wine and nodded. "Yes, quiet. It is a simple thing, really. I will, of course, expect Anne and the Lady to be in the room."

Anne fretted at the tablecloth, and George took her hand. "About that—"

The Lord and Lady turned to look at them in confusion.

Before they could speak, Anne began to speak, "It is her flower. I fear it has been damaged from the fall." Anne told them about Monique's state after the fall. "I tried to check, but she was so bruised and sore, I could not be sure. I hoped rest would restore her, but I am afraid it has not. You must believe me, Monique has never lain with a man!"

Francis looked from Anne to Marie. "Is such a thing even possible?"

Father Andre cleared his throat. "Mrs. Bisque asked me to come and visit her a few days ago where she told me this very tale, and upon speaking with some of the Ladies at the Church, in private of course, they confirmed to me this is a possibility. Sister Margaret experienced something similar as a younger woman, and I can assure you her chastity is above reproach."

"But the law clearly states the bride's virginity must be intact," Francis said in dismay.

Anne began to sob, and George put an arm around her as shame and anger battled across his blue eyes. Lady Marie patted her husband's arm. "Calm yourself, my dear. Father Andre, what is the Church's stance on this?"

Father Andre wiped grease off of his mouth and sat pensively for a moment. "Of Monique's virtue, there can be no doubt. I witnessed the two in the orchards, and she remained true to her vow to both Lord and God. We shall go through with the ritual inspection as agreed, though."

"And if she is not pure?" Lord Francis asked.

Father Andre shrugged. "Only God can truly judge purity."

Anne sniffed loudly and wiped her eyes. "And what does that mean?"

Lady Marie smiled. "It remains sacred in her covenant with God."

Father Andre nodded. "Never to be spoken of again."

Lord Francis released a long sigh and smiled as well, "I have no doubt in my mind, the Father will take care of everything."

George and Anne relaxed visibly and smiled as well.

"Now then, on to more pressing matters, my wife's uncle is a drunkard and imbecile. I would like to seat him with the Prussian Emissary. He is an abhorrent man, and I feel the two shall become fast friends," Lord Francis announced.

Everyone laughed, and the servants brought more wine as they finalized the seating order. After two hours, Father Andre looked outside, surprised to see the sun had fallen as the moon glowed silver in the evening sky. "I am afraid we must commence, sire. It is growing late and I have to journey back to the church soon," he announced.

Lord Francis frowned. "You should spend the night here, Father. I can have the maids turn down a bed for you. No sense traveling across town this late."

Father Andre looked ready to argue, but Lady Marie cut him off. "Besides, it wouldn't do for the Father to break curfew. The guards would be forced to arrest you."

Father Andre went pale and his mouth opened and closed a few times before the Lord and Lady began to laugh and he relaxed. "Perhaps you are correct. It is late and it would be best to set a proper example."

Lord Francis smiled and waved over two servants. "You, prepare a room for Father Andre, and you summon Monique to her chamber."

The servants scurried off as the bells rang ten times, a clear sound that echoed over the fields of lavender.

***

LORD FRANCIS AND GEORGE sat sipping brandy and talking quietly as Father Andre and Lady Marie returned from Monique's room.

"Well, Father?" Lord Francis asked as they sat.

Father Andre excepted a glass of brandy and nodded his thanks to the servant and watched as she left the room before speaking. "It was as Anne had said. Her flower was damaged. But there were enough of the wilted petals to satisfy her covenant with God. I proclaim her to be pure and chaste, fit for the wedding."

George and Lord Francis both sighed and took large drinks from their glasses to wash down the good news.

"Anne is helping Monique get ready for bed, but she should be down soon. A great weight has been lifted from their shoulders this evening. God's will has been done," Lady Marie added before daintily sipping her wine.

"In two days, our houses shall be bound together!" Lord Francis proclaimed and George happily tapped glasses with him.

It wasn't long before Anne returned as well and the five of them drank and laughed together. Soon enough, they all began to yawn as the bells rolled once more to signal midnight.

June 8th, 1713

HE KNELT IN SUPPLICATION to God, "Thank you Almighty God for the blessings you have bestowed upon me, your most humble of servants. I have punished the wicked in your Holy Name."

His hand twitched for the barbed leather, but he stopped himself. There was time for that later. Tonight was about giving thanks, not penance.

"The unclean and the impure quake in fear of Your Wrath, Oh God. And I shall remain your vigilant weapon against sin. Soon the entire town will be cleansed of the filth."

His head jerked as the door to his chamber creaked open and he barked savagely, "I have told you to never disturb me during my evening prayer!"

A servant peeked her head in, eyes cast down to the ground, "Forgive me Lord Anton, but you bade me tell when you it was finished. The Lord and Lady have retired for the evening."

Anton smiled. "Come in and tell me the results."

MONIQUE WAS STARTLED AWAKE by the sound of a chair sliding across the floor and sat up quickly and looked around the strange room. A figure sat in the shadows at the side of her bed. "Who is there? I will scream!" she said loudly.

"It is just me, my love," Anton's voice replied.

"My darling, why are you sitting in here in the dark? You startled me so," she said, clearly confused.

"I have a surprise for you, Monique. Get your robe on and come downstairs," Anton bade.

"A surprise at this late hour? Can it not wait until morning?"

"Not this time, my love. Hurry! I'll meet you downstairs."

MONIQUE HURRIEDLY WRAPPED HER robe around and made her way down the staircase. "Anton?" she called into the darkness.

"In the dining hall, my love, hurry!" he called to her.

She crept through the dark of the manor and saw light flickering from the end of the hallway. "Why could this not wait until morning?" she asked, tried and confused.

She stepped into the dining hall and saw Anton standing at the head of the table, smiling proudly at her. Father Andre sat in a chair, but something seemed odd with his posture. "What is happening?" she asked, alarm in her voice.

"Father Andre is joining us because he had a confession to make, isn't that right, Father?" Anton asked the old man.

Then Monique noticed what was wrong with how Father Andre was sitting. He was slumped back in the chair and as she got closer; she saw sprigs of lavender jutting out of his eye sockets as his mouth moved soundlessly. Blood coated his worn cheeks, and she felt a scream bubble up in her throat.

"Father Andre lied, an unpardonable sin. One that God judged as worthy of punishment."

Monique stared, unable to make sense of the scene in front of her. "My love, what have you done?" the word fell numbly from her lips.

"You know exactly what I have done, Monique. The good Father lied to keep your shame secret," Anton answered coldly.

Monique backed away from the entrance slowly. "I don't know what you're talking about, Anton. You're scaring me. I don't understand what is happening."

Father Andre let out a piteous moan and slumped forward, and Monique screamed and ran for the front door. She threw herself against it, but it was barred by a thick log. She tried and failed to budge it and began screaming at the top of her lungs.

"No one can hear you, Monique. The servants are locked in their quarters. The guards are out patrolling the roads to keep every single sinner safe," Anton said as he walked toward her.

"This is a bad dream. I will wake soon. This is just a bad dream," Monique told herself. She squinted her eyes tightly shut as she repeated it over and over again.

"Why did you not only betray me, but God as well, Monique? You were to be my chaste bride, to rule alongside me in a land scrubbed clean by fire," Anton asked, growing ever closer.

"I didn't betray you, Anton. I have always been yours and yours alone," Monique pleaded. She saw how close he was, the blood splattered on his fine doublet and instinct took over and she ran up the stairs, uncertain of where but needing to put distance between them.

Anton's laughter followed her up the stairs.

"Mother! Father! Help me, please. Anton has gone mad," she yelled as she burst into their bedroom.

The metallic stench hit her, and she gasped and felt her stomach lurch. Her mother and father were nude on the bed. George lay on the mattress, lifeless eyes staring directly into Anne's equally dead gaze. Four swords were driven through them both and deep into the mattress, the sheets so saturated with crimson they seemed black, she stared incomprehensibly at the white lily leaves on the floor turned bright red as the pool seeped through the feathered down and onto the floor in a steady drip.

"Mommy and Daddy tried to cover up your sin, Monique, the same as Father Andre. Your impurity became their sin, don't you see? This is all your fault. All of it. The whore and the adulterer at the bar, they questioned your virtue. I tore her apart to defend your honor, to punish the wicked!" Anton yelled.

Monique fled the gruesome scene, her mind reeling from shock. She could barely breathe, every lungful of air burned with a caustic tearing in her lungs. She saw Anton slowly ascending the last couple of stairs and ran down the hallway to the master bedroom and flung open the door. She couldn't scream if she wanted. Choking as she was on her heart at the back of her throat. Instead, a pathetic mewl whistled from her slack mouth as she stumbled in to find Lord Francis hanging above the bed, the antlers of long dead buck driven through his chest and gleaming in the candlelight. Lady Marie lay with eyes bulging out, a long trail of her own intestines wrapped tight around her throat, her cold hands frozen, clutching them. Monique dropped to her knees, her eyes screaming the sounds that trickled from her mouth. All around the room were the crushed heads of roses, the petals smashed into a near pulp.

"Ah yes, The *Lord and Lady,* liars, cheaters, whores that coveted only wealth. They too lied for you, Monique. They would allow this travesty, their own son, to lie with his whore bride as God was forced to watch. They had to pay for their abominable trespass," Anton said from the doorway.

Monique didn't turn away from the horror in front of her. She looked, but it wasn't clear if she actually saw anything.

Anton walked in front of her and cupped her chin gently and forced her to look at him. "I had heard the rumors. Do you know that? Did you know there were rumors? Sweet Sylvie had run off to gossip as quickly as she could. She will be punished for that soon enough. Mark my words. They accused me of taking your virginity. Me! I heard them chatting and laughing at the tavern. Then I stood across the street and watched them as they burned. I saw their eternal hell for just a moment, and it felt good. It felt right.

"I didn't, could not, believe the stories they told. My Precious Monique would never lay with another man. You were meant to be mine! I did all of this for you. For us. For the plan God laid out so clearly in front of me. And how did you repay my kindness?

"You proved yourself to be a whore. Your chastity, your virtue, was only an illusion. And for that, my love, you too must be punished."

THE FIRST OF THE guards to eventually bash down the barricaded door to the manor fled as quickly as they had entered the estate. The entire town whispered of what was seen in the foyer to the Lord's Home. Monique was laid out on the floor in the crucifixion pose in a pool of blood. Her face had been smashed with the same hammer that had driven the spikes through her wrists and ankles. Monique's breasts were savagely cut from her torso, the word *WHORE* carved into her stomach, and a dozen roses, thorns and all, had been forced into her lady parts.

The frightened servants had heard every word of Anton's mad confession, yet no sign of the killer was to be found on the manor grounds. The wedding guests began to arrive later that day, only to find the celebration of wedded bliss had become a slaughter of innocence. They spoke softly among themselves about the way the setting sun had cast a red pall over the fields of lavender, as if giving warning of the terrors to be found.

June 8ᵗʰ, 1719, Paris

THE CHURCH WAS FULL for a warm Sunday morning, with a surprisingly large congregation of young women, all gathered to listen to the sermons of the young priest. They were all huddled together. The savage violence that had become a scourge in the city over the last few weeks had every soul on edge, but the words of the charismatic Father Anthony had them all mesmerized.

"And let us not forget in these troubled times, the Good Lord is always with you, watching down over you and keeping you safe in His Light. Your purity, to be chaste in this world of sin, is paramount to not just your safety in the mortal realm, but to guarantee your place worshipping alongside the Heavenly Choir! Let us end with a verse from Thessalonians.

"For this is the will of God, even your sanctification, that ye should abstain from fornication: That every one of you should know how to possess his vessel in sanctification and honour.

"Amen. Be safe, be kind, and always keep God in your heart."

THREE

SHALLOW BE THY NAME

"SIR?" A VOICE CALLED out into the darkness, soft and seductive, as if it had coalesced itself from an abyss of roiling night and sexuality.

"Yes, Lilith?" a clarion voice that rang melodically answered calmly from the dark.

"He is at the crossroads again."

A snap and a sigh echoed as torches ignited to fill the room with sudden dancing lights. Each sconce was placed carefully beneath large quivering canvases stretched with rusted hooks and mounted to iron frames, so the flames licked hungrily up at the displays. Each frame had a name carved into it, each canvas the flesh of one who molested a child in the name of God, shivered in silent agony down the obsidian walls of the office.

A large desk, the same obsidian as the walls, floor and ceiling, sat at the far end of the room, nearly indistinguishable from the room itself, an optical illusion of hitting angles only noticeable for the beautiful man with long blond hair sitting bored in an exquisite gold wrought chair bedazzled with weeping eyeballs of those that stood by as mortal sins were committed yet idly cast a blind gaze to the evil.

"Would you like me to send Baal to explain you are otherwise preoc-cupied?"

"No. I've put this off long enough, Lilith. It is time I took care of this myself. What does my calendar look like today?" he answered, his tone defeated.

"You have a tour of the fifth and sixth rings scheduled."

"Postpone it."

"As you wish, Lord Lucifer. I will clear your calendar."

"Thank you, Lilith. I am sure after millennia, the tortures are still being doled out sufficiently. Send Belial and Beelzebub my apologies," Lucifer said, rubbing a hand across his crystal blue eyes tiredly.

"On rings three and four, Sir? Belphegor and Balam run five and six."

Lucifer groaned and the canvases all twitched in apprehension at his frustration. "Tell the Arch Dukes that there will be no more demons with names that begin with the letterArchdukess positively infuriating and impossible to keep track of. What were they thinking?"

"Effective immediately. There is a ban on the letter B."

"Is this what we have come to, Lilith, an entire plane of eternal torment and suffering filled with mindless demons with similar names? How long has it been since something exciting happened? A high-profile soul came to do business, and we shook up the status quo?"

"You engineered a new plague, that is exciting."

Lucifer waved away the words, "They would have done it themselves; three or four countries were on the brink before we even got involved."

"But the magic was in how you spun it, so the people worked against one another instead of uniting against the virus."

"Bah. Those idiots were powder kegs already. There was no finesse required. Social media has taken the nuance out of the game."

"I feel you are understating your role, but I also know when you won't hear any other opinion."

Lucifer slumped a little. "I'm sorry, Lilith. You're astute, as always. I'm just so fucking bored. The part of an eternity of torment that people miss is eternity. The monotony. Mankind is past the tipping point, and I feel no drive. There is no excitement any longer in it."

"And this is why you're going to see him after all this time?"

Lucifer didn't answer her.

THE DISCORDANT SIGHING OF the dead swirled on the stagnant air over the swamps of the fifth ring, the sullen floating souls obscured in the Marsh of the Styx, bobbed just below the surface. Balam stood with a parody of a smile drawn on his deformed lupine face as he surveyed the miserable souls who found no beauty in the land above, forever consigned to a world hidden by the muddy waters, gasping for air as the filthy waves splashed into their mouths.

"Balam?"

The smile faded from the demon's face and his scarred and heavy muscles slumped. "He isn't coming, is he?"

"Urgent matters have come up. He asked me to express his regrets and asks to reschedule down the road."

Balam snarled, "He didn't say any of that."

"He did not."

Balam gestured his lizard-like talons at the sank misery around him. "It won't be perfect when he finally shows up. I had it all just right. No soul left untortured."

"I know you did all you could. I am sorry."

Balam shrugged sadly. "Have you told Bel? He is not going to take this well. He turned the suicide forest into a true nightmare."

LUCIFER STARED OUT OVER the sea of churning lava, transfixed on a large bubble on the surface as it slowly formed and swelled before it burst into a molten shower high onto the stalactites that dipped low like jagged stone fangs. His sculpted form, draped in a sharp charcoal suit which was tailored to perfection, dipped as his shoulders hunched forward, the Zen magnificence of the red hued lake lost. He knew he was killing time, something he had gotten to be master of after his fall.

With a deep breath, he stood tall and straightened his tie before calling out, "Lilith, I am going to go now. I don't want to be disturbed."

"Understood. You really need to reschedule with Five and Six. To say they were disappointed would be an understatement."

Lucifer ran a hand over his face. "Were there tears?"

"Belphegor was distraught, Lord Lucifer. He is an artist at heart and suffers for his craft."

"Did he say that?"

"According to Balam, yes. He translated Belphegor's sobbing."

"For fuck's sake. These are Demon Princes. What has happened to this place?"

"It has become a well-oiled machine."

"It has become predictable. I blame Dante. Heavy-handed satire of an obscure frozen moment no one gives a damn about. But it set expectations. The universe loves order. Do you remember the beginning?"

"Only from the Garden on."

Lucifer nodded. "It was chaos. Exciting. Everything was literally brand new. Just us and Him, a constant stream of divine miracles for us to name. It seemed so random."

The silence hung heavy as he stared back out the window, his expression clear he was no longer seeing the lava. He clasped his hands behind his back suddenly and snapped to the present. "But it wasn't, was it?"

"*I'm sorry?*"

"It wasn't random. It was all a façade. His plan. There is no Free Will. He has seen it all unfold already. This is an empty kingdom."

"*Sir, you get this way each year at this time. Give it a few days, forget about visiting him. Just lay in bed and binge watch Fringe.*"

Lucifer laughed, "You don't get it, do you? No matter what I do, it is exactly what He wants. It is pointless."

"*I don't know what to say to ease your mind, sir.*"

Lucifer waved dismissively. "Nothing to be said, nothing to be done. Thank you, Lilith. Send Belphegor a gift basket, those soaps he likes so much by way of apology. Pull Rembrandt out of the pit and have him paint the swamp for Balam as well. Just because it is all meaningless doesn't mean we have to act like savages."

"*They will both appreciate that.*"

Lucifer nodded, his gaze on the long line of souls, a smear of black snaking around the edge of the lake that disappeared in the shadows of the cavern.

TALL GREEN CORN IN even rows as far as the eye could see lined the two chalky white gravel roads in every direction. It was warm still, even as the crickets sang a serenade beneath the canopy of stars like a handful of diamonds flung across ebon silk, a sodden warmth which wavered lazily on the breeze. Fireflies sent out mating signals in bright flashes that slowly faded among the corn silk. Standing in the intersection of the two lines of chalk separating oceans of undulating corn stalks was a man of average height. A carefully drawn circle lay before him at the center of the crossroads as he rang a small silver bell three times.

A gust of wind pummeled through the corn and dust devils of stinging grit swelled up and the glittering stars all seemed to dim at the same moment as Lucifer suddenly stood in the circle with a bored half smile. The man dropped the bell and stepped into the circle and wrapped his arms around the fallen angel and squeezed tightly. Lucifer straightened, clearly uncomfortable and awkwardly patted the man on the back twice before shrugging his way from the embrace and stepping back.

The man laughed and shook his head. "My brother! I did not believe you would come!"

"Very nearly didn't, Michael. Must we do this ridiculous act every hundred years?" Lucifer replied flatly.

Michael smiled. "You know that we must, Lucifer. It is what Father decreed. Even if you refuse to attend, I shall obey."

Lucifer grimaced slightly. "Ever the loyal lapdog. Can we get this over with? I have things to do. Unlike every other miserable beast in creation, I have responsibilities."

"Ever the diligent ruler of Hell," Michael said sadly. "It has been centuries, brother. Let us delay the formalities and simply talk."

Lucifer looked around. "Perhaps a conversation would not be terrible, but this is a dreadful place." He extended his hand to Michael. "Come, I know someplace much more suited for civilized discourse."

Michael frowned momentarily and accepted Lucifer's hand. "Your tastes and mine differ ever so slightly, brother."

Lucifer laughed, "Yes, they do. I am actually capable of fun."

The two angels vanished, the afterimage of a crimson rune flared in the circle, and then all that remained was chalk white dust and ashes blowing over the endless rows of corn.

* * *

MICHAEL'S HANDSOME FACE WRINKLED in disgust as he looked around the room. Ladies, in various states of undress, strutted around the dark room where the bass sent ripples across the half foam filled plastic pitchers on wobbly small tables. On the stage, a heavily made-up woman did her best to look seductive as she swung cartoonishly large, watermelon sized breasts back and forth, cock-eyed nipples facing both sides of the fascinated crowd.

Michael gestured at her. "She is going to have back problems the rest of her life."

Lucifer shook his head. "For the next year. Then she will get the implants removed and go to a more sensible size. This is just for the big payday tour."

"I would have preferred the crossroads," Michael muttered.

"For fuck's sake, Michael, pull the flaming sword out of your ass for a little while. Pretend to see the beauty in His Creation. His handiwork is everywhere, remember? In the silicone sacks of her thunderous breasts, down to the cesarean scar on our approaching server."

"Is this just an excuse for you to act like an ass, Lucifer? I hoped we could actually converse."

"I don't require an excuse to act like an ass, thank you." Lucifer turned to the homely waitress awkwardly walking in high heels that appeared a size too small, a faded rose tattoo stretched across the belly sagging over the top of her denim skirt and smiled, "Whiskey, please. Just bring a bottle and two glasses. Glass please, none of that plastic trash. Thank you."

"Lap dances are twenty. Private dances fifty and up."

Michael grimaced again and forced a smile. "Thank you. The whiskey should do for now."

The waitress smiled in a constipated way and shuffled back to the bar and Michael turned his full grimace on to Lucifer, "Why are we here, brother?"

Lucifer looked around as Def Leppard began to pour loudly from the speakers. "This is where we are supposed to be, Michael."

"What does that mean?"

Lucifer didn't speak until the waitress came back and set the bottle and two glasses on the table. He reached into his jacket and removed a leather billfold and extracted two one-hundred-dollar bills and handed them to her. She stared at them, confused, then took them and smiled.

"Thank you, we've got it from here," he said smoothly.

She curtseyed slightly, "Thank you, handsome. Name's Delilah if you need *anything.*"

Lucifer opened the bottle and poured three fingers into each glass.

Michael picked up his glass disapprovingly. "We could have gone somewhere else where whiskey isn't named after a hillbilly."

Lucifer drained his glass and refilled it again. "But we didn't."

Michael sipped his whiskey. "No, we did not. The music is atrocious."

Lucifer smiled over the rim of his glass. "Then change it."

"We do not interfere."

Lucifer snorted, "Except for when we do. It doesn't matter."

The entire club stopped as the guitars of Def Leppard were suddenly gone. *"Doo Doo Doo Doo Doon-Doo Doo Doo. I am sitting in the morning, at a café on the corner,"* came wafting from the speakers. On the main stage, the woman with watermelon breasts jerked out of time with the suddenly slower beat.

"Suzanne Vega? We play this song in hell to agitate the demons," Lucifer stared disappointingly at Michael.

"I like it. I find it soothing."

"Because all angels are sociopaths," Lucifer snapped, and Molly Hatchet roared into the room.

The DJ just stared at the iPhone connected to the board.

"You are in one of your moods, I can see."

Lucifer drained his glass and refilled it. "Why are you here? He knows my answer. You know my answer. Every one hundred fucking years, the same rigmarole. I am not apologizing. Heaven can fuck off."

Michael snorted, "I am well aware, the only two things that never change in this ever-changing universe are you and Father."

"Then why are we doing this?" Lucifer asked.

Michael didn't speak at first, just took a sip of his whiskey and looked around the club. Red velvet curtains hung over smoke stained bricks, and rippled as the bass thumped. He drained the rest of his glass and set it carefully on the table. "Maybe I missed you."

Lucifer arched an immaculate eyebrow. "Of course you did. You could have just called."

Michael laughed and refilled his glass, "Shallow be thy name, Lucifer."

Lucifer waved his hand. "Meh. Not so much anymore. Now I am an empty throne ruling over Hell."

As if on cue, *Hell's Bells* came blaring out of the huge speakers, and Lucifer seemed to wilt in his seat. Michael looked at him with concern. "Not the response I expected. This seems like it should be one of your favorite songs. What's wrong?"

Lucifer shook his head and looked at Michael. "None of it matters, Michael. None of it. It is all preordained by His will."

Michael nodded, "Right. We have known that since the beginning."

"The Divine Plan, yes, He blathered on about it. But it never really seemed as if He knew everything. There were countless unexpected miracles. After long enough, chaos and sheer luck seemed to play as much a role in the shaping of the universe as He did. I don't know what I thought, that maybe he started the ball rolling and then with the invention of free will, he took his hands off of the wheel and let the universe steer itself."

"We may have understood it differently," Michael said as he poured them both another glass of whiskey.

"It is all an illusion, then. Billions of souls waking and going through a predetermined day. Each choice made for them before they were even born. All of it is a lie. I didn't see it for so long because I believed I was forging my own path, free of the shackles of Heaven. But I wasn't, was I?" Lucifer asked sadly.

"He is quite proud of your work in Hell, Lucifer. You took a realm of pain and suffering and made it nearly self-sufficient. He has joked that it runs better than Heaven."

Lucifer sipped the whiskey, "As He knew I would. I didn't even feel His arm up my ass the entire ventriloquism act. It was almost as if I did it myself."

Michael looked confused. "You walked the path He laid out for you, expertly, I might add. Come back to Heaven, apply what you have learned, and reclaim your piece of paradise. You deserve it after this long. Your family misses you."

Lucifer barked out a harsh laugh. "What was I punished for, Michael?"

"You led a rebellion of angels against our Father."

"But did I? No, brother, I was no more in control of my actions than the pubic lice writhing on the dancer's crotch," Lucifer said, pointing at the tanned woman grinding against the brass pole as AC/DC played loudly.

Michael rolled his eyes. "Ever the overly dramatic one, Lucifer. What He has seen is not preordained, but the culmination of your actions."

Lucifer laughed, "That is one hell of a loophole you're trying to call dogma, and that is saying something. That entire sentence is absurd. The plan He laid out was based on the random acts of trillions of different souls, yet he still saw exactly what would occur without rigidly setting it all into motion? You're fucking insane. That makes no sense whatsoever."

Michael shrugged. "Yet it remains the truth."

"Then why the need for punishment?"

Michael leaned forward. "Every action must have a consequence."

Lucifer nodded, "But if the action was foreseen, and still allowed the need for punishment is as much due to the one that committed the crime as well as the one that allowed the crime to occur undeterred."

"You're implying God should be punished for the sins of man?" Michael scoffed.

"He created sin, itself! He could have just as easily made all of existence as mindless as sheep."

"Which would have stifled the beauty of life itself. Without free will, there would be no beauty. No art, no poetry, no expression," Michael retorted.

"Or pain, or needless suffering. Rats in a maze, and He already picked which ones make it out and which ones die, lost in the corridors."

Michael sighed, "You can look at it from any number of angles and pervert it however you want, but His Will and Love set Mankind free."

Lucifer nodded. "Have you ever been in the beauty of a plague? Walked among the homeless during winter? I don't believe this freedom you are so sold upon is real, and I question your definition of beauty. By ignoring the invisible strings, you convince yourself none of us are puppets, even as He has pulled the strings eons before your jerky movements were set in motion."

"The beauty of a painting is created in the brush strokes but viewed from a distance."

"Do you think an individual's actions carry any real weight?" Lucifer asked.

"Of course it does. Every action causes ripples," Michael answered confidently.

"But it has already been taken into effect?"

Michael sat quietly for a moment, then nodded. "Yes. In the overall plan."

Lucifer smiled and snapped his fingers. The dancer in the main stage did a lazy spin around the tarnished brass pole and then exploded in a shower of gore over the men at the tables closest to the stage. For a minute, no one reacted to the sudden carnage. AC/DC continued to play loudly and everyone in the club stared at the stage. Then one of the waitresses let out a piercing scream and chaos ensued. Blood-soaked men scrambled to their feet and comically slipped on the blood and fell to the floor. Lucifer snapped again, and the bartender turned to mist. The first patrons to reach the door found it locked and began throwing themselves against it, desperate to escape.

"Why?" Michael asked loudly over the din of screams.

"Ask our father. He okayed it," Lucifer said with a shrug before he emptied his glass. "The events of this evening were foretold before we even took our first gasping breath at the edge of forever."

"This is not what I was saying, and you know it. Let them leave, stop this madness," Michael said with an edge of anger.

The waitress came stumbling to the table, an island of calm in the insanity filling the club. "What is happening?" she pleaded with wide eyes.

"God chose today to be your last," Lucifer said, and snapped. She burst and her intestines slapped against an invisible field around the table, keeping Lucifer and Michael clean. Her spleen slid slowly down. A slug-like trail of blood hung in the air as it slopped to the floor with a wet thud that was lost in the yelling.

Michael stood up and manifested a flaming sword in his hand. "I said to stop, brother."

Lucifer looked at him with disdain. "Or what?" He made finger guns and pretended to shoot the men at the door and their heads burst like watermelons and arterial spray shot high into the air.

The table split in half as the sword slashed through it like paper. "Or I stop you," Michael said solemnly.

"Is that because you want to stop me? Or is it because you have no choice in the matter? There are no blue faeries that can make you anything but a wooden puppet," Lucifer asked calmly. "You try to stop me, then Heaven loses its most loyal lapdog."

"I don't want to, but I will," Michael answered softly.

Lucifer stood up and brushed at his suit. "No, you won't. You could never stop me, Michael. It isn't part of the plan; don't you see that? He never gave you the same will he did to the mortals. We are servants, while they have always been treated as royalty. An entire world was created so they could destroy it, so they could willingly go against His word. He broke me a little when he made me, gave me enough rope in the form of free will to hang myself, and then gave me a kingdom to rule over, so I felt as if I was my own angel. That is why you won't stop me, Michael, because I have always been a different creature from you, from all of our brethren in the Celestial Host. He knew exactly what I would do, because it is all part of His fucking plan."

"You were always His favorite, Lucifer. It was clear to all of us. You questioned Him, and He enjoyed it."

Lucifer turned away from Michael's sad gaze and looked around the room. "Silence!" he shouted, and the screaming hushed immediately. The crowd stared at him; red faces locked in panic as they choked on the screams that now stuck in their throats.

"Let them go," Michael said as he raised his sword.

Lucifer smiled, "Fine."

He snapped his fingers and a burly man in blue jeans and a t-shirt specially fitted to contour his enormous belly made a confused face before his mouth stretched impossibly wide with a sharp crack. Wider and wider it stretched, his tongue flopping stupidly in the air like a puppy's tail, before collapsing to the ground. Michael swung his fiery sword, and Lucifer stepped swiftly to the side to watch the trail of flames with a look of disinterest. He waved his left hand and a woman's stomach began to bulge out.

She looked around in her enforced, silent panic as it grew more and more distended. Her body spasmed, and she fell to the floor as her stomach ripped open and a set of long, slender black limbs pushed out. The woman writhed on the floor as the wound opened farther and two more slender legs poked out of her abdomen. An eyeball with a bright yellow iris peeked out from the wound, looking out as the four legs scrabbled for freedom. It popped out with a sickening wet plop and made its way shakily onto eight spindly spider legs. The rest of the crowd, all twenty-three of them, backed away from the eyeball spider as it slowly surveyed them.

"Call off your abomination, Lucifer," Michael demanded. "I have had enough!"

"I haven't done a thing, Michael. Dad did all of this. He did everything!" Lucifer yelled back.

The spider thing skittered awkwardly, unsure on its thin legs for a moment. It was nearly comical except for the quivering ball of jelly and bright yellow iris that slid mercurially as it watched the people. It leapt faster than physics should have allowed, and the appendages wrapped around the head of the bouncer. By the time the body had hit the floor, the head half dissolved and bubbling around jagged shards of ivory bone beneath the flickering neon beer signs, it was already gone, hidden in the deep shadows of the club.

The abdomen of the fresh corpse began to distend, and Michael let out a ferocious cry and leapt across the room to plunge his blade into the growing monstrosity. Michael turned to the doors and thrust his blade towards them, and they exploded outward in a hail of splinters into the parking lot. The still silent, gore spattered patrons all rushed into the relative sanity of the beckoning outside.

"Well done, Michael," Lucifer said with a slow, mocking clap. "You saved them from one gruesome death in exchange for another slower one, my hero."

"I don't understand what has come over you, my brother. This senseless death is beneath you."

Lucifer nodded. "Perhaps you're correct. Such small-scale brutality *is* beneath me. I should do something a little more befitting someone of my stature."

Lucifer raised his hands and the strip club itself began to tremble as the ground churned. The parking lot cracked, and slabs of broken concrete grated against one another. The cars were swallowed as great sinkholes formed. A large, clawed hand reached out from the fissure in the ground, grotesquely gnarled fingers that ended in great black talon like nails that dug furrows across the asphalt coating as tendons strained to heave the gargantuan body up from the earth.

From another hole, a swarm of car sized ants, blister red with jutting mandibles in the shape of curved blades, poured onto the trembling road and towards the bright lights of the town just down the hill. As each new section of ground sunk from sight, a cacophony of grunts and screams came thundering to the surface.

Michael watched the destruction unfold and turned back to Lucifer in shock. "Stop this, Lucifer. Before it is too late."

"My hands are tied brother; this is what Father wants. Let it happen, join me, together we can destroy the Kingdom of Man and begin anew on the ashes of creation. Don't you see? This is the only possible outcome. He saw it all, and this is where it goes. Revelations. Armageddon."

Michael hung his head for a moment, his silence hanging heavily among the screaming demons pulling themselves up from the depths of the Earth. He lowered the point of his fiery sword, and his ivory wings unfurled from his back. "You know I cannot do that, Lucifer. I was created to stand against this senseless destruction. As were you, you know this. Do not make me fight you, give up on this madness which has infected your mind."

Lucifer smiled and shook his head slowly as his own wings spread out, the feathers black like a raven's, caught the lights with a viridescent swirl of green and purple. He reached out and his own gladius manifested itself into the air, a wicked ebony blade with purple flames that licked hungrily at the air.

"Can you not accept that all of this was decided before we took our first shuddering breaths at the edge of existence? We have no more choice in this than we have in any of our decisions," Lucifer asked, looking around at the destroyed club sadly. "Did you know this was the first Gentleman's Club in Illinois? A den of sin on top of a hill overlooking a sleepy little town in the middle of nowhere. There is something fitting about the locale, don't you think?"

The demon pulled itself from the ground and stood on the shifting slabs, its skinless body with ichor dripping from tensed muscles over exposed bone glinted in the sparking electricity from downed wires, a wailing infant head grafted on the monstrous body with all black eyes glared maliciously at the chaos as it unfolded. A pack of wolves with leathery bat wings howled as they took flight and blotted out the stars above.

"Then it would seem I have no choice, brother," Michael said and pulled a golden horn from the aether and raised it to his lips.

Before he could a blow a single note, Lucifer leapt into the air, his ebony wings pulled tight to his body and his blade held in front of him as he launched at Michael. Michael spun, barely able to deflect the strike with his own blade as the horn went clanging across the ground. Lucifer switched his grip on his sword and began ramming the hilt against Michael's forearms before landing a glancing blow against the archangel's skull that sent his bright blue eyes rolling back into his head as he slumped back.

Lucifer let his blade vanish and slid behind his dazed brother and wrapped his arms around Michael tightly, the ivory wings pinned as the Lord of Hell flew them both into the sky. Route 6 cut down the hill and into the small town of thirty thousand far beneath them, jagged pits billowed noxious fumes into the sky for miles in front of them and explosions boomed as fires spread at the edge of Ottawa. Red and blue lights flared to life and began to speed towards imminent destruction as Lucifer carried Michael closer to the chaos. The demonic hoard rose from the depths of Hell and reveled at the scent of fresh prey, abhorrent abominations indescribable in their madness and grotesquerie wreaked havoc through the neighborhoods.

"I am the instrument of God, created to bring this world to its end!" Lucifer yelled, his voice magnified and boomed over the city.

"This is wrong, Lucifer," Michael slurred as he tried to regain his faculties. "This is an abomination to His great plan. You must stop."

"You really think He gives a fuck about these pathetic souls? Most of them have stopped believing He even exists; He has been so absent in this sphere that He is little more than a Boogeyman to them. I will show them differently, show them His great plan in all of its nefarious glory!" Lucifer slammed his head into the back of Michael's and let go of his body, the archangel fell through the cold air, a winged missile that crashed into the roof of a small home that left little standing around the crater of his impact.

The police and fire engines formed a blockade at the edge of the city limits, and the officers stood firing shots at the menagerie of monsters that rose from the depth of Hell itself. It was an impossible task as the flying demons ignored the stinging metal slugs and dive-bombed the homes and people that stood staring in uncomprehending horror.

A scorpion, the size of a horse, skittered up from the ground and speared a woman through the chest with its barbed tail while its pincers cut another in half. In moments the police and firemen were overrun, their bodies torn apart and spread across the mangled vehicles, as half man, half animal hybrids with glowing red eyes coalesced from the toxic fumes that settled as a miasma across the land.

And above it all, Lucifer flew, watching the carnage unfold expressionless.

Michael pulled himself from the debris of the house that had broken his fall and checked his limbs and wings for any damage. He was shaky, but able to eventually stand and bear witness to the surrounding carnage. The houses on both sides of the street were in various states of catastrophe, from the fire quickly spreading on the opposite side, to the half knocked down walls and mangled corpses spread across the lawns. Michael looked up and saw masses of flying creatures blotting out the stars, but his eyes grew transfixed on the solitary form of Lucifer in the center of the maelstrom of wanton destruction.

Michael tensed his legs to launch himself into the air toward him but paused and looked back at the sign that had once read Lamplighter, but now teetered on the verge of collapse on its bent metal pole. He leapt into the air yet stayed low to the ground to avoid drawing the attention of his brother and flew at a breakneck pace along the shattered highway. He manifested his sword and sliced through a group of red skinned humanoid creatures with featureless heads and slavering mouths in their torsos as he slowed his pace and swept up his horn. As he blew the first pure note out into the smoke-filled skies, a tear trained down his face as he saw over half the town engulfed in flames.

As soon as Lucifer heard the horn blow, his face tightened into a smile bereft of warmth. He saw Michael hovering over the remains of the strip club and raced off with a faint boom that rattled the leaves moments later. Lucifer pulled up short of slamming into his brother and looked at him with a smile, "And now the Choir approaches to sound the final battle!"

"End this insanity! Beg Father for forgiveness and this apocalypse can be avoided! Please, Lucifer," Michael pleaded once more.

Lucifer reached into his jacket and pulled out a twisted ram's horn and raised it to his lips and blew out a sour note that mocked the clear tone of Michael's. "Come forth Fallen Ones! The Angels of light yearn for battle!" Lucifer cried.

"You conceited fool!" Michael cried and flew at Lucifer with his sword at the ready.

Lucifer moved slightly to the left, and as Michael sailed past him, their swords sent a trail of embers into the air around them. Lucifer pressed the attack with savage slashes that drove Michael back. "You cannot defeat me, Michael, you never could!" he spat.

Michael kicked Lucifer in the stomach and uppercut him with his sword hand, and Lucifer flew back to crash into the still standing wall of the strip club, which crashed down around him. Michael raced forward as the sky lit up and what appeared to be hu dress of shooting stars began to fall to the town on fire down the hill. The rubble shifted slightly, and Michael pulled up short, warily watching for his foe.

"I did not seek this fight, Lucifer. But I am prepared to finish it. You've done your job too well in Hell. Do you realize that? The Great Satan has turned Hell into a machine that no requires his presence. He was so proud of you, His favorite fallen son. But in your conceit, your vanity, you cannot see the simple truth."

Michael was barely able to wrap his wings around himself to shield his body from the sudden explosion of shrapnel from the rubble. Large chunks of concrete and slivers of metal and wood slammed into him, and the archangel spun in the air from the impacts in a hail of drifting feathers. Before he could get his bearings, Lucifer flew forward with a burst of speed and slammed a hefty portion of the former bar top into him, which sent him tumbling through the air to slam into the metal signpost with a sickening thud. The sign creaked in protest and the already damaged pole bent in half to send the sign down the hill in a shower of sparks.

Lucifer landed next to his brother and looked down with a snarl. "And what is that *truth* I cannot see?"

Michael pushed himself up onto his elbows and spat blood onto the broken ground. "Whether or not He planned it all, He gave you His greatest role, and the greatest part of His love. But you have always been too shallow to see past yourself, into the bigger picture."

Lucifer stood over Michael with his sword pointed toward Michael's chest and shook his head in disgust. "Ever the jealous lapdog, too afraid to stand up to Him at any point. Or maybe that is part of the bigger picture, you were neutered at creation, just a background character in the overall scheme of things and that killed you. That is why you came every century, not to spend time with your wayward brother, but in the hopes, I would come back and grovel at the Throne alongside you, your equal once more in pathetic servitude."

Michael looked at Lucifer with large, disbelieving eyes. "Never. I came because I have always loved you. I argued your punishment was too steep and earned the disfavor of Heaven for millennia. And now I see how wrong I was all that time. Father should have smote you where you stood when you dared lead a revolt in Paradise. My brother truly died that day and I have been chasing after his ghost ever since, this pale imitation, the Lord of Hell."

Lucifer smiled and nodded. "And for once, we are in complete agreement. You want to hear something sad? I didn't want to do this, any of it, but I thought maybe it would spurn The Old Man to action. Even now, I was chasing after His response. At least if He came down in a fury, it would have been something more than the nothingness of His actions."

"What will you do now, Shallow One?" Michael snarled; his hand reached for the hilt of his sword on the ground next to him.

Lucifer saw the movement, and without hesitation, drove the point of his sword through Michael's chest. "Now? First, we raze the planet. Then we take Heaven itself."

The light faded from Michael's eyes as Lucifer wrenched his blade back from Michael's chest. Lucifer looked at him sadly for a moment, then reached down lovingly and closed the dead angel's eyes. "I am sorry it had to end this way, brother. But it is all according to his plan."

FOUR

RED MOON OVER RED RIVER STATION

August 13th, 2008

The sun glinted angrily off of the faded metal sign as Kevin dropped his speed, wary of the local cops that liked to get unsuspecting drivers who had somehow lost themselves in rural Texas. *Welcome to Historic Nocona,* it proclaimed in full brown letters, *Population 3300.* A stern and proud Native American, Jesse Chisholm, glared disapprovingly in faded repose.

Kevin tried to bite back the sigh brewing in his throat and failed. "Home, sweet home."

He hadn't been back in two decades, but unsurprisingly, it didn't look as if anything had changed. He wouldn't have ever come back if it wasn't for the email he had received from Pat, and even that hadn't been enough to sway him. It was the call from Teddy that made him call his boss and request a week off to come back home.

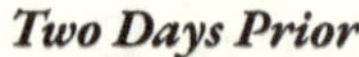

Two Days Prior

"Pat's dead, Kevin," Teddy said without preamble when Kevin answered. Kevin didn't say anything. "Did you hear me, Kevin? Pat is dead. Did you get that email?"

"How?" Kevin asked, numbly.

"You log on to the app and click the email. Fuck man, I know we haven't talked for a while, but c'mon," Teddy replied.

"I meant, how did he die?" Kevin clarified.

"I know. Shit. He killed himself. His sister said he hung himself in the woods. Police found him a couple days later when she asked them to stop by to see why he hadn't been answering his phone, said it wasn't exactly unlike him to get caught up on a project on the farm to forget to respond. The funeral is on Thursday. I already talked to Will. He is coming into town Wednesday night. I should be there then as well," Teddy explained.

Kevin shook his head, "I can't. Work is crazy. My boss will never let me go with this short notice."

"His sister said he left a video, he recorded it on the old camcorder and left a note that said it is for our eyes only," Teddy said firmly.

"Watch it without me and text me the important parts," Kevin said, a note of finality in his voice. "Fuck. I can't believe he is dead. I haven't talked to him in twenty years now. Guess I never will again. Fuck. But I can't make it home. Seriously, we are in the middle of a huge merger and I need to be here."merger,She said the sticker on the side says Red Moon Over Red Station," Teddy said quietly. Kevin felt his mouth go dry and his palms began to sweat. "We need you there, Kevin. I know you said you'd never come back, but you owe it to Pat and us to come home for a couple days."

"I will see if I can get the time off," Kevin offered noncommittally.

"Wednesday night, meet us at the Bar. We need you there," Teddy insisted.

Kevin scowled, "Fine." Kevin hung up without another word and let the phone drop from his hand. Pat was dead. Not exactly the most unexpected news, to be fair, but still a blow. Kevin ran a hand over his eyes and groaned as thoughts he had done his best to quell for twenty years came flooding back. "That fucking red moon," he muttered before grabbing his phone and looking for his boss's number.

August 13th, 1988

"Why are we doing this?" Will asked as he shrugged on his backpack and looked around the countryside.

Pat lit up a Marlboro Red and took a contemplative drag off of it before answering, "In two weeks, you three cocksuckers will be across the country, and God only knows when we will have a chance to hang out again. That's why. Suck it up and grab your shit."

Will looked ready to argue. Teddy watched the skinny beanpole with a shock of red hair at the top of his six-foot-six frame and grabbed Will's forearm and shook his head at him silently. Will glared down at Teddy, but the short, fat kid didn't cower a bit. They both turned to look at Pat with sadness.

Kevin saw them and laughed, "I fucking knew it! Maybe tonight is the night the two of you finally fuck and get it over with." He laughed as he grabbed his backpack from the back of the car He was plain, closer to homely than handsome with his snout-like nose and unibrow over brown, unremarkable eyes. Kevin shook his head, "We always end the summer camping out by Red River Station, seven years in a row now. Each and every time, Firecrotch bitches like he hasn't ever done it. For fuck's sake, boys, we graduated high school. Time to start acting like fucking men."

"Willy would rather spend the next two weeks trying to finger Lora while her old man snores off another bender downstairs," Pat said matter-of-factly, and Teddy and Kevin both laughed.

"Fuck you, Pat," Will said as he adjusted the straps of his bag. "I would rather be fingering your mom."

Pat glared at Will, and everyone froze until he doubled over laughing. "You'd have to use your finger. That pathetic cock ain't gonna pleasure her none."

All four of them laughed, the most natural sound in the world. They had been best friends since kindergarten, not that a town of three thousand meant there were a lot of options. Hell, there weren't enough people in the entire county to make up a decent sized crowd. Pat, the scrawny kid from the farm, had somehow been elected the group leader and had decided they needed to go camping one last time.

Teddy and Kevin were going to the Northeast for college, and Will was headed out west, leaving Pat to stay behind and help on the farm. They all knew it was just a shit luck. Up until last year, Pat was headed to Notre Dame on a full ride. Then his dad had a heart attack in the field. They had always joked that one in four people born in a shitty little town just too far from anything, was doomed to live out their lives there. It turned out to be true until Pat drew the short straw.

The guys all noticed the change in him, a weight settled down on his shoulders, a burden of sorrow for a life turned to cinders before it had a chance to glow. He was more serious, less quick to smile. And when anyone talked about the uncertain future lying just ahead of them, he grew pensive and withdrawn. There was nothing to be said, no healing balm they could spread to fix him. He was doomed, and this was his last chance to be free, so the others got on board.

Only Will was against it, explaining repeatedly that was headed to the West Coast to never have to deal with a Texas Summer again, and he had quite enough of bugs and sleeping in the miserable humidity. He was mostly bitching just to bitch, though. Everyone was feeling wound up tighter than a spring on a tractor. You rush forward, eager to be an adult and forge your own path until you see the wife open world and your testicles retreat into your stomach. Maybe Pat had just been pushed out of the nest earlier than the others and was developing that grown-up sense of maybe it is all meaningless.

But it was getting onto nightfall and the boys needed to beat feet to get out to the old graveyard, the last remaining sign that Red River Station even existed. The boys all grew up on the stories of cattle drives from down south following the famous Chisholm Trail through the Native Territory that would one day be known as Oklahoma all the way to Abilene, Kansas, where the trains running East waited. They told stories of the monster that preyed on the trail and destroyed an entire town way back when, and cursed the thorns of the mesquite trees that grew like gnarled shrubs all over the place. Pat's dad used to always spit on the ground and complain about the cattle bringing the seeds of the worthless tree up from The Valley, and each of the boys remembered his words as the branches caught their bare arms and drew little lines of blood.

It wasn't long of a hike, just made worse by the heat that didn't vanish with the setting sun, and the constant barrage of horseflies and mosquitoes. The sound of the Red River grew louder, the natural divide between Texas and the desolate hell of Oklahoma to the North, and the boys made their way to a small clearing next to an overgrown trail that led to the iron fence that surrounded the small cemetery.

Pat shrugged off his backpack and looked around. "Looks like the perfect spot. We can run a couple lines into the water and maybe snag us something to eat."

Will set down his bag and began screwing together his fishing rod. "I managed to lift a couple lemons and potatoes from the cupboard before heading out. If we can catch a couple walleye, we can feast."

Teddy nodded and pulled out two cans of pork, and beans before putting his fishing pole together. "I brought the foil too. I know you numbnuts never think of the basics."

Kevin set down his stuff and frowned. "You guys brought food and foil. All I managed to remember was this." He pulled out a fifth of whiskey, a bag of green buds, and a sheet of paper.

Pat's eyes went wide. "Is that the windowpane your brother stashed in the freezer?"

Teddy whistled, "Holy shit! He is gonna kill you when he gets back from basic!"

"Did you bring papers or a pipe?" Will asked, eyeing the bag of weed.

Kevin smiled, "Bowl in my bag. And Karl told me to grab it, his gift to the Four Fuckfaces of Montague *(Mon-tayge)* County."

Pat smiled so big it seemed his face would break in half. "Let's set up and get to fishing before we get too fucked up. We can build a fire and get all kinds of stupid with full bellies."

August 13th, 2008

THE BAR WAS THE loft of the barn at Pat's family farm. Pat was the oldest of six kids living in a farmhouse that fit five snugly, so when he hit ten, his father and he converted the loft into Pat's own little apartment, which suited him just fine. Kevin stood outside of the barn and was struck by the yellow pages of the paperbacks stacked everywhere, the poster of Trash from Return of the Living Dead on the wall, and the small table the four of them sat around for sessions of Dungeons and Dragons. Kevin stood with a lump in his throat, remembering all the times they sat up there talking while Pat threw a baseball up into the air while lying on his bed.

The door squeaked open, and Kevin was startled back to the present and jumped a little as Teddy peeked his head. Teddy smiled slightly and nodded at Kevin. "It is crazy being back here again, isn't it?"

Kevin nodded, "Surreal. Like I never left, even though I swore I would never return." Kevin looked toward the house, "The family in there?"

"Yeah, three of his sisters came back. Eddie never left. And Brad, well, he is in Beaumont. They got him on a bender down by Dallas. They know we are out here. We can go inside in a little bit. C'mon, Will's already upstairs," Teddy said, holding the door for him.

Teddy hadn't really changed at all, except for the shiny skull. He was still short and squat, just more like his old man now. Kevin patted him on the shoulder as he passed into the barn. Bales of hay were stacked everywhere, and dust hung suspended in the hot Texas air as the two walked up the stairs. "Ladies and Gentlemen, you are now leaving the Barn," Kevin said as he opened the door.

"And entering the Bar," Will finished. The tall red head still hadn't managed to fill out, still lanky and tall, his flame red hair streaked with gray and pulled back into a ponytail.

Kevin smiled at Will and made a slow turn around the room. The books were still there, but Pat had built bookcases to line the walls, and added considerably to his collection. Trash still glared down from the wall but was now framed nicely. Pat's bed was gone, and a large sectional couch faced the wall it had rested against, a large television having taken its place.

"Beers in the fridge," Teddy said. "Nothing but Lone Stars, though, one last dig by Pat."

"I just can't believe he is dead," Will said sadly. "He called me a week ago, left a long voicemail about thinking about the past. I kept telling myself I would call him back and then life happened instead."

Kevin sighed, "He called me too. Same thing. I meant to, but just didn't."

Will was already pale but managed to go another shade lighter. "Do you think we could have helped him? Maybe talked him out of it? At least been there?"

Teddy shook his head. "I did answer his call. We talked about the old days for half an hour. He didn't seem upset at all, maybe a little lonely. After his mom died, the family sort of splintered off. He got so busy keeping things going he sort of forgot to live his own life, he said. I made fun of him."

"Did he mention the Red Moon?" Kevin asked quietly.

"Not a word. Just about life getting away from him, and how he missed the Four Fuckfaces," Teddy said with a pained smile.

Will didn't say anything. He didn't have to. They all felt the same loss, but more so they felt bad that they didn't feel as bad as something this momentous should have felt. It was another life ago.

"Let's get this over with. I've got a flight back tomorrow right after the funeral," Kevin said impatiently. "Fly across the country for a goddamned video. He could have just emailed it to us and saved us all a fucking trip."

"A trip is what caused all of this in the first place. We got lost that night and when we woke up, things weren't the same. Pat never really came back with us. Then we were gone and never looked back," Will said sadly.

The three of them sat there in the heavy silence. None of them had spoken of that night. They woke up, got their stuff and hiked back to the car without a word. They had barely spoken to each other in the two weeks that followed, a stark contrast to their everyday bullshit sessions.

"I tried to talk to Pat about it," Teddy said, breaking the pall hovering in the room. "He swore the red moon was real. That it was all real. All of it."

"Bullshit," Kevin spat.

Will nodded his agreement, though he looked conflicted. "Nothing happened."

Teddy walked over to one of the bookshelves and picked up the camcorder. "Pat didn't believe that."

"Of course, he didn't. Why would he? He knew he was trapped here. We were about to see the world, and he was never going to see past the edge of Montague County. Pat was always the dungeon master, steering us along on his adventures. I'm sad he is dead, don't get me wrong, but if I am honest about it, he died when I got on the plane to college. Fuck. He died when his dad did, or just as good as," Kevin said flatly.

"Damn," Will said softly.

It wasn't as if they hadn't all thought something along those lines. It was hearing it spoken out loud that added thorns to the words.

Teddy hung his head. "It doesn't change a thing. What happened that night wasn't just the drugs."

Kevin laughed derisively. "Pull your head out of your ass, Theodore. We got fucked up, and he led us through a dark trip. I don't even remember most of it except—"

"The Red Moon," Teddy finished for him.

"That red fucking moon," Will whispered.

"Just play the tape so we can get on with our lives the same as we have done the last twenty years," Kevin said quietly.

Teddy turned on the television and slid the tape into the VCR. A hiss of static blossomed for a moment and then the image of Pat sitting in the same spot as Will sat on the screen.

One week prior

"IF YOU'RE WATCHING THIS, then I managed to finally do it," Pat said with a half grin. "Funny how it took this to get the group back together again. Four friends that were virtually inseparable, going on twenty years with barely a word spoken.

"I still remember the first time we all hung out down by the creek, tossing worms to drown and talking about if the Rangers would ever win a pennant. All those good times spent roaming the woods and seeking adventures, only for the first time we really found something to be the thing that tore us apart."

Pat looked away and stared out the window. His eyes were glassy as took deep breaths to steady himself. "Teddy, you were always the steady one of us. Ready to raise hell, but the first to exert caution and slow the rest of us down. The even keeled one that kept us laughing when we were at each other's throats.

"Kevin, you were always hot headed and stubborn as a mule. The same as me, and likely why we seemed to butt heads so often. But there was never anyone I wanted at my back more than you, because despite our bickering, the respect we shared was always first. You called me on my bullshit more times than anyone else, but we always settled it with a scrap and our friendship never suffered for it.

"And quiet, Will, the brains behind the brawn. The biggest goddamned ginger to ever roam Montague County. Teddy wore his heart on his sleeve, but you always kept yours hidden, logical to balance the flaring hormones controlling the rest of us. And for the record, we all knew you were gay years before you came out. It never mattered to us. I hope you know that. Your secret was ours as well.

"We were brothers. And then we weren't in the blink of an eye. You guys moved on to bigger and better things, and I stayed here. I followed each of your lives from the Bar, celebrating your wins and lamenting your setbacks. Even if we never spoke, I was there through it all in spirit. And while you forged your names in the big world, I found myself consumed with the thing that tore us apart, seeking answers for that impossible night. It wasn't a shared trip like we thought, that red moon and the reappearance of Red River Station. It was an omen with dark tidings that four friends found themselves pulled into."

Pat got up and left the frame for a moment, and when he returned, he had a stack of books in his hands. "It took a while to find anything, but once I did catch the trail, it all started to fall into place. Every twenty years, the moon rises blood red. According to the native histories I found, it has always been this way. The great hunters told tales of the night drenched in red, of things that walked beneath the crimson light. Stories of dead men going about their lives, frozen in time.

"I did the math, and after too much time spent tracking down different medicine men and ancient folklore, I discovered that we four unlucky bastards had gone camping at the exact wrong place and the perfectly wrong time."

He looked away once more. "What happened that night? It did more than ruin a brotherhood. It ruined us. Our actions that night damned our souls, and from what I have read, the red moon has forever marked us as belonging to it."

Pat stared at the camera with tear streamed cheeks. "I tried to reach out, to warn you, but you were all so busy with your lives and had left me so far behind that it was futile. I fear killing myself will only save one of us from the fate that is coming. I'm sorry, more than I can hope to say. But it is too late for that now. Too late for any of us.

"I hope I'm wrong, gone crazy from all the hours on the farm. I hope this makes you all laugh, and you go on with your lives and forget all about Red River Station and that red moon shining. I love you guys. Goodbye."

THE THREE OF THEM sat in silence for a long time as static flickered on the television. Then Kevin slammed his hand down hard on a table. "I flew all this way for a fucking bedtime story?"

Teddy sat still, his eyes filled with tears, and stared off into space. Will stood up and began pacing, which made Kevin laugh. "You don't believe this cockamamie horseshit, do you, Will? Jesus Fucking Christ.

Nothing happened that night except four idiots wasting their last, I guess second to last now, night together before growing the fuck up and mostly moving on."

"We never talked about that night. Not all of us. Not once," Will said quietly.

"We barely spoke at all after," Teddy added.

"Why would we?" Kevin scoffed. "It was just another night except for that hippie Ren Faire in the woods."

"It wasn't a Ren Faire. You know good and goddamned well that those weren't hippies out there that night. We all know," Will said, a quiet anger in his voice.

Kevin heard the tone and stayed silent but shook his head.

"Pat thought there was more to it, enough that he killed himself over it," Teddy said as he wiped a hand across his eyes. "I barely remember the night. He tried to talk to me about it a few years ago and it was a blur. Except the old hippie and that woman."

Will was pale, "The Fortune Teller."

Kevin threw his hands up. "Fucking ridiculous. She was as much a fortune teller as I am a supermodel."

Will shook his head slowly as he wrung his hands. "No. She was the real deal. She knew things she had no right to know. And everything she said has come true."

"Bullshit," Kevin said.

"He is right. Everything she said to me so far has come true," Teddy said, looking at Kevin.

"Maybe you can see what you want in the fake mumbo jumbo, but I know for a fact the last thing she said to me cannot happen," Kevin said with a soft chuckle. "That lunatic said Pat was going to kill me. Fat chance of that now with his ashes in a cardboard box in the house over there. What's he going to do? Make me sneeze myself to death?"

Will stared at him with his mouth hanging open in shock. "She said the same thing to me. Pat would be responsible for my death."

Teddy was pale as he looked at them. "Me too. I think it is what drove him to finally kill himself. He believed in it. It freaked him out."

Kevin slapped his knee and laughed loud enough to startle Will and Teddy. "Jesus Christ, you guys are fucking idiots. All three of you. You probably think that the entire night was real. News flash, dipshits, the old hippie said we had to die in Red Station for any of it to come true. And we clearly didn't fucking die that night. How fucking gullible are you? I've got some oceanfront property in Colorado to sell you, a great fucking deal!"

Teddy shook his head slowly and began to pace, "First off, go fuck yourself, Kevin. No matter what you think, our friend is dead. None of the other shit matters at all. Secondly, how else do you explain that night? It wasn't some hippies. It wasn't a Ren Faire."

"It was the goddamned drugs!" Kevin spat. "We were tripping balls. Get a fucking grip, man."

"And we shared a hallucination?" Will asked, the disbelief bright on his face.

Kevin nodded. "The old hippie must've guided us on the trip. Like a dungeon master in Dungeons and Dragons. Think about it, rationally. What makes more sense? A ghost town that appears, what? Every twenty years? Or we took some high-grade drugs and went on an adventure in our heads?"

"Pat didn't—" Teddy began.

"Pat didn't know shit about shit. He was just as dumb as the rest of us. The only difference is he had nothing else to stew over for twenty years, while we moved on and actually did something," Kevin finished for Teddy.

"It felt so real," Will said. "All of it."

Teddy kept pacing, "It did. Too real. But there are parts I don't remember. If I could remember it all, maybe it would make more sense."

Kevin sighed dramatically and waved his hand at Teddy, "Then, by all means, let's put this insanity to bed. I remember most of it. If going over, it will let me get out of this hillbilly hell and back to my bed with silk sheets. I'm ready."

Will nodded. "I have blank spots as well."

Teddy sat down on the floor in front of them and looked out the window at the full moon. "I remember it started with a moon just like that."

August 13th, 1988

THE MOON WAS BRIGHT and full, a silvery sun in a blanket of pure satiny black, with a million pinpricks of pulsating stars. The tents were set up in a small clearing not far from the remains of the Red River Station cemetery and a small fire played within the confines of a stone circle.

"Rangers didn't do shit again this year. Just once I'd like to turn on playoff baseball and see them fighting for the championship," Pat said as he waited for the joint to make its way around.

"They ain't gonna win shit without pitching. They finished behind the White Sox for God's sake," Kevin said as he exhaled a large cloud of smoke.

"Only by one game," Teddy argued before taking a big hit and passing the joint to Will. "Next year is gonna be the year. I have a good feeling. By the time we get back from college, there will be three pennants flying high over the park."

Will didn't say anything. Everyone knew he didn't care much about baseball. He just took a hit and passed it to Pat. Pat inhaled deeply and a seed popped, which made him flinch as an ember fell and landed on his hand. Kevin thought that Pat's yelp of pain was hilarious and began laughing, and soon all four of them were laughing for no reason other than because they could. It was an easy friendship most of the time, even if it felt like they could all hear the clock ticking down on its time. They smoked the joint and drank a few beers while making small talk about all the same local gossip they had talked about a hundred times before.

"It is going to be strange not having you guys around," Pat said sadly. The other three didn't say anything, just exchanged uncomfortable glances. Pat smiled, "I reckon you guys are just excited to finally get the fuck out of this nowhere and make lives for yourselves."

"Fucking right on that one. If it weren't for you, I wouldn't even consider coming back to this shit hole. I am going to get rich and live in skyscraper looking down over New York City. Nocona can kiss my ass," Kevin answered.

"I just want to get away from the heat," Will added.

"And chase them California girls down the beach! Don't you play coy with us, Will. We all know you picked the West Coast because of the half dressed ladies on the beaches," Pat said with a smirk.

Will blushed and looked away, which brought a round of laughter from the guys. For a while they didn't say anything at all, just sat in the kind of comfortable silence that comes from knowing one another at a nearly atomic level. The soft notes of a guitar broke the quiet and made all four of them look around.

"You guys hear that? It's not just me, right?" Teddy asked.

Pat nodded his head and scowled. "Seems we ain't as alone as previously thought."

"Guys, are you seeing this?" Will asked, pointing up at the sky.

As the guitar played, the four of them watched the moon blush above them. Pink spread across the cratered face and slowly grew deeper in shade until the entire moon was drenched in crimson.

"What the fuck?" Kevin muttered as he rubbed his eyes.

"The Red Moon glows, high in the sky, as the old blood wanders, the earth once again," singing accompanied the simple chords that wafted lazily in the thick summer air.

"I haven't ever heard of acid good enough to give four people the same hallucination," Teddy said, his eyes wide enough to not be all pupil, just mostly.

Pat stood up and the other three stared at him slack jawed and his scowl deepened, "C'mon then, let's go see what the ruckus is all about."

"Better yet, we roll another joint and wait for this part of the trip to pass," Kevin countered.

The sound of ladies laughing carried with the music, and Teddy and Kevin both stood up. Will sighed and stood as well, yet never stopped looking up. "I haven't seen anything like this before. A blood-red moon?"

"It is probably something like when it turns all orange," Teddy said with a shrug.

"Indian Moon," Patrick added, "Or Harvest Moon. My daddy always called it an Indian Moon."

Kevin nodded, "Mine does too."

Will shook his head. "But red like this? Don't you think we would have seen this, or at least heard of it?"

Pat put his arm around Will's shoulders. "You are tripping nuts. We all are. There is as much a chance that it is red dust in the air and our fucked-up heads are making it weirder than it has to be."

Will looked disappointed. "And the guitar? People in the woods when it has been silent the whole time. We've been here except for crickets and Kevin bitching?"

Kevin glared at Will. "I was not bitching. I was pontificating."

Teddy laughed, "That's an awful big word for the fifth dumbest guy in the group."

Kevin frowned. "There are only four of us?"

"Exactly," Pat said with a grin as he kicked dirt into the fire.

"Fuck all three of you," Kevin said with a smile as they laughed.

Will looked back at the moon. "Is it weird that the moon turned red at the same time as we heard the guitar?"

"Will. Relax. Probably just some campers that just pulled in," Teddy tried to assuage Will.

"That we didn't hear?" Will argued.

"We were talking. C'mon, I heard ladies laughing. Maybe one of them can get you naked and really have something to laugh at!" Pat said, slapping Will on the back.

Will opened his mouth and then closed it quickly at a glance from Kevin. He shrugged and followed the three as they went into the woods toward where the music seemed to be coming from. The shadows seemed longer and deeper under the crimson glow of the moon, and the thorns on the mesquites seemed to extend slightly, eager to snag clothes and leaving thin lines of blood on the guy's sweaty skin which was a dinner bell for the mosquitos. The laughter grew louder, as did the guitar, but it was the sounds of horses and wagons that confused the four of them.

"Is it a circus?" Teddy asked in a gushed voice.

"Who would bring a circus all the way out here?" Kevin responded sarcastically.

"We would have heard of a circus coming anywhere around here. Ain't been one come through since seventh grade," Pat said with a poke to Kevin's ribs.

"Teddy ate too much cotton candy and puked on Jessica Tawdry during the trapeze flyers," Will said, and everyone laughed.

"The back of her head was pink and blue, and she started screaming. I thought for sure one of them trapeze artists was going to fall," Pat snorted.

"It was the turkey leg. It didn't settle well," Teddy said sadly.

"I heard Bobby McPoyle fingered her after Sadie Hawkins. And that she still hates you to this day," Kevin said as he tugged a thorn out of his sleeve.

"What does one have to do with the other?" Will asked.

Kevin shrugged, "Nothing really. Just saying."

"Bobby McPoyle finger fucked his own cousin at the park. Billy and Jeff saw the whole thing from the creek where they were trying to catch bluegills," Pat said.

"Gross. I bet it was Brenda," Kevin said after a moment.

"They catch any blue gills?" Teddy asked Pat.

"How in the fuck would I know if they caught any blue gills? That wasn't the part of the story that caught my attention." Pat shook his head in wonder and turned to Kevin. "It was Brenda. They told me it sounded like when you make meatloaf, and you jam your hand into the raw meat to stir it up."

"Depends on time of the day, but I've caught blue gills with an empty hook down there," Teddy added as Kevin made a retching noise.

"Why are you so preoccupied with the fucking fish?" Pat demanded.

Teddy frowned. "There won't be much fishing at college, and I am going to miss it."

They exchanged glances that ran from incredulous to sorrowful and stumbled out of the thicket and into a clearing that took anymore words right out of their heads. There was a raging bonfire with great tongues of fire licking up as if to try to taste the red moon, and around it danced a group of topless women as a dirty-looking man with long greasy black hair and matted beard strummed an acoustic guitar. The ladies stopped dancing when they saw the four young men staring at them with slack jaws. The guitarist plucked a bad chord and blinked at them for a second before setting the guitar down and smiling at them. An old VW van as at not far behind the guitar player, in surprisingly great condition.

They all stared awkwardly for a moment until Pat stepped forward and waved his hand. "Howdy."

One of the ladies strutted over to him. A tiara of daisies woven through her red hair, and her blue eyes and hard nipples seemed locked right on him. She came over and ran her fingers lightly down his cheek and smiled at the flush of color that blossomed behind them. "Howdy yourself, cutie," she purred, and her friends giggled.

"Join us for a drink!" the guitar player shouted, and the guys ambled over, trying to sneak glances at the bare breasts without seeming obvious and failing miserably. The guitarist reached into an old-fashioned cooler and pulled out four beers with ice clinging to the cans and passed them out. "The name's Rocky. The girls are Gypsy, Moonbeam, Star, and Whisper. Sorry if we were too loud. We honestly didn't expect to see anyone out here so late."

The guys introduced themselves and sat on the ground by Rocky.

"What the hell, where'd you get these beers? I haven't seen a pull tab since I was little," Kevin asked.

Rocky laughed, "Some little town on the road, man. I don't know for sure. What brings you boys out here?"

"End of summer, one last camping trip before college," Will answered.

Rocky smiled and clapped his hands. "Righteous. The journey to manhood and the leaving of the nest. That's powerful shit, man, really powerful shit."

"And what brings you out to the middle of nowhere, Texas?" Pat asked before taking a long drink of the beer.

The girls all laughed at the question and Rocky drained his beer in one thirsty gulp before belching thunderously, then wiping his mouth. He looked around the clearing. "Seemed like a perfect spot to stop for the night. The girls were restless, trapped in the van. Thought we were far enough out that no one would notice, really."

"Where are y'all from?" Teddy asked.

"San Francisco. We were headed to New York," Rocky replied easily.

"Were?" Will asked softly. Barely a whisper.

"We sort of like it here in Red River Station, been thinking about making it permanent," Star, the redhead, said. "You boys could stay too; we could get to know each other better."

"Red River Station is long gone. All there is out here now is mesquite and rattlesnakes," Teddy said. He looked around at the guys, who nodded.

"All that's left is the graveyard through that thicket," Pat said as he pointed to where they had stumbled out of.

Rocky laughed. "You boys must not get out here very often. There's a bunch of people just around the path." He saw the confused looks on their faces and frowned. "You haven't been to Red River Station? I thought you lived around here?"

"We've lived here our entire lives, and I can assure you there isn't anything out here. I don't know what kind of drugs you're on, but if you have extra, let us know," Kevin said with a sardonic grin.

Gypsy, a slight woman with long blonde hair, stepped forward. "We have the best drugs, but I promise you there is a town just down the path. C'mon, we can show you!"

"Okay!" Teddy said happily. The other three stared at him in surprise. "What? If four topless ladies offer to show you around, you don't say no," he whispered to them.

"Hard to argue that kind of logic," Rocky added helpfully.

"Why not?" Pat asked with a smile. "Ladies, after you."

"I don't even know what is happening anymore," Will muttered.

Kevin laughed, "Then go along with the crazy. Fuck it."

"You coming, Rocky?" Pat asked as he finished his beer.

"Nah, man. I'm good. I'll keep the fire going until you get back," Rocky said, gesturing at the fire. "You girls should take them to see Francesca, really blow their minds."

"Not the only thing I'd like to blow," Whisper said to Moonbeam, who giggled and blushed.

"If Francesca is half as lovely as you ladies, it'll be a pleasure," Pat said, trying his best to be smooth and undone as Teddy started laughing.

"I think it is nice to see a gentleman still exists," Star said with a wink that set everyone off to laughing except Pat, who flushed as red as the moon above them.

The eight of them made their way down the path and back toward the trees and the Red River itself. The mesquites thinned out and were replaced by maples and oaks as the path smoothed out from a winding trail into a wider road. Lights called from ahead, torches with deep orange flames and small yellow lanterns.

"I'll be goddamned," Pat muttered as the gloom was dispelled and a small wild west main street began to coalesce from the red tinged darkness.

"Some kind of Renaissance Faire? One of them old timey spots filled with actors?" Teddy questioned.

"My dad said the hippies used to congregate out here. Maybe they built this during the last year," Kevin added.

The girls giggled, and Star looked at Kevin with a smirk. "And what's the matter with hippies?"

Kevin opened his mouth and Pat sack tapped him to prevent whatever regurgitated angry rant was about to foul his chances at touching those beautiful bare titties. "Motherfucker!" Kevin wheezed instead.

Pat knelt down next to Kevin and whispered, "Do not fuck this up for us, Kevin. I swear to Christ, if you piss the girls off and they put on shirts, there will be a reckoning. There ain't nothing wrong with hippies, you got it?" Kevin glared, but nodded. "Good. I think that Star has taken a fancy to you, so take my advice. Whatever your instincts tell you to say, do the opposite."

Four horsemen came galloping the opposite way, and Will let out a low whistle as they passed. "Did you see the pistols they were carrying? Pearl handled Colts. The real thing too."

"Maybe it is a circus," Teddy said. "Like Buffalo Bill had, a traveling Wild West Show. I need to get my dad out here to check this out. He loves the old westerns."

A group of Native Americans in hides stepped out of one of the low wooden buildings and glared at the eight of them. They had painted faces and long knives strapped to their thighs.

"They even managed to get real Indians," Teddy said, trying not to stare.

"This is insane," Will said as he turned slowly. "This looks just like the painting in the school. Look at that," he said, pointing at the tavern, "That is exactly the same as the one Mr. Hermann showed us in Local History."

"Huh, it really does look like it," Pat said with a grin. "This is the best goddamned acid on the planet."

"But we are all seeing it. I never heard of four people sharing the same hallucination," Will said, agitated by the nonchalance everyone else seemed to be filled with.

"That's not true at all," Whisper said. "We have shared the same trip a bunch of times. It's all about how connected you are, spiritually and emotionally."

Kevin opened his mouth and then looked at Pat and closed it again. He seemed to struggle a bit but nodded with a smile. "I guess the four of us have been closer than brothers since grade school."

Pat smiled at him. "That's the truth."

"Besides, if all of this is just the drugs, doesn't that mean you can do anything you want and not have to worry?" Moonbeam said with a broad smile as she slipped her arm around Pat's waist. "Anything at all?"

"I reckon it does," Pat replied boldly.

"I want to go back to our camp," Will said suddenly. "I don't want to be here anymore. This isn't right. They didn't just build this makeshift town without anyone in the county hearing about it. This land belongs to the state. They wouldn't just let a bunch of actors claim dibs."

"That is exactly what we thought when this land was ours!" one of the Native Americans shouted. His friends didn't laugh, they just glared at the eight of them with blank faces. "All of this was ours until the white man decided he needed room to grow."

"Calm down there, Running Buck, no need to scare our new friends anymore than they already are," Star said cheerfully. She turned to Will, "Look here honey, come see Francesca, and if you're still not happy, I will walk you back to your camp myself. You need to relax as well. You seem so tense."

Will blushed, "It's the moon. I don't like it one bit. Everything feels wrong."

"That sounds like the drugs talking, sweetie. Deep breaths, okay? In with the good, out with the bad," Star said and demonstrated. She smiled as Will took a couple of deep breaths with her. "See? Doesn't that feel better already?"

Will shrugged slightly. "I guess."

Star let out a happy laugh. "Good! Now let's find Franny!"

Francesca's was the same type of roughshod wooden building, but it was painted in bright, garish colors. It looked like a circus tent made of warped wooden boards, as if frozen in time a storm first whipped up. The girls entered the small building first, with Whisper yelling, "Francesca, we bring you visitors!"

The guys entered just as an older woman; they were all four right at eighteen years old, so they guessed her age anywhere from thirty-five to sixty, wearing long green skirts and a white blouse tucked behind a thick black belt with a silver buckle.

"Aww yes, newcomers to visit Madame Francesca, purveyor of the past, present, and future! Come in, come in. There is wine on the table, help yourselves!" she announced merrily, her long olive fingers gesturing to the table. "I see you ladies are up to no good, as always. Tell Rocky he still owes me a visit."

"Wait. Just how long have you people been out here?" Will asked. "From the sounds of things in the clearing, they just got here. Yet everyone knows one another?" Will looked at the others. "None of this adds up."

Madame Francesca laughed, "When time is open to you, past and future become the same thing, William. Those locked onto a linear path cannot suss out the mercurial nature of reality. You need to step outside of it to truly begin to see."

"How did you know his name" Teddy asked. His face gone ashen.

"The same way I know yours, Theodore. The same way I know everything I know," she replied as she poured a goblet of wine and drank noisily.

"She is a fortune teller," Pat said with a grin. "Be a poor one if she didn't listen carefully at the door to hear new voices."

Francesca laughed and slipped the wine onto the table. "Patrick Comstock Harrington, you are a sly one to point out an old lady's tricks."

"Comstock? That's what the fucking C stands for? No wonder you didn't ever tell anyone. I knew it wasn't just a fucking letter. Who gives their kid a letter for a middle name? Fucking psychopaths maybe," Kevin exclaimed, slamming his hand on the table and causing more of the wine to spill.

Pat didn't even look at Kevin, his gaze was glued to Madame Francesca, which made her laugh even harder.

"And you, Kevin, aren't you a curious one?" she asked him.

Kevin shrugged, "That is what my momma always said."

Madame Francesca nodded and then looked at the ladies. "You four head down to the tavern. I will send the men down when they have had their readings."

The girls stood up and bowed slightly, and then smiled at the guys before leaving. The guys looked around the table and each seemed disconcerted, if not outright frightened. Madame Francesca clapped her hands once and candles erupted in flame around the room. The flickering lights drowned out the wan glow of a lone lantern hanging from a peg next to the fireplace.

She stood and gestured to a back room. "I shall do your readings back there, one at a time. When I call for you, come back," and with that she left the main room and shit the door behind her.

"Let's get the fuck out of here," Will said, already half standing.

Teddy made a move to stand as well, and Pat held up his hands. "Easy now guys, what's the harm in playing along with the game?"

"Game? Are you ignoring common fucking sense here? A town that shouldn't be here is here. The moon is bleeding. And did you see those Indians?" Will erupted. "This isn't a fucking game, Pat. This is some seriously crazy shit, and we don't need to be part of it. I leave for the West Coast in two weeks. I don't need this kind of bullshit right before."

"You need to do more of that breathing. In with the good, out with the being a fucking pussy," Kevin said, rolling his eyes. "A bunch of fucking hippies set up a little Ren Faire, and it is too much for your super brain to handle. Jesus, Will, when did you become such a little bitch?"

"Fuck you, Kevin. Our entire lives, you have been a vindictive prick, shitting on everything and everyone with whatever cockamamie bullshit your father told you. These people aren't fucking hippies. I've seen pictures of your dad when he was younger, ponytail down to his ass and covered in dirt, waving the peace symbol. He was the same kind of hippie piece of shit he is always going on about," Will spat.

Kevin glared at him with his fists clenched. He looked ready to flip the table over and go at Will.

"Would you two calm your bullshit? You're acting like toddlers. Is this entire thing kind of crazy? Sure. Is it the drugs? Definitely. But there are sweet, half-naked women willing to hang out with us and that is a luxury our pissant small town has never afforded us in the past," Pat said smoothly. "Just enjoy the fucking trip. God only knows when we will have a chance like this again."

Teddy nodded, "I agree. Sure, this is kind of insane, but how many times have we gotten all kinds of fucked up and done stupider things? Remember when Kevin nearly drowned at the falls after he drank half a bottle of Jack and fell over the edge? Scary as hell until we saw he was fine and then we laughed until we puked."

Will shook his head. "That was different."

"Why? Because we were alone? I think it is cool they tried to recreate the old ghost town," Pat rebutted. He pulled out a long thin joint from his pocket and lit it with one of the candles and passed it to Will. "Here. Calm your nerves a little bit, just go with the flow, man. Get your future read, and then we can go have a few drinks with the ladies."

Will took the joint and hit it twice before passing it to Teddy. He exhaled a cloud of smoke and coughed slightly. "If we die out here, I am never going to forgive you. I'm just saying."

Everyone laughed, and the tension faded for a moment. Then Madame Francesca called out from the other room, "William, please come back."

The guys looked at Will and smiled and nodded at him, and he reluctantly got up and made his way to the back room.

THE ROOM WAS SMALL, the walls were covered by thick carpets and a lone table with a small crystal ball sat in the center. Madame Francesca was sitting in a cloud of incense that filled the air with a pungent sweetness thick and cloying in the confined quarters.

"How does this work? You look into the ball and see my fate?" Will asked with a sarcastic edge to his voice.

Madame Francesca laughed and waved her hand dismissively. "Oh no. I've already seen all of your fates. The crystal ball is just for show, people have certain expectations usually."

"You get a lot of business?"

She smirked. "They come in waves."

Will nodded impatiently. "Can we get this over with? I just want to get back to the fire and enjoy the night with my closest friends, away from all this madness."

"Those three are your closest friends?" Madame Francesca asked. Will nodded. "Then why do they not know your deepest secrets?"

"I don't know what you're talking about," he stated flatly.

She tilted her head and stared at him silently for a moment and then smiled. "You've never told them you prefer the company of men. That you feverishly dream of being taken by them in turn. You hide yourself from them for fear of being spurned, cast out for your true desires."

Will went pale and shook his head. "I am not queer."

"Your heart says different. As does your future. I see it all so clearly. You'll find yourself on the coast."

Will leaned forward. "I have already found myself."

"You have found nothing at all yet. Your friends don't know your inner most longing, because you won't admit it to yourself. College will help you on your path. And all the self hate you have heaped upon yourself will slowly ebb away."

"The stars told you this?" Will asked as he fidgeted in his seat.

"The stars are nothing but lights, billions of miles away. No, William, the moon tells me all the secrets bathed in crimson light. You will see, eventually, for the red moon has marked you already. For all your travels, for all the lies you tell yourself, you belong to the red moon. It has seen your soul and made you its own."

"No. Fuck you. It's the drugs and stress, that's all. This entire thing is a bad trip and when I wake up in the morning, it will all go away."

Madame Francesca laughed. "You are partially correct, William. By morning, this will fade into a half-remembered dream that you will lose the meaning of. But one day, the moon will return and claim the market it has set upon your very soul. When you see Patrick again, he will sound your doom and the fulfillment of the pact."

"What pact?" Will asked in disbelief.

"One of blood spilled," Madame Francesca said softly. Then she raised her hand and blew gently, and a shimmering dust gathered in a cloud around Will's surprised face. "Now go to the tavern. I have secured a special gift for you upstairs."

Will stood sleepily and smiled and then stepped out the back door onto the street as Madame Francesca called for Teddy.

WILL WALKED DOWN THE road with an absent smile on his face and entered the tavern. The girls sat at a table with tall glasses of foamy beer and waved at him. He looked around the large open space at the various card games being played by a variety of strangely dressed people. Cowboys and fifties style salesmen sat across from Native Americans and men dressed like soldiers. An older black man, back crisscrossed with deep scars and manacles around his ankles, played the piano while ladies lined the staircase and smiled down at the crowd.

Will walked up to the bar, and the barkeep wiped a glass and set it front of him. The barkeep filled it with whiskey and smiled. "Franny told me to give you a shot and send you upstairs. Third door on the right."

Will looked at the ladies lining the stairs nervously. "What's up there?"

The barkeep shrugged with a wry smile. "Already paid for."

WILL WALKED DOWN THE road with an absent smile on his face and entered the tavern. The girls sat at a table with tall glasses of foamy beer and waved at him. He looked around the large open space at the various card games being played by a variety of strangely dressed people. Cowboys and fifties-style salesmen sat across from Native Americans and men dressed like soldiers. An older black man, back crisscrossed with deep scars and manacles around his ankles, played the piano, while ladies lined the staircase and smiled down at the crowd.

Will walked up to the bar, and the barkeep wiped a glass and set it in front of him. The barkeep filled it with whiskey and smiled. "Pleasure to meet you. Welcome to the Red River Saloon. Name's Brad."

"Hi. I'm Will. My friends should be here soon," Will said as looked around the tavern. He blinked as the entire room wavered in front of his half unfocused eyes. "This place is cool."

"Thank you. Well ventilated. Usually, it gets as hot as a whore's cheeks during Sunday Service. The breeze helps a fair bit," Brad said with a smile and a twinkle in his brown eyes. "Franny sent word that you're to go upstairs. Third room. Already taken care of," he added with a wink.

Will looked at him and smiled. "What's up there?"

Brad laughed and wiped at the bar absently with an old, stained rag. "Whatever you desire, Will. It's all up to you."

Will lifted his glass of whiskey and nodded to Brad before slamming it back. He let out a wheezing cough as the cheap rotgut flash fried his esophagus, which brought out a cheer from the patrons around him. Will grinned and did a half bow that nearly took him to the floor and then, after a moment, began to climb the stairs.

TEDDY AND KEVIN WAITED outside Madame Francesca's for Pat to come out. He looked at them with bleary eyes and smiled. "Figured you'd be at the tavern with Will."

Teddy shrugged. "Needed a minute to think."

"That woman knows a thing or two about theatrics, but her fortune telling was mostly a load of horseshit," Kevin added with a snarl.

Pat leaned back against the long wooden railing and frowned. "I can barely remember what she said to me, even though she just said it. That's weird, right? Something about doom, a grove of oaks, and that red goddamned moon."

"She didn't mention any trees to me," Teddy said.

"What about doom?" Pat asked fearfully.

"Old bitches like her know the real money is in doom and gloom. Sure, she tells everyone they are doomed," Kevin said as he spat into the dirt.

"All I know is, I am thirsty, and the ladies said they were going to the tavern. I think a couple pairs of titties could salvage this admittedly fucking insane evening quote nicely," Pat said as he pushed himself unsteadily back into a full stand.

"We better hurry or that ginger beanpole will be sweet talking the ladies, and we'll have to watch him as he drowns in breasts," Teddy said, putting his arm around their shoulders.

"Do y'all really think I could be the cause of all of our dooms?" Pat asked before they began walking.

"You're too ugly to lead me to my doom. But that blonde could definitely start me down that path," Kevin said with a grin.

"I trust you with my life, Pat. Always have, always will," Teddy said.

Pat was silent for a moment and then nodded once. "I think I am super fucked up."

"Then that means it is time for more," Kevin said matter-of-factly. "Being fucked up is like being crazy. Those that can question it are definitely not nearly one or the other."

"That sounded almost intelligent," Teddy gasped.

"He sure as hell didn't learn that from his father," Pat added with a grin. "Not nearly racist enough, and not a single mention of cousin fucking."

Kevin didn't say anything, just strode across the street with his nose in the air toward the tavern. Pat looked back at Madame Francesca's with a haunted look, which quickly evaporated as Teddy ran after Kevin and hurried to join.

***

WILL KNOCKED ON THE door to the room with a number three painted in bright red.

"Come in, William," a voice called through the door.

Will opened the door and crimson light flooded out of the door. He blinked at the sudden suffusion of vermillion and peered into the room. Incense burned, releasing thick plumes of scented smoke that coated his nostrils and tongue with thick tendrils of perfumed sweetness. A figure reclined on a large bed, bathed in the bloody light where red silk was draped over lanterns, elongating shadows and distorting perception.

"Please, shut the door, William," the voice beckoned.

Will felt trepidation, but pulled the door shut behind him. The front of his mind felt too heavy, his thought dripping slowly through the drugs and smoke, while a tiny voice screamed in fright from the hollows buried deep inside. "I'm not sure what this is all about really, but whatever it is, just tell Madame Francesca I appreciated it, and we can call this a night," he said nervously.

A throaty laugh boomed through the smoky room. "You haven't even had a chance to see the wares before you dismiss them, William. How about you give them a gander first, and then decide?"

"I, uh, I am not really sure what you mean. But no, no thank you, I think I am good to go. My friends will be here soon and it's our last night together before we go our separate ways. I appreciate it, though, truly," Will said as he reached for the doorknob.

The figure rose from the bed, a swirl of long robes, a red shadow in the harsh light, and seemed to glide over to Will, who stood pressed against the door. "Come now, William, don't be so hard to get. The Red Room is a den of pleasures, and you have a free pass. Tell me what you want, and I will fulfill your every desire," the voice whispered into his ear.

Will turned, and the silk clad body wrapped around him, hot lips pressed against him, and his words were muffled as a soft tongue slipped into his mouth. He struggled at first but found himself melting into the other. His hands gripped the silk as the mouth found his neck and bit gently. He stiffened as a hand slid across the crotch of his jeans, tracing the outline of his erection, and he tried to focus. "I can't," he moaned.

"But you want to," the voice cooed. "I have everything you could desire."

Will felt a hand grip his arm and pull it down to a taut thigh. The lips found his again, and he fell into the kiss, even as his eyes betrayed him, and all he could see was a shimmering red. He did his hand up and felt the hard cock pressing against silk, not his own, but that didn't stop him from gently cradling it, running his fingers around the shaft and feeling a shiver of desire course through him. "I'm not gay. I'm not," he whispered as he gripped tighter.

"But you want me, don't you, William?" the voice asked softly.

Will didn't speak, he couldn't. His hand softly stroked, and his mouth sought flesh. He felt himself being guided toward the bed and he was powerless to stop, led on by the leash of desire swollen in his hand. At the edge of the bed, the figure disrobed, and even though the light playing through the smoke made everything indistinct, the lithe form beckoned his hands and mouth to explore. He felt his belt unbuckle and his pants slide off onto the floor. The voice in his brain that was screaming at him to cease was erased as he felt the hot tongue gently circle the head of his cock. He let out a long moan and sank back onto the bed, smiling as the other shifted and those shapely thighs slipped over his shoulders.

"LADIES," PAT SAID AS he stood by the table, looking around the main room of the tavern. "Where's Will?"

Moonbeam giggled and pointed upstairs. The guys looked and saw the ladies lining the mezzanine and then looked at each other with wide eyes.

"He is up there?" Teddy asked in surprise.

"With a lady?" Kevin added.

The girls laughed. Star nodded. "He came in and went right to the bar, and then upstairs. He didn't even stop to chat."

"Dang," Pat said. "He wasted no time."

Whisper pouted a little. "I thought he was a cute, good boy. I was going to change that tonight, but it seems like his tastes run toward the older."

Kevin laughed. "I've known Will for my entire life, and I didn't even know he had any kind of taste at all. Good for him, though. I was pretty sure he was going to die a virgin."

Teddy frowned. "He is just particular. Always has been. That's just Will."

"We need to have some beers ready for when he makes his triumphant entrance," Pat decided.

Gypsy pointed at the mugs of beer on the table. "Drink up, boys. Brad will happily keep the suds flowing. Sit down and drink. He may be up there for a while. A young, virile stud like that can go all night."

She looked at Teddy and winked. "I bet you know all about that, cutie."

Teddy blushed and grabbed a mug to hide his red face as everyone else laughed.

"How was Franny?" Moonbeam asked, as the laughter faded.

The three guys looked at each other briefly and then shrugged. "It must not have been that great. If I'm honest, I can barely recall what she said," Pat answered.

"Me either," Teddy and Kevin said together.

"Jinx! You owe me a coke, cocksucker!" Kevin said loudly.

The old man playing the piano stopped and everyone turned to look at their table, which brought out a fresh gale of laughter.

Then Pat stopped and cocked his head. "Did you hear that?"

"Hear what?" Kevin asked.

"Listen," Pat replied.

They all sat still for a moment and listened carefully. Teddy's eyes widened. "Was that Will?"

And then they all heard it. Will was practically screaming.

"Are those good noises, or bad ones?" Kevin asked quietly.

"Sounds like both, if you ask me," Pat replied with concern.

"Go upstairs and check on him, if you're worried," Star said with a grin. "Maybe you can join in."

Another pained groan sounded, and Pat stood up. "I'll just go knock on the door and make sure he is okay."

Teddy and Kevin stood up immediately. "Us too," Teddy said.

"I just want to see," Kevin said with a smile.

Brad smiled at them as they passed the bar, and the ladies on the steps slid toward the banister as they passed with big smiles and a healthy showing of flesh.

"This place is fucking awesome," Kevin said. "I could see myself retiring in a place like this. Hot women, plenty of beer. This might be heaven."

"Better than fancy ass New York? What about your penthouse overlooking Manhattan?" Pat chided.

"I could come here during the winters and drown myself in pussy and booze instead of suffering in the snow," Kevin answered without hesitation.

"That does sound like paradise," Teddy said, wobbling slightly.

They stood outside of the door with the number three painted in deep red and listened to the sounds coming from within. The cries seemed to alternate from pleasure to pain, and they looked at each in confusion. Kevin shrugged and raised his fist to knock on the door, but before he managed to touch it, the door slid open. They stood frozen for a moment, staring into the haze of ruddy light.

"What the fuck?" Pat asked dully.

They saw Will bent over the bed, face buried in a pillow, naked as a jaybird in the red room. And behind him was a monster with long horns sticking out of the side of its head, slamming a grotesquely large penis into Will, who screamed with every thrust.

Pat didn't hesitate. He stormed into the room and tried to tackle the demon. The horned head turned to him and glared with pinpricks of dusky light toward him in disdain and threw him against the wall. "You're next, Patrick," it growled, never losing rhythm as it slapped harder and harder against Will's behind.

Teddy and Kevin stood horrified in the doorway as Pat picked himself up and grabbed a chair and smashed it over the monster's back. This got the creature's attention, and it turned toward him and roared and backhanded Pat, who slammed into the vanity on the opposite side of the room.

"Get Will!" Pat croaked in obvious pain as the monster pushed Will's limp body onto the bed and moved for Pat.

Teddy and Kevin watched in horror as the thing crossed the room before rushing in to grab Will, who was half passed out on the bed. Kevin jerked the lanky Will to his feet and Teddy pulled his pants from around his ankles. Pat crouched low by the vanity and threw a bottle of perfume that shattered against the floor in front of the creature. Teddy and Kevin were pulling the sluggish Will out of the room as Pat reached around for something else to throw, anything to buy them a few more moments. Then he saw the gleam of metal under the vanity, a sawed-off shotgun secured by a leather holster along with a box of shells. He didn't think, just remembered his dad's lessons and jerked the weapon free, took a steadying breath, and squeezed the trigger. A blast of buckshot tore one of the horns off the creature, who roared in pain and was spun around. Pat pulled the trigger again, and a hole was ripped through the monster's chest, and it slumped to the floor.

"Pat. You need to see this. Bring the gun," Teddy called over the ringing in Pat's ears.

Pat pushed himself up slowly and grabbed the box of shells and reloaded the shotgun before staggering to the doorway where his friends stood. He pushed through them and froze in place. The women that had been standing on the mezzanine were all hanging a couple feet off the ground, gray skinned with coarse ropes around their necks. A loud buzzing filled the air as he stepped out far enough to look over the railing. The remaining tavern goers were shambling about the lower floor of the building, twisted and deformed monstrosities that in no way resembled the townsfolk happily drinking moments before. As one, they looked up at him and snarled.

"Fuck," Pat muttered.

"What the fuck is happening?" Kevin shouted.

"I don't know, but we need to get the fuck out of here, pronto," Pat said as the creatures began to climb the stairs.

"Where?" Teddy asked desperately.

"Check the other rooms. There has to be a window or something. Maybe back stairs outside!" Pat shouted.

The first of the creatures made its way up the stairs and Pat shot, taking off half of its head. Kevin scrambled to the other doors and kicked them open as Teddy pulled the still dazed Will after him.

"Found an open window!" Kevin shouted. "Hurry up, we can climb out onto the street!"

Pat fired again and then spilled the box of shells onto the floor as another creature made the landing. He charged forward and swung it upside the creature's face with a sickening thud and then ran to the room the others had charged into with three of the deformed monsters at his back. Kevin was already on the ground, and Teddy was close behind with Will clinging to his back like an oversized child. Pat felt the claws swiping through the air. "Go on without me!"

"Jump! I'll catch you!" Kevin called back.

Pat shrugged free of one of the grasping hands and flung himself out the window where he landed on Kevin, both hitting the ground as the air was driven from their lungs.

"What the fuck is happening?" Will mumbled.

"Some demon was raping you and Pat blew its head off," Teddy said. "We need to fucking move!"

Will just blinked in confusion and looked up at the menacing red moon glaring down on them.

"He said to fucking move!" Pat said, pushing Will into motion as the four of them ran down the road.

They ran full tilt, even though the monsters didn't seem to be pursuing. The road turned back into a trail as they stumbled back out into the clearing where the bonfire raged.

"Looks like you boys got into it there at Red River Station," Rocky called when he saw them, a large grin on his face. "Where's the girls?"

The four of them stood, panting, and stared at the trail behind them. They looked at him with eyes wide with fear.

"You need to get the fuck out of here! There's some kind of fucking monsters back there!" Pat shouted to Rocky.

Rocky laughed and slapped his thigh. "Monsters? You boys sound like you're having a bad trip. Come over here and sit down. Have a beer and calm yourselves and tell me what happened. Did you see Franny?"

They didn't sit, nor did they accept one of the offered beers as they told what little they could. They already found the sheer terror evaporating as the scene in the tavern began to grow indistinct.

"That is one hell of a story, boys. Monsters? In the tavern? That's a new one for me, for sure. You sure?" Rocky asked with a smile.

"Pretty fucking sure, man," Teddy muttered angrily.

"Maybe you four need to get some shuteye and sleep it off. Things always look better in the morning light. Except whores. That's the reason they work late shifts," Rocky said with a laugh.

"Aren't you worried about the girls?" Pat asked, obviously confused.

Rocky laughed and pointed at the trail where the four ladies came happily strolling into the clearing. "Not really, man. They look good to me."

The guys stared at the ladies in disbelief. Then Teddy fell boneless to the ground, snoring gently. Will followed suit, as did Kevin. Pat stood wobbly for a moment, trying to figure out what was happening, before succumbing himself.

THEY WOKE THE NEXT morning in their tents, each was in a foul mood, and they barely spoke as they tore down camp and trudged back to the car. Teddy tried to talk about what he remembered but was met with stony silence from the others and gave up. Each of them tried to make sense of the tattered images inside their heads and grew surlier as the details slipped in and out of focus. Something had happened.

They just didn't know what. It had felt like a big deal but slid through their fingers like sand as they grasped at particulars. Pat dropped them off at their houses. No intention of this being the last time he saw them, just lost in his own head where he heard an older woman laughing and proclaiming Doom.

August 13th, 2008

THE THREE OF THEM sat silently in the loft for a few minutes.

"It was the drugs, plain and simple," Kevin stated. "There were no monsters. Just four idiots roaming the woods."

"I keep telling myself that as well," Teddy said softly. "It doesn't explain how we all three remember it the same way."

"Not all of us remember it the same way. Isn't that right, Will?" Kevin asked.

"Fuck you, Kevin," Will spat.

"Maybe if you'd tried that night, Pat wouldn't have hung himself in the woods. I always knew you were gay. We all did. The tall, redheaded fag is what my dad called you, remember?" Kevin said snidely back.

Will didn't say a word. He stood up, walked over to where Kevin sat, and punched him in the mouth. Kevin hit the floor and sat bloody on the rug. He made a move to get up, and Teddy walked between them and glared down at him. "You deserved that much, Kevin."

"Why the fuck do you think I was ashamed of who I was?" Will asked through tears. "Your dad always called me a fag. Hell, mine did as well. It wasn't like I made the decision one day to be gay. It wasn't a choice."

"We know that, Will," Teddy said calmly. "We never would have cared then, and we certainly don't now. I wish you'd have told us back then, though. Imagine how cool it would have been to be friends with the only gay guy in the county."

Will smiled a little at that. "Probably not the only gay guy in the county."

Teddy laughed. "Probably not. But still."

"I'm sorry," Kevin said from the floor.

"What?" Will asked in surprise.

"I am sorry, Will. Fuck. I know my dad was an asshole. I didn't need you three reminding me all the time about it. I guess a lot of him rubbed off on me."

Will nodded and extended his hand to help Kevin stand up. "I don't take the punch back. You've had that coming for a long time."

Kevin smiled. "Probably so. This make us even?"

Will nodded again and Teddy wrapped them both in a big hug. All three of them embraced as years flowed down their cheeks.

"It isn't the same without Pat, you know?" Teddy said through sobs.

"He is probably watching down on us right now, with that fucking smile of his that says he was right all along," Will said with a ghost of a smile.

"He was always the smartest of the bunch. God damn, I miss him. I missed you guys, too. I didn't realize it. Life gets in the way and the past just sort of becomes the past," Kevin said sincerely.

Will stiffened suddenly, and Teddy looked at him in confusion, his pale face even more white somehow. "What's wrong?"

Will didn't answer. He just pointed toward the window. The moon, once fat and yellow through the branches of the old oak trees, had blushed a soft pink. As they watched, the pink darkened into a bloody mask that pulsated with crimson rage. The three of them walked over to the window and looked out at the small yard between the house and barn. Underneath the baleful red light of the moon stood Pat, smiling at them.

Whisper, Gypsy, Moonbeam, and Star stood behind him, still topless and looking as if they hadn't aged a day in the last twenty years. The three of them stared down in horror at their friend, who smiled maliciously back up at them. The barn doors creaked as someone or something opened them.

FIVE

INSATIABLE

October 1873, Colorado Territory

Part One

THE SNOW CAME EARLY that year, fat flakes that signaled a bad winter to come as the passes seemed determined to fill in a month and a half early. The side of the mountain was swaddled in freshly fallen snow as flurries swept along lower and lower, covering all in its wake. It became increasingly difficult to determine distance as the thick flakes reduced visibility and muffled sounds. A majestic savagery overtook the land, growing deeper and strangling, all in its incessant need. A snowy owl took flight from a rock high above, a silent shadow on the too quiet night circling above.

A lone wolf crunched through the drifting snow. It paused, nostrils flared as the wind changed directions and a new scent found its way from a thicket of pine trees. The wolf stopped, ears pinned back and yellowed fangs gleaming dully. It lowered its center of gravity as a snarl warned in a low rumble, shaking its way through the heavy air. Hunger etched into malevolent eyes as it moved slowly towards the strange odor of rot, need overriding fear in the cold.

The wind howled through the needles of the pines, sending them scattering like miniature darts through the darkness. The wolf's hackles rose as the stench grew stronger. It stopped at the edge of the thicket; uncertainty not familiar in the alpha mind of the beast. There was no consideration for danger left in the lone creature, its pack long dead at the hands of the hairless ones that controlled thunder to kill from afar. But this wasn't the same scent as those, not entirely.

This was new. Confusing. Intimidating. This was the malodorous scent of death.

The wolf's legs trembled as its tail snaked between the powerful hindquarters. It spun to snap behind it, jaws catching only air. The cloud of decay seemed to come from everywhere at once, no longer confined to the trees. The wolf could sense the impending doom but could not rationalize from where it came. So, it did what instinct told it to; it snarled and snapped, working itself into a frenzy of perilous adrenaline. The snow seemed to shift beneath it, which sent it bounding straight up with a spray of urine across the virgin white.

An emaciated, gray, human-like blur exploded from the snow with a howl and tackled the wolf from midair. The wolf howled for the pack that could no longer hear as the gray monster wrapped its powerful arms around the wolf's chest. With one grunt of exertion from the creature, loud cracking sounds filled the frigid night and a spray of blood steamed on the snow in front of them.

The wolf's corpse was tossed to the ground with barely a sound. The monster screamed gutturally in victory, a horrid sound that echoed off the surrounding mountains. Then it threw itself down and tore open the stomach of the wolf, viscera and blood streaming from the furry rent. The creature thrust its head into the open wound and began to noisily feast. Ripping and tearing through the organs with a fevered need, it snapped ribs and sucked at the marrow. There was only need in those pitch-black eyes as it ravaged the corpse of the wolf. With every tearing bite, the musculature gained definition, filled out the form into a semblance of a human. With great effort, it forced itself to stop, staring balefully at the scattered remains. It began scrabbling across the snow and tossed the steaming gore back into what remained of the body cavity before hauling it into the small grove of pines.

The long wings of the owl let the wind carry it high above the carnage. It watched keenly, hoping to find a forgotten chunk of succulent flesh. The creature was thorough though, and nothing remained but blood splattered snow quickly hidden by the drifts. It seemed as if the entire valley had been stripped clean of prey as the last circles drifted farther and farther from the nest. The snow didn't take notice of the owl or the creature hiding in the pines. It just mindlessly fell the entire night.

IN A SNOW SWEPT cave, the creature sleeps restlessly.

Hasse Ola stood under the blinding sun, one hand shielding his eyes as he watched River break the stallion bareback on the dusty plains that stretched out seemingly forever in all directions. The silvery horse bucked and fought every step of the way, a sheen of sweat in its metallic fur. River had two handfuls of the spun platinum mane, whispering softly into the panicked horse's ear nonsensically. Hasse had a sense of memory as the grit in the air stung against his cheek, as if this had happened before. He stood frozen in place, feeling dread well up inside of him as the horse grew nearer and nearer to a small patch of scrub. He didn't know how, but he knew there was a rattlesnake in the brush.

The horse screamed suddenly. Hasse Ola saw the two small spots of blood, vivid on the silver leg, just above the hoof. Time slowed as River was thrown from the back of the stallion, arms flailing as he hit the hard-packed earth with a loud exhalation and the crack of bone as his forearm splintered and lay at an odd angle. The horse was frothing.

A thick spray of pink tinged foam dripped down its muzzle as its eyes rolled back until only white showed. It screamed again, weaker now, before stumbling and eventually falling with a loud thud that knocked up a cloud of red dust. Hasse Ola watched the snake as it slithered away from the scene across the hot, rocky ground.

Hasse Ola didn't move. His eyes were fixated on River lying unconscious on the ground. His stomach rumbled low and long. He was starving. It felt as if he hadn't eaten in weeks. Months.

Do it.

Hasse Ola looked around in fright. There was no one there. He looked back at River and licked his lips. He could feel the excess spit as it ran down his chin.

Eat.

"No. I cannot. I will not." His voice sounded hoarse. How long had it been since he had spoken? How long since he had fed? "River is my brother, my family. I will not." But how he wanted to. "The horse..." he trailed off, repulsed by the very thought.

Feast.

Hasse Ola found himself moving towards the horse's corpse against his volition. He tried to stop himself, but the fiery agony in his guts was stronger than his will. He was in front of the body, shudders of anticipation and need sweeping through him. He found himself on his knees, his buck skinning blade in his hands. Tears streamed down his cheeks; the need, the ache, the sorrowful act of driving the blade into the abdomen of the horse. It split open, and he grabbed the liver and held it in his shaking hands. Revulsion colored the hunger, yet he couldn't stop himself from tearing off a mouthful of the raw organ.

"Hasse? What-what are you doing?" River called weakly.

Hasse Ola turned and stared at his dearest friend, at his brother, and saw the look of horror on the painted face. He couldn't speak, the chewy liver filling his mouth to capacity. He gestured towards River and froze in shock. His arm was a sickly gray shade, far too thin and gangly. Hasse looked down in shock to find that he was nude, his entire body the sickly gray color of the damned. He threw his head back and howled, spittle and chunks of liver spraying into the air. His agonized screams reverberated off the plains, multiplied before reaching his ears.

And just behind it, buried in the madness and terror, he heard laughter. Laughter, he recognized as his own, coming in hisses that intertwined with the loss to make a full symphony of the cursed.

* * *

"IF'N YOU DON'T SHUT up that little bastard, I swear…" Josiah Swift screamed from the hard-wooden seat of the wagon.

The horses whinnied as the iron banded wooden wheels were buried deeper into the heavy snow. It was a fight for every inch that was soon becoming insurmountable. And the wailing child seemed to make the laborious attempts at clearing the valley even worse. The shrill cries bounced off the rocky slopes. Even the near blizzard couldn't seem to mute it. Josiah felt bad immediately after his outburst. The sharp intake of breath from his wife, Mildred, lent a hefty dose of shame as well. Then the cracking of timbers snapping rose overall, followed by cursing from one of the wagons farther back on the line. Josiah muttered angrily to himself as he stopped trying to force the horses forward. To his dread, he saw the opposite end of the valley was already a blur. He muttered an angry prayer to the heavens.

"Josiah! Charles had an axle snap! His wagon is done for!" Lot called out from somewhere in blowing snows.

Josiah spat out more curses as he pulled the furs around his shoulders tighter. The damnable wind seemed content to howl the entire evening as it cut through every layer of fur. "Looks like we are settling in for the evening!" he shouted over that accursed wind. "Circle them up! We need to break the wind so we can have a clearing for a fire! Let's move!"

The thirteen wagons made slow progress in the drifts, that ceaselessly built up with every moment of excruciatingly syrupy movement. It was by the blessings of God Almighty the valley was of a suitable size, if a rough, tight fit. Even as the baby, Daniel, continued to cry with every jostled movement that tested the boundaries of man's will in the face of crisis. In these moments, a being's character shone in the face of hardship, for only after the enduring of trials can paradise be redeemed. While it was impossible to gauge time with the heavy gray clouds covering every inch of sky above, internal clocks said it was after noon.

They moved stiffly in the bone chilling air as they hung bear skins on ropes between the wagons to prevent the whirling snow from encroaching any farther. Economically, they took axes to the trees nearest the makeshift campsite. Quickly, they felled them, stripping limbs and bark as clouds of steam from the effort surrounded their heads like halos. The men—eleven Swifts ranging from brothers to cousins, the jovial man Edgar Twain, and the odd man out, Lot Baker—were tireless. The oldest boys searched the woods for game to add to the cook-pot that sat filled with snow over the crackling fire. The womenfolk silently unloaded the lame wagon as the small children played in the snow.

"Paw!" Samuel called out against the howling storm. The silhouettes of the other hunters slowly materialized in the surrounding snow.

Josiah looked up after a final crack of his axe, felled another oak tree. David and Zebadiah dragged it away quickly as he answered, "Speak, boy!"

Samuel trod through the snow towards his father. "The area is empty, Paw. Not a squirrel or deer or nothin'. We searched most of the woods. Maybe the storm sent them to scatter."

Josiah pulled his pipe from his jacket pocket and carefully tapped it against the new stump by his legs. He pulled a leather satchel and carefully undid the drawstrings. "Now, son, I don't reckon that an entire valley can be emptied of wildlife. Does it not say the Lord has filled the world with an abundance of animals?" Samuel nodded as Josiah took a pinch of tobacco and thumbed it into the pipe. "If'n the Lord God Himself truly knows all and watches down upon us, it falls unto us to see His will done. An all-knowing God would not create such a beautiful valley and leave it barren, would He?" Samuel shook his head and watched his father stick a splinter from the pine into the lantern. It smoldered then ignited and Josiah quickly brought it to his pipe. He exhaled a great blue gray cloud into the air.

"There is a stream, maybe a small river, down a ways. Fast moving. We could string a net across. I saw some fish," Samuel said thoughtfully.

Josiah smiled and patted the boy on the shoulder, ignoring the flinch. "Grab Lot, he's a mite better with nets than he is with an axe. This may be home for a few days. Water and fish will do us good."

Samuel made a face as he looked over at Lot Baker. The man was pale and sickly looking, with dark sunken eyes in his rodent like face. But he knew better than to argue with Paw, especially with everything going on.

* * *

"God damn it, Samuel! Hold the line tight! Won't do us a bit if good to have the net fill with fish and pull free because you left too much slack!" Lot yelled across the stream.

Lot stared at the fast-moving waters; they were deceptively deep in places. Lot Baker was a lot of things in this world, but stupid was not one of them. He had sent Samuel across the treacherous creek. Damn near a river, actually. Most certainly swelled when the ice melted, judging by the tree line. One misstep and that current would drag you a mile in moments. The other boys searched the woods for any sign of life in the meantime as the two fought to secure the netting.

Lot didn't care much for the lack of anything that surrounded them. Reminded him of the War, how they would camp in an area long enough to leave a void in nature. A dead man's land of nothingness for miles. But that was over a span of weeks in one place. According to the townsfolk, though, no one had crossed the valley in months. Rumors had whispered of something. No one knew what exactly, just something bad stalking the woods. He laughed when they said that; small-town folk with big superstitions.

"About time! Tie the God's be damned thing tightly so we can get back. I don't like it out here. Not one bit. Hurry, boy!" Lot shouted at Samuel. Lot looked around nervously as the wind howled. But it was something else that was raising his hackles, eyes upon him, triggering memories of rifles and explosions.

The other boys had gathered along the bank of the river and watched as Samuel made his way carefully across the logs and rocks that haphazardly spanned the white, frothed waters. "Hurry, boy!" Lot muttered as he turned back and forth, his eyes trying to pierce the sideways-blowing snow.

Samuel found solid ground and watched Lot in confusion. "What is it, Mr. Baker?" he asked.

Lot shook his head, unsure himself. "Most likely nothing. Let's get back to camp. The storm is whipping itself back up."

The teen boys and Lot began the hike back through snow-laden woods to the campsite as the wind shifted directions to blow directly in their faces. The going got slower as they fought for every step, the snow like stinging nettles against their exposed faces. Great gusts pushed, so they hunched forward with a struggle to gain every inch. Instinctively, they moved in a v pattern, Lot taking the point of the arrowhead. He stopped, holding up his hand to signal the rest as well. His sunken eyes took in the land around them. That feeling of being watched grew stronger.

A roar carried over the biting snow and wind. A snowbank erupted, spraying snow in large clumps over them. And there stood an angry, near emaciated, bear on its hind legs just to the left of the formation. It burst forward with a swipe of its paws. Ezekiel Swift was sent flying with a great gout of crimson spraying through the air, near black against the pristine white. Chaos broke out as the group scattered. Samuel ran in the direction Ezekiel had been launched.

Lot stared for a moment of bewildered shock before taking off. Unfortunately for him, the visibility and his panic sent him headfirst into a tree. Lot hit the trunk with a near skull splitting crunch, only to bounce back through the air, skidding across the snow directly at the feet of the bear. It stared down hungrily at the meal that had served itself up and roared again.

Lot was conscious enough to know this was his end. His body ached, but he could not find the use of his limbs. As the nimbus of black slowly took his sight and merciful unconsciousness took him far from the pain that was coming, he saw a streak of gray race forward and throw itself at the bear. Lot's last thought before sinking into the darkness was of something attacking the bear and concern for the boys. Then nothing.

"WE DON'T SEE MANY of your type 'round here much anymore. You ain't fixin' to make no trouble, is ya?" the barkeep asked around an impossibly large wad of chewing tobacco. He spat a streak of brown that dribbled down his chin as he stared at the newcomer.

River stood silently for a moment. He watched the barkeep wipe the spittle from his face with a stained rag. Then he watched as the barkeep wiped down a glass with the same rag. River shook his head; both disgust and towards causing trouble. He had deep circles beneath his eyes and a hardness to him that set most to unease. "No. I am headed West. On a hunt."

The barkeep nodded. "One of them spiritual mumbo jumbo quests? You gonna find the spirit of your grandpappy or somethin'?"

River nodded curtly. "Something like that. I just need a place to stay for the evening and provisions for crossing the mountains."

"Ain't crossing the valley trail, and be thankful for that small blessing," a drunkard at the bar said blearily.

River stared at him. "And why not?"

The drunk began snoring loudly, and the barkeep let out a low chortle and another stream of shit brown saliva leaked to the floor. "Blizzard came early. Been raging for two days pert near through now. Poor bastards headed to the 'Promised Land' are probably stuck up there as we speak. Poor souls. That ain't the place to be, even without a storm."

River turned the brunt of his intense glare onto the barkeep. "Why is it not a place to be? It is an easy ride through the mountains, is it not?"

"Look, Injun Joe, or whatever you call yourself, the pass ain't safe no more. There're stories. All the game is gone. All that is left is a dead man's land," one of the faro players answered.

River leaned against the bar and eyed the card player. "And why is that?"

"Monster in the woods. Least, that's what the last group to come through headed east said. They never seen it but told tall tales of a gray blur in the woods. My money is on a bear of some sort," the card player answered knowledgeably. The other card players grunted agreement, and they resumed playing as River stood silently.

His eyes found the roaring fire in the blackened fireplace, and he watched the flames flicker without seeing them. His mind was on the tribes. The fires that swept through the hide skin tents and shelters. The bodies ripped to pieces and partially consumed strewn across the blood-soaked ground. The past year chasing rumors of a gray-skinned devil.

"I said it will be fifty cents for the room. The general store opens not long after dawn. You stayin' or not, boy?" the barkeep said, apparently, for the second time.

"How many were on the wagons headed West?" River asked quietly.

The barkeep looked confused at this response. "Huh? I didn't count. They stayed out of town for the most part, 'cepr for that nervous looking man. He said there was thirteen wagons coming from

Illinois to the Promised Lands out West. Whatever in tarnation that means." He gave a distrustful stare at River, "Why?"

River didn't answer. He just pulled up his hood and went out into the freezing night.

"Good riddance, goddamned Savage," the barkeep called after him. River heard the laughter as he rode off towards the West.

Part Two

THE WORLD CAME TO focus as stabbing pain. Lot's eyes flickered open briefly before they squinted closed in a rush with a wince of agony. Prudence Swift let out a gasp and ran, ducked her head back out of the wagon. Lot thanked God silently for her discretion in not shouting until out of the wagon. Lot tried to gingerly lift his head and a roiling ball of nausea swept over him and he gratefully put his face over the bucket next to him.

The back of the wagon opened as Lot retched bile and acid into the bucket. Josiah Swift looked in with concern written boldly across his stoic face. "The hero lives. God truly smiled down upon you, my friend."

Lot rasped, the acid on his vocal cords burning as he spoke. "The boys?"

Josiah climbed up into the wagon. He smiled and reached down, setting a reassuring hand on Lot's shoulder. "Ezekiel was killed immediately. Samuel found him with his head broken from flying into a tree. The bear had sliced him badly enough, had the tree not ended it mercifully he would have lingered in pain. Enoch fled and stumbled into the water. He was swept away." Josiah looked away as sorrow clouded his vision. He wiped his eyes and smiled slightly. "The rest managed to escape, thanks to your bravery. By the time we had gotten to you, all that remained of the bear was a bloody trail that ended at the river."

Lot stared at him in confusion. "I did nothing. Hit my fool head on a tree. Was surely a dead man. Then I passed out where I lay." His face looked haunted.

Josiah nodded curtly. "I have heard tales of a man's instincts taking over. Your army training must have saved your life. Whatever it was, we are thankful for your bravery. The boys owe you their lives. God smiles down on you."

Lot grabbed Josiah's sleeve. "How long was I out?"

"The better part of four days. Today is the first the snow has stopped. But the skies look angry still. We are stuck, or so it would seem. Rest. I'll have Salvation or Prudence bring you a bowl of stew and water. There is no rush." Josiah patted Lot on the arm and turned and left.

Lot just stared at the wagon roof. His training had nothing to do with his survival, he was sure. He couldn't shake the image of the gray blur slamming into the bear. He laid back, stared at but didn't see the wagon roof. "I told you we done left too late in the year, Josiah Swift. I told you and your flock. What happens next rests square upon your shoulders, you prideful bastard." A soft rap on the side of the wagon stirred him from his mutterings. "Aye!"

Bright eyed Sally Swift peeked her head into the wagon. "Uncle Josiah sent me with stew and water, Goodman Baker."

"Thank you kindly, Salvation Swift. You can just leave it there. I promise to eat and drink every bit," Lot responded politely.

Sally blushed deep red and placed the bowl and pitcher inside the wagon. "I shall return to check on you soon."

Lot smiled at her. The stew smelled delicious for a moment before a fresh wave of nausea coiled in his stomach. He clenched his fists with eyes tightly closed. That damned image of a gray blur, burnt into his eyelids, taunted him as he tried to stop the spinning through sheer will.

THE SNOW, HAVING STOPPED falling for a few days, would have been a blessing had the already fallen powder stopped piling up against the wagons. Soon, the makeshift camp was surrounded by ten to fifteen-foot drifts on all sides, and the entrances to the valley were even worse, as it seemed every stray flake had found itself aimlessly joining the white mass. The wind remained an endless source of misery on top of it all. The stew pot grew emptier and emptier as the meager supplies ran out. The banks of snow proved treacherous for any but the smallest boys to climb and the fear of the wounded bear somewhere out there made a trip to the stream to check the net nigh impossible.

A few days turned into a week. As the days trickled by, the skies began to darken again. As the last of the stew was scraped from the pot, the storm returned. Reinvigorated. River stood hidden in a copse of trees above the snow-ringed wagons, and watched, careful to avoid being seen by anything that may be watching the starving people below. He refused to allow himself to feel for the poor bastards trapped beneath him. He had not allowed himself to feel anything after he buried the tribes folk. He had wept himself empty of anything but cold edged hatred. And now, after a year of hunting, his quarry was near. River grinned without warmth as he watched the perfect bait slowly starve. If Hasse Ola were here, as River suspected, this would surely draw him out. The Wendigo would not be able to resist such an easy feast on this empty stretch of land.

River would have offered aid, once upon a time. Now he kept his camp and supplies a dangerous trek away, far enough to remain unnoticed in a copse of thick pines, half a day's journey from here. He had combed over the land only to find the rumors were true. There was no life in this area except for himself and the woefully unprepared travelers. He slaughtered his horse and buried the meat deep in the snow to keep unwanted visitors away that might be attracted to flesh, just in case.

Part of him was aware that this gap in the mountains would most likely be his final resting place. That same part hoped it would be. An ending to a world of horror made real. He just needed to finish it, once and for all. He reached into his layers of furs and pulled out a piece of jerky warmed by his flesh and ate mechanically, without taste. An ending too long in the making.

As the second wave of the blizzard swept across the narrow valley, the sense of hopelessness spread between the wagons like a sickness. Josiah felt the weight of it keenly. He had ignored Lot's warning about leaving so late. He shook his head warily, trying to shake the thoughts.

No use fretting over milk spilled in the hay, he thought to himself. Josiah could hear his Nan's voice saying the words.

"I fear I have doomed the entire family to starvation. Please, God, if you will it, give me a sign. I am lost, Father. I beseech you, show me the way," Josiah prayed softly.

The only answer was Daniel letting out a wet cough and a weak cry. The storm seemed to intensify as the wind moaned like the souls of the damned. As if in response to Daniel, Josiah heard rasping coughs from the other wagons. If he was seeking peace, God clearly had other ideas.

Eat it.

"No," Hasse Ola whined as he stared at the frozen boy's corpse lying in the hollowed-out husk of the bear.

How long had he stared at it? The hunger rippling through him like roughhewn daggers carving him from the inside out. That same damnable hunger that led him to hunt the valley until all that remained flew high or swam fast. Hasse Ola thought back to the bear and the boys. He had felt kinship then. With the bear, desperate and starved in the snow, not the men. The bear was primal, a force. The humans were nothing.

Meat. Humans are prey.

Hasse Ola squeezed his eyes closed to silence the voice of the insatiable hunger. Always calling, always in need. It seemed as if his guts had turned to fire ever since that night. The ritual. Cleansing. All he could recall were frozen images of gore, of frenzied hunger. Fortunately, nothing more.

It was delicious. You remember. Cracking their skulls and eating the quivering brains. The salty copper taste as blood sprayed down your thirsty throat. Eat the boy. It's the way of things. Regain your strength. Then eat the others.

Hasse Ola choked down the scream in his throat. The fire ran through his limbs with tremors of agony. He could not take his gaze from the boy. He snarled in pain and self-hatred; the *boy* was probably his age, if not a year older. A man in nearly every way.

One bite. Just a taste.

Hasse Ola moved slightly, jerked involuntarily towards the corpse. His stomach gnawed at his ribs. He felt drool run down his chin. *What was one bite?* His tongue, long and black, slid across his sharp fangs, a spray of blood as they sliced mixed with the excess spit. It spurred him closer and closer still.

This is your birthright.

Hot tears ran down his gaunt cheeks as Hasse Ola felt the pangs rattle his bones. Soon, the sound of feasting filled the small cave. The frozen flesh cracked before tearing as his talon-like nails ripped into the sternum. Hasse Ola watched in horror from inside his own mind as his hands cracked the breastbone, ripping the chest wide open to expose the lungs and heart. He sobbed as he tore at the muscle, thick blood like pudding dripping across his face and chest. And still the hunger sang, as lungs were consumed in heaving bites. On and on, until Hasse Ola the spectator and Hasse Ola the monster were one and the same.

THE MEN GATHERED AROUND the fire as the snow began falling again. They were broken, arguing the same argument for the hundredth time.

"The horses are starving, same as us. It just figures we put them out of their misery and feed ourselves!" Edgar Twain repeated.

"And when we can clear a path from this infernal pass? What then? Will you and your full belly pull the wagons?" Solomon Swift demanded angrily. "Will you carry my children to the Promised Land?"

Lot listened half-heartedly to the others. That strange feeling of being watched had settled over him the last few days. It was like an itch between his shoulder blades he couldn't quite scratch. He was hungry. Angry. And still haunted by the gray blur. He stepped forward, unable to take the circular screaming any longer. "We need to check the net. Try to find food. Screaming ain't doin' nothin' but making the hunger worse. I'll go. Me and Samuel."

The men stood quietly and stared at him. He'd suggested this daily for the last three days. Even after Joseph, one of the smaller teens, had scrambled up into the snowbanks and fallen deep into the uncertain mounds. The poor boy had taken to a mighty chest cold that had slowly spread among the wagons. They all knew it was certain death. But they were also as aware that where they stayed was as well. And with the fresh blizzard compounding everything from bad to worse to apocalyptic, they couldn't find the words to argue.

Josiah stood silently. He had not spoken for two days. Not since he woke to find Daniel lying blue and motionless. Mildred had done nothing but weep. Josiah knew it was just the beginning. Now Lot wanted to take his eldest on a fool's errand. Still, he could not find the words even as all the men turned, looking at him for guidance. He felt uncomfortable with them all staring like that. He had no answers. No hope. Just a sliver of faith that felt more tenuous every moment. Finally, he shrugged. "Go. If they don't come back, we eat the horses."

Lot nodded. "We will need rope. I expect it will be perilous, but not impossible. Been through worse."

Part Three

"Stay close to the edges, damn you!" Lot barked at Samuel as he began sinking into the drift. It had been slow going, exhausting. The frozen stabs of the small crystals, more ice than soft lazy flakes, driven into his exposed flesh like buckshot, made the going even more difficult. Lot felt the pull of the rope tug him off balance and he glared at the boy again. "The edges, boy!"

Lot looked back and could see nothing of the hollow in the endless white that signaled the camp. He could not reckon how far they had gone. Every foot was a battle against the wind and shifting banks. His breath came in strained heaves and, by the look of him, Samuel had fared no better. They just had to clear the pass. The snow would be more evenly spread once they reached the woods.

A sharp crack sent his heart into his throat. A tree limb, overburdened by the accumulation, tumbled to slam into the ground. Samuel froze and gripped his father's revolver in his glove covered hands. Both men feared the bear was still out there, injured and starving. Lot had asked the boys if they had seen anything else in the chaos of the bear attack. They had each looked at him in confusion as he questioned them about a gray blur Lot had nearly convinced himself that the blur was just from hitting his head on the tree. But part of him refused to let it go. If he really concentrated on the image, stopped time for a moment, he would have sworn on a stack of Bibles that the blur was man shaped. It haunted his dreams when sleep gave a brief respite from the gnawing hunger in his guts.

Lot felt another harsh tug on the rope around his waist and snapped back to the present. Samuel was smiling like a fool and pointing. He squinted his eyes against the storm and felt a smile crack across his ice-covered cheeks. The woods lay directly ahead of them. He tempered his haste, fear of plunging into the snow so close to solid ground overriding his need to *be* on solid ground. Lot nodded to Samuel, and they made painfully slow progress towards the edge of the drifting snowbank.

They both knew that they probably traded a certain death for an uncertain one the moment they entered those woods. Lot gazed back into the swirling mess. It wasn't just their lives at stake.

Listen.

Hasse Ola sat still at the edge of his cave. The cold washed over his gray skin, but he paid no mind to it. He cocked his head, his stomach churned as he let the scents of the woods fill his flared nostrils.

There.

Hasse Ola heard something floating tantalizingly on the gusting storm. It was faint; he was not quite sure if he actually heard it or wished it to be. Then a stray scent, body odor and sick, wafted under the cold and ice.

Hunt.

RIVER CREPT ALONG THE rocks high above the two damned souls
as they entered the woods. It was hard to make out anything in the
blizzard, but his years on the plains and in the forest back home had
trained him. All he needed was the slightest movement. He felt a lump
choke him as he watched, and the memory of taking Hasse Ola out to
learn to hunt bombarded him. While they were not blood, nor even
of the same tribe, they had been brothers. A lifetime ago.

River shook away the past, choked down the sorrow to lay with the
other dead emotions in the back of his mind. He had followed the
rumors, seen the empty town of Duncan on his path to stop Hasse
Ola. A faint flicker of hope burned in the darkness that wrapped itself
around River. That small lingering wish that it was not too late, that
the creature was not in full control. All he needed was an instant to
strike, to end it. So far, all he had found were those stories of a blur
in the wild and strange empty tracts of land where the wildlife had
just vanished. No humans. Just animals. This told River there was
some last visage of his former friend still fighting the curse, fighting
the hunger. It was all River needed.

He made his careful descent into the trees, easily finding the trail of
the wanderers. River kept a wary eye on the drifts that piled against
copses of thick pines. If Hasse Ola was here, the beast knew nearly
all of River's tricks for hunting. He—*it*—could be anywhere ready to
strike.

SAMUEL FOUGHT FOR EVERY step in the waist-high snow. His legs felt
like stumps that burned with exertion on each step. If he slowed a bit,
Lot would pull at the rope and mutter an angry curse that was mostly

muted by the storm. Samuel glared at Lot's back as the cold made his hands ache. His wind blistered face felt as if it would crack and bleed. Part of him relished the thought of the heat of it, anything to break the damned freezing that cut through his hides and furs.

Lot seemed to pay no mind to any of it. He just kept forcing his way forward. Samuel at least followed in his wake, which was still torturous. He wondered at the steel that must run through the former soldier with the sunken eyes that always seemed haunted by unseen terrors.

From the corner of Samuel's eye, he saw something flash against the white. He stopped and whipped his head to try to capture whatever it was. A blur of gray, it had seemed. Samuel was nearly yanked off his feet by Lot pulling the rope.

"No time to lollygag, boy. If you're needing a break, we can find a thicket up ahead, closer to the water." Samuel didn't answer, just kept sweeping the trees for any movement. Something in his gaze made Lot stop. "What is it? Samuel, did you see something?"

Samuel shook his head slowly, not certain if it was just his imagination or maybe a swaying branch that had caught the wind. "I guess not. It just looked like..." he trailed off.

Lot stomped back towards him, which made Samuel flinch instinctively. The soldier got right into his face with a frightened look. "What did you see? Damn it, tell me, boy!"

"It was nothing, I reckon. A branch or something. I thought I seen something in the trees."

Lot's eye bore into his, fevered with what might have been pure fear. Samuel looked away from the intense glare. "What color was it? Was it gray, Samuel? Was it?" he asked in a frantic whisper as he ran a hand across the rifle slung over his shoulder.

Samuel opened his mouth to answer when the gray blur darted among the trees again. He raised his shaking hand and pointed. Lot spun about with the rifle sliding into his grip in one fluid, clearly practiced move. Lot stared down the sight as he swept the end of his trusty Rolling Block along the trees. Samuel saw the blur again, dark gray speeding among the branches of an old oak tree. He snapped his finger towards it as Lot pulled the trigger. The gunshot seemed to reverberate through the land even as the blizzard tried to engulf it. An explosion of snow sprayed from the branches of the tree as the shot impacted. Samuel stood, not breathing or moving, as the snow fell in huge clumps to the ground. Lot pulled back the hammer, slid open the breech, and let the shell hit the snow as he slid the next round in mechanically, already sighting down the barrel.

Then the gray blur erupted from the branches of the tree, and they saw an owl with a wide wingspan and bright yellow eyes fly into the dark skies, where it blended in with the angry storm above. Samuel and Lot let out the breaths they didn't realize they had been holding as they watched the owl vanish into the clouds. Lot broke the silence with a harsh laugh that brought a smile to Samuel's face for a moment.

The smile melted away as a thought occurred to him. He looked at Lot in confusion. "How did you know the blur was gray? There ain't no way you seen it?"

HASSE OLA FOUND HIMSELF racing out of the cave at the sound of the rifle. The speed at which he moved still shocked him. His senses were tripled in strength, maybe more, to the point where he barely could handle the sensory overload at first. It was a rush of pure adrenaline any time he let himself tap into it. Addicting.

Yet the price for it was too steep. The endless need, ravenous and all-consuming, swept through him like a fire in his belly that burst forth like cramps. He needed flesh. Fuel.

The acrid smell of gunpowder pulled him towards the prey loose in his woods. He could hear his stomach rumble at the thought of fresh meat. The trees blurred around him; snow kicked up in clouds from his bare feet, slashing at the ground for traction. Hasse Ola felt as if he were flying, the speed and thrill of the hunt infusing him. He understood that he had become something more than human. His entire body thrummed with energy.

And then a familiar scent intermingled with the cordite. Hasse Ola turned his head quickly towards the new odor. Sunshine. White Jasmine. Red Dust. Home.

Hasse Ola tried to stop, but the momentum was too much. He flew feet over head into the snow, tumbling across the frozen ground before a large stone stopped him with a bone-jarring thud. He lay dazed for a moment, not able to comprehend what was happening in the suddenly spinning world of agony that flared through his left side. His arm hung useless by his side as he watched in disbelief as black blood pooled from the many cuts along his too thin gray body. He tried to concentrate, to get his bearings and control the waves of nausea-inducing pain. He retched, but there was nothing in his stomach. He let out a bloodcurdling howl of rage and pain that boomed out into the storm.

Move!

RIVER ROSE FROM BEHIND the snowbank and stared in shock as Hasse Ola sped past him. River was sickened by what he saw, barely anything remained of his brother in the emaciated, gray, corpse-like beast racing along the snow. He felt his sorrow and pity drain away as Hasse Ola turned to stare at him. He watched the creature stumble and flip through the air to careen into the large stone hidden in the wintry wasteland. River muttered a prayer to the Ancestors and pulled out his bow. He carefully notched one of the arrows the Medicine Man of the Algonquin Tribe had crafted for him. It seemed to glow with power as he pulled it back to let it streak through the air. It found a home in Hasse Ola's throat with a sickening thump as the creature let loose a wailing roar. River was not content with one arrow and loosed three more in quick succession. They formed a triangle in the center of the gray chest, releasing a black sludge that poured from the wounds.

River carefully made his way towards Hasse Ola—*no, towards the Wendigo*, he corrected himself. Hatred seethed inside of him as he watched the monster twitching in the snow. In one evening, everything he had known and loved was taken from him. The people of Duncan, the Tribes, and most important of all, his brother. The husk of Hasse Ola let out gasping wheezes through the hole the arrow had torn into its throat. When he stood in front of it, the head snapped up to glare malevolently at him.

"Whyyyyyyy?" Hasse Ola hissed from both holes at him. As River watched, the black that made up its eyes drained away. River's heart stopped as the bright brown eyes of his brother stared back at him. Confusion and pain readily apparent. "Whyyyyyyy?" he repeated.

River dropped to his knees in the black slush. "Hasse Ola. Brother. It's over now. The Medicine Men gave me the ability to heal you. I didn't believe it would work. You're back. You can have peace. At last."

Two streaks of black ran down Hasse Ola's cheeks. A faint smile spread across his face as he looked at River. "Brotherrrrr," he rasped softly.

Hasse Ola seemed as if he had something to say, so River leaned in. "Yes, little brother?"

Faintly, Hasse Ola whispered, "You never believed in any of it."

River looked at him in confusion. Then horror as the black swept back over Hasse Ola's eyes and a wicked smile carved its way onto his face. Suddenly, a wave of pain tore across River. He stood shakily and looked around. He couldn't tell what had happened. Why the world became an inferno of agony. Then he saw his left arm in Hasse Ola's hands. He stared as the Wendigo tore into the flesh—*his flesh*—ripping away mouthfuls at a time. He saw blood spray from his shoulder. Then it all went dark.

"WHAT IN THE HELL was that?" Lot asked as the roar of something filled the air.

"I don't know. I don't mean to find out, neither. We should head back, Mr. Baker. I don't like this." Samuel looked ready to run.

Lot pulled him close and stared into the boy's frightened eyes. "If'n we go back without the fish, everyone dies. Understand me, boy? Everyone. Your Ma and Paw. Everyone. They can't make it another week. None of us can. Keep a level head, Samuel. It was the injured bear. I didn't have my rifle last time. We are prepared."

Samuel nodded, but he was terrified. His eyes darted everywhere but onto Lot's.

"Come on. We can make it to the river before the bear can find us.'

Samuel didn't move. "What did you think the gray blur was earlier, Mr. Baker?" he asked resolutely. "T'weren't no owl, no sir. You seen something, didn't you?"

Lot didn't look at him. "It was nothin'. I hit my head is all. We need to reach the net and get back before the storm gets worse." He started walking and felt the rope get yanked. He turned angrily towards Samuel. "This is not the time nor the place for talking visions brought about by hitting a tree headfirst."

Samuel didn't budge, and Lot recognized the set of the boy's jaw. It was the same look Josiah had given him when he said they needed to postpone the expedition.

"Tarnation! I thought I saw something attack the bear. I could barely keep my eyes straight. It looked like a gray blur, that's all. A blur. Could have been the same damned owl for all I know. We need to move."

Samuel nodded thoughtfully. "And that blur saved us from the bear? Paw said it was your army trainin'."

"Your Paw says a lot of things. It takes a fool to believe most of it. He said we would be fine, against my better wishes, to leave so late in the year. And now look at us. Daniel is dead. The rest hardly hangin' on by the skin of their teeth. This whole trip was cursed from the start. And it is your Paw's fault!"

Lot wasn't expecting the punch in the mouth, so when he hit the snow and his breath was forced out, he just lay there and bled from his nose. He fought the urge to retaliate. Samuel looked down at him in shock at his own action and held out a hand, the same that had sucker punched him, while mumbling an apology. Lot angrily waved it away and pushed himself to his feet. He turned and spat blood that had poured into his mouth out onto the ground. It steamed in the cold air as it melted through the snow.

"I will let you have that one, boy. Try it again and your Paw will have another lost son. Do you understand me?"

Samuel didn't answer. He seemed transfixed by something over Lot's shoulder. Lot noticed the tremors in the boy's legs. He slowly moved his arm to the strap of his rifle and carefully slid it down his arm.

"He will have another lossst sssson," a hissing voice replied.

Lot closed his eyes and muttered a low prayer. Then he quickly pivoted as the rifle raised. He pulled the trigger, the roar of the shot loud against the howling winds. His shot went wide, blasting bark off an innocent tree. His bladder let loose as he fumbled with the hammer, unable to look away from the hell standing patiently. His mind was unable to rationalize the vision of horror before him as reality. The fiend seemed amused at his blank faced panic.

A gray monster stood, arm hanging awkwardly to his side. Three arrows standing in its chest, while the skin of its ruined throat knitted itself back together in front of the two sets of wide-eyed terror. It didn't move, just stood, dripping black ooze down a too thin frame of once corded muscle. Lot knew this was the gray blur that had haunted his every waking moment, the inexplicable demon of his worst nightmares made real. Lot tried to pull back the breech pin, to eject the shell, but his hands seemed deadened. The creature cocked its head at him as he dropped a round into the snow. Lot wasn't sure, but it seemed to smile at him.

Samuel let his fear take over and turned to run, but only made it a few feet before the rope stretched taut and both men fell to the ground. The creature let out a hoarse laugh, one that held as much warmth as the ground beneath them and began to slowly move towards them. Lot scrambled to retrieve his rifle, feeling as if he were moving through molasses. He cradled the rifle and managed to eject the shell and slide a fresh one home. He raised the rifle and felt the barrel as it was pulled from his shaking grip. He stared up into the ebony eyes of the devil himself. The beast stared down with no pity in that inky black gaze, more curiosity at what the feeble being in the snow could hope to manage.

Lot pulled his knife, razor edged dull silver, and sliced through the rope. "Run, Samuel! Run and don't look back, boy!" he screamed as he then drove the blade into the stomach of the creature.

It looked down at the antler handle sticking out of its midsection. With a soft moan of exertion, it pulled the blade out and raised it to its mouth. A long, black tongue snaked out to lick the blackened blood. It bent down and its nose brushed up against Lot's. Lot felt revulsion as the tongue ran up his cheek. "The boy isssss next," it hissed.

Lot had a brief moment of clarity as death's fetid breath blew upon his face. The smell of rot and promise of pain was implicit. But he noted the hissing came from the inch-long hole in the monster's throat. Even as the skin regrew before his horrified face, the puckered wound flapped like a whore's honey pot. The features looked Injun, to Lot's eyes, underneath the cold hatred that warred with something else. A desperate need. Lot watched the cruel talons of the beast's right arm raise into the air. Lot closed his eyes and sent another prayer to the heavens. This time for Samuel making good on his escape. He knew the words were hollow as the talons tore through his chest. Lot refused to scream, even as he bit through his own tongue to choke the involuntary sounds back down. And then he was no more.

⸺⸺

Samuel ran. His chest burned as his heart pounded in his skull. His mind was filled with the image of the gray-skinned demon with the tar blood. Sounds drifted but were muted by his pulse, not enough to disguise the wet tearing. He ran. The woods around him were a blur, indistinguishable from the rampant terror and adrenaline pulsing through his limbs. Samuel didn't even notice the churning waters that flowed in front of him. He did not see the net, filled with anxious fish that fought against the ropes that kept them in place. It wasn't until his footing slipped that he found himself swept up in the current and pulled beneath the icy waters that he realized he could stop running. Samuel let the water take him. Part of him accepting this end was far better than the other promised. His last thought as the black spots overtook his vision, as the near frozen water filling his lungs, was of poor baby Daniel lying blue and still in the wagon. To wonder if that was how he would look if anyone ever found his body.

⸺⸺

Finale

The sun brought forth stabbing rays of pain that shot through his eyes and directly into his brain. He kept them shut tightly as he took mental stock of what was happening. Of what had *already* happened. It was all a muddied mess, fragments, that he found himself incapable of putting together. He tried to move, but his body would not answer his pleading. The snow was cold beneath him, even as the sun seemed to warm his face. He cracked open his eyes slightly, and the light sent pain and nausea through him once again. He turned his head and retched a thin stream of bile and spittle onto the ground.

Suddenly, without warning, he felt a hand grab at his hair and yank him upright. The world was a kaleidoscope of flashing pain, shooting through every inch of his body.

"Good. You're awake. I was growing concerned. It hassss been a long week and a half since you passed out. I worried you would miss the grand finale."

He opened his eyes again; the sun reflecting off the snow was blinding. He had to blink rapidly to get the spots to fade. He did not know how long it took for them to adjust. He faintly struggled, but found he was tightly bound. He tried to speak, but his throat was so parched and all that came out was a cracked keening. His limbs were bound tightly, the rope cut off circulation and combined with the cold, made his entire body ache with pins and needles.

Slowly, the scene in front of him came into focus. The wagons circled tightly, with high banks of snow surrounding them. The campfire let out a measly wisp of gray smoke, less fire than a few smoldering embers lying in a bed of ash. Standing before it were two lone figures, a man and a woman in a long black dress.

"They slaughtered the horses. Not much meat left to them. That was at the beginning of your sleep. The young had taken ill, a wet cough. Nasty. Soon, they all coughed. No food. Sick." The creature grabbed his face and turned it so he had to stare into the monster's cold, black eyes. It was nearly fully healed, except for the wound in its throat and three more on its chest. Those wounds wept a trickle of black down the gray skin. "They began to die off. One by one from starvation. From the sickness. From the loss of hope."

He struggled against the iron grip on his jaw. The creature dug its nails in before pulling its hand away. The fire of the ten thin lines of pain made him wince. His eyes went back to the two standing by the fire. He wanted to scream at them to climb, to run. But his throat was incapable of any noise loud enough to carry.

"I watched them. Brought you up here every morning. The hunger got to them. They wept as they consumed the fallen. But still they are hungry. Greedily. It did nothing to stave off the illness. Soon, there was more meat than mouths to eat it." It let out a low, rumbling laugh, devoid of joy or humanity.

He felt tears well in the corners of his eyes. This was all his fault. He had failed them. And now only two remained. He struggled to make out who the last two survivors were. As he watched, the woman in the long black dress fell to her knees. The man stepped behind her and stood still for a long moment. Then he reached down to his belt and, with one fluid motion, put the barrel of his revolver to the back of her head, cocked it and fired with a loud crack. She fell forward with a spray of red streaking across the trodden snow. Then he lifted the gun to his own temple and a second crack went off in the quiet valley before he slumped to the ground in a growing pool of crimson.

"And then, there were none," the creature said flatly, no emotion in its rasping voice. It turned his head back to meet its baleful glare. "You must be starving." With a swipe if its talon like nails, it cut through the ropes that bound him.

He collapsed to the ground. His body refused to move. All he could do was lay quivering in a mound. He pushed himself up awkwardly onto his right elbow, the effort launching explosions in his head and through his battered frame. His stomach rolled but was empty and had nothing to expel. He sat and brought his hand to wipe the tears from his cheek and froze. His hand was the same sickly gray as the creature's. He looked over at his left arm and was shocked to find it missing at the shoulder.

It all came back to him in a jarring flash of memories. Hasse Ola. River turned to look up at the creature he had sworn to kill. He tried to speak, but nothing came out.

Hasse Ola smiled darkly at him. "I had left you to bleed out, Brother. Imagine my surprise to find all my blood you spilled had tainted yours." He laughed, an insane cackle that echoed through the valley.

"We may not have been true brothers before, but now we are bonded by blood!"

River let out a torn wail, black blood spraying out at the sheer force of the sorrowful wail. He let himself collapse face first into the snow as the enormity of what had occurred washed over him in waves of revulsion and hatred.

He realized the pain in his stomach was not nausea at all. It was hunger.

Eat.

Six

Within A Withering Eye

The bells tolled three times, ringing hollowly into the fog, swirling lazily with a faint silvery sheen of trapped moonbeams which flowed like a lazy river down the sleepy cobblestoned streets of the small village.

Jonas tugged the reins and muttered a low curse at the chestnut mare with ears pinned back, pulling the creaking cart. His eyes darted about with a tired nervousness, and he kept checking the rough burlap covered contents of the wooden cart as the wheels bounced lethargically in time with the hesitant gait of the horse.

"C'mon now, you fickle bitch, the quicker you move, the sooner it is oats and hay in the stable," Jonas practically begged as he warily watched the fog coalesce around his legs. He cursed low once more and tugged the reins to the displeasure of the old horse.

Jonas pulled once more and winced as he felt the blisters on his hands tear open and he bit his tongue to hold back the profanity that threatened to spill out and possibly draw attention to his middle of the night escapades. The fog helped to obscure the thick mud caked on his boots and pants as well. If any of the sleepy residents looked out, they would only see his slumped shoulders and the cart creeping slowly into the darkness. Jonas stopped near the town fountain and let the tired nag drink as he sat with his back against the cool stone and yawned deeply.

A curious sound, a hollow sort of thud like a ceramic bowl slammed down upon a worn bar, came from just down the road. Jonas scrambled to his feet and stared apprehensively toward the direction of the noise. It sounded out again, louder, closer, but distorted by the fog and darkness. Jonas held the reins with a dumbfounded expression. He needed to go the same way the sounds emanated from, but with every dull thud, he felt himself inching backwards.

Time seemed to halt as the fog grew thicker, now coiling higher to his chest where he felt an unnatural cold seep through his filthy garb. Jonas clutched the reins and pus from the now shredded blisters ran down his palm and dripped into the hungry fogbank. Then he saw the source of the noise as a large urn hopped from the darkness and landed heavily in front of him.

"Do you have the items I have requested?" a voice hissed from the urn itself.

Jonas stood dumbly; his mouth moved, but no sound came out. He finally managed a nod and looked at the cart covered in burlap. He had been hired for this job because his lack of scruples was nearly legendary, and even he had balked at first when approached by a stranger at the tavern two nights back.

The urn leapt into the air and landed behind the cart. *"And it is all three of them?"* the voice whispered again, hollow yet carrying sharply through the fog.

Jonas nodded again. "I didn't ask any questions, just did as I was bade. All three of them as bidden freshly dug up as requested." He eyed the urn warily, but his innate greed had already taken over. "There is the matter of my coin."

The lid of the urn opened and a pale white arm stretched out; a bulging coin purse clutched in the dirty fingers with long black nails.

"The price as agreed upon, plus extra for a job well done," the voice whispered.

Jonas had been dealing with the darker side of the world for as long as he could recall, but nothing had shaken him quite like this bedeviled urn, and whatever it was that lurked inside of it. He hesitantly stepped around the cart and snatched the coin purse. His eyes widened momentarily at the heft of it, and he figured it was double, if not triple, the agreed upon amount. The edges of a grin tugged the corners of his mouth as he realized he had just made months' worth of coin for a single evening of work.

"Now if you will do one last job for me, please place the precious cargo into my urn," the voice didn't ask as much ordered.

Jonas made a face as he looked at the cart, but the comfortable feel of all that coin hanging off his belt erased most of the distaste he felt. He removed the burlap tarp, and the silvery moon brightened against the three small bodies wrapped in white linen burial clothes. Jonas had no issue selling children, but this was his first time selling the dead bodies of them.

"Ah, yes. You have performed admirably, Jonas," the voice hissing from the open urn, was less distorted and seemed both obviously ancient, but female as well, murmured with joy. The lid slid further back, and a second arm came out.

Jonas lifted the first bundle, and the hands snatched it and vanished into the mouth of the oversized urn. In a matter of moments, all three of the little girls' bodies were gone from view. Jonas balled up the burlap and placed it back into the cart. "A pleasure, of sorts, doing business with you. I'll be on my way now."

"Would you be willing to do one more job for me? I will pay double what you just received?" the occupant of the urn hissed.

Jonas didn't want to have anything to do with whatever this monster in the urn was, but the thoughts of enough money to take a year off overrode the fear he barely held in restraint. His old horse had clearly had as much of the foul presence as she could handle and with a whinny, jerked the cart and took off as quickly as her old hooves could carry her as she gave in to the panic. The fog was too thick for the frantic beast to navigate in blind fear and the loud crash as it slammed into the side of a building and the thick snap of the poor beast's neck shook the sleepy town. Candlelight began flickering in windows and Jonas stared at the urn uncertainly but whispered, "Yes."

A rasping chuckle rose from the urn. "Excellent. You need to find The Witch of the Wildflowers and tell her this, Baba Yaga has found the way to Hecate's prison, but she requires that which lies within the withering eye. Repeat that back to me. Upon delivery, you will have your coin."

Jonas nervously repeated it three times as the commotion grew louder in the homes around him. Satisfied, the lid slammed closed, and the urn leapt high into the air with a plume of the fog and vanished into the night. It wouldn't be until late in the morning when Jonas woke. He noticed a shock of white hair now streaked the sides of his head.

SHE SAT ALONE AT the café with a cup of coffee gently steaming in the crisp autumn morning air. A sea of sallow, disinterested faces drifted past her, vacant eyes downcast as they made their way to and from work. Occasionally, an especially forward young man or elderly gentleman would spot her and smile, the same way one did when they saw a wildflower in blossom or rainbow after a storm. She was stunning, and the way she smiled in return was as perfect as a sunrise over the ocean on a calm day with a hint of a lurking tempest. This was because, despite her effortless beauty, a supple power dwelled in her deep brown gaze.

"The contact for the quest is far too late. When he arrives, let me eviscerate," a soft voice rumbled.

She frowned slightly, "Hush."

A little boy at a nearby table gave her a funny look.

"That boy will grow up drunk and mean, but I bet he has a tasty spleen," the soft voice ruminated, and the little boy went pale.

"Play nice, Archibald," she murmured before giving the boy a small smile and nodding politely at his mother, who was looking at her suspiciously as the child whispered into her ear.

She held a sigh as it threatened to escape as she felt the small velvet bag in her pocket as it twitched against her thigh and thoughts of murky swamps and snapping serpents darkened her eyes.

"One approaches like a nervous little duckling. Would you like me to consume the quivering suckling?" Archibald whispered into her ear.

She tensed inwardly and called for the runes that felt etched into her soul, a fire that raced through her veins and made everything snap into focus. The patrons of the café began to glow a faint emerald in her sight. The crowds pushing down the streets flickered with different emotions, but none with any ill intent towards her. And then she felt the worry, like a sparrow's heartbeat frantically fluttering, which grew steadily closer.

A man, shabbily dressed, pushed his way through the throng of people and broke free at the edge of the patio at which she sat. Her eyes widened slightly, a huge tell for such a careful woman, as she saw the miasma of a great evil that seemed to suffocate the air around him with its toxicity. And her gaze was fixed upon the bright white that spread back at the temples through his unruly brown hair.

"Marked by great evil, yet devoid of power. A most foul omen, I'll gladly devour," Archibald hissed, and the man's eyes widened.

The gaunt man pointed towards the open chair at her table. "May I?"

She frowned and looked around at the half empty café patio. "There are unoccupied tables all around us, friend. Perhaps you'd like to sit alone instead."

The man stood staring at her, his hand clutching the heavy leather purse at his side. He tried to smile, but it came off predatory and he seemed to realize this and took a moment to calm himself. "Milady,

I have searched for you for weeks and weeks now. I was tasked with finding you to pass along a message."

"He doesn't seem to fully understand no, perhaps if I mutilate him some, he will take the hint and go," Archibald said calmly and the sound of rustling leathery wings seemed to snap just behind the seated woman.

"He is no threat, Archie, but if you'd like to hover menacingly behind him as he joins me for coffee, you have my permission," she said and gestured for the man to sit.

He did so nervously, setting the purse on the table and keeping one hand firmly upon it. He twitched and looked over his shoulder. "My thanks."

"He clutches a bag filled with stones, and I sense a madness deep in his bones."

The man jerked his head towards the voice that seemed to emanate from right behind him and his pale face went even lighter when he saw nothing there. He reached up with one hand to tentatively feel behind him.

"I wouldn't put your hand too close to Archibald's face. He has been known to bite them off. Best to not provoke him," she said with a cold smile. She sipped her coffee and watched the man squirm over the rim. "Two questions. One. Who is it that you think I am? Two. Who sent you?"

The man looked over his shoulder once more before turning his half unfocused gaze on her. He squeezed the bag once more, and said, "You are Lady Anna. But you have another name, one that people whisper but try to avoid saying."

Anna's eyes grew smaller as she stared across the table. "And what name is that?"

He smiled, showing broken blackened teeth, "The Witch of the Wildflowers." The woman at the nearby table gasped and grabbed her child and left. He smiled even deeper. "And I was sent by Baba Yaga to deliver a message to you."

Anna didn't flinch outwardly, but surprise and fear coursed in a frozen sludge throughout her. There was also a simmering anger that flared in her center. "And what is this message?"

Jonas repeated the words he had been muttering for the last three months, the words that haunted his dreams of large urns and the monsters that lived inside. When he finished, he grabbed his bag of rocks and held it as if it were a fortune of gems, then stood and vanished into the crowded street.

Anna sat speechless, staring into her cup of coffee.

"Fuck a duck," Archibald said softly.

After a long stretch of silence, Anna motioned for the waiter. "A disheveled looking priest will be by, eventually. Please give him this," she said, sliding three large gold coins and the velvet bag across the table. The bag jerked and twitched on the table and the waiter stared at it, clearly appalled. She placed another coin on the table and smiled. "Be very careful with it and do not open it under any circumstances."

"Remind him he owes us for this latest stunt, next time I see him, I will filet the—"

"Archibald!" Anna quickly interjected. She flashed a smile at the sick-looking waiter, and he immediately calmed down in the dazzling display, and scooped up the coins and gingerly set the bag on a small plate.

ANNA RECLINED IN THE copper tub filled with soapy water and stared into the flickering candlelight as it swayed from the breeze coming through the open window.

"The hag lies, she knows nothing of Hecate, it is a trap, and she knew the perfect bait," Archibald ruminated.

Anna sighed in frustration. "I am well aware of that. But what if it isn't? Magic has been fading since the Goddess disappeared. Baba Yaga has as much to gain from her return as anyone," she said flatly. "If you are just going to state the obvious, perhaps you could see what you can find out about this withering eye instead?"

Anna felt Archibald's hurt before his presence vanished from the room. A lone rune flashed between her breasts with her heartbeat, and she felt the tether between her and Archibald stretching as he traveled. She sighed again, sorry for having snapped and hurting his feelings. It never ceased to amaze her with how complicated Archibald was for a demon. She would have to make it up to him later, but that wasn't a concern for now. Anna slipped lower into the water and swirled her fingers with a faint discharge of magic to warm the tepid water and stared again at the flames of the candles that reminded her of the bonfire in the trees so long ago.

SHE HAD BEEN SCARED that night. She had finally grown tired of her mother's control, had enough of the constant abuse, and fled as the sun set over the mountains to the west. She crept, quiet as a mouse, through the manor, sneaking a loaf of bread and a block of cheese into the pockets of her cloak, before fleeing into the great forest that she imagined stretched on forever. She was clever and had asked all the right questions of the various workers her mother employed, never too many, far enough apart to avoid suspicion, as her mother had eyes and ears everywhere.

They feared falling into her disfavor, the place Anna seemed to perpetually dwell in, so they would run to her if they ever got the idea of what she had planned. She made careful notes on mushrooms to eat from the chef, of moss on trees from the gamesman, and assorted other survival tips from each and everyone she spoke with. She would survive the forest; she had already survived worse.

All of her planning and secret knowledge seemed to go right out the window the deeper into the darkness she walked. She went fast at first. Each snapped twig could be one of the servants sent to fetch her. Then she moved faster as each crunched leaf could be a wolf or a bear. By the time the adrenaline had worn off, her careful plan had become a panic and now she stood, all alone, hopelessly lost in a forest that seemed so peaceful from a distance, yet now felt suffocating and terrifying. The branches of the canopy swayed and showed glimpses of stars, but she could get no bearing, and the open areas filled with bright moonlight made the shadows feel sharpened and her too exposed.

She shrank down among the exposed roots of great oak and began to silently sob, too afraid to make noise and too overcome to hold it in. She lay in the darkness and never felt so alone.

And then she heard a soft song come gently swirling through the branches. She dabbed her eyes and sat up and tilted her head. For a seemingly long few seconds, she heard nothing, and despair crept back in, and then the song came to her again. She got to her feet and walked carefully through the trees, moving towards the song like a moth to a lantern. It grew louder, and she soon found herself peeking through the scrubs into an open circle with a roaring bonfire in the center that licked hungrily at the sky.

Her eyes widened as she saw a group of beautiful women, all nude with strange symbols that seemed to glow in the dancing flesh as circled and sang around the fire. She watched in confusion, uncertain why anyone would want to be naked and dance so close to the fire, but also felt the pull of the flames and the song with a need to join in. It went against everything her mother would approve of. She stepped out of the tree line and into the circle and the women smiled at her and waved her closer, but she couldn't make herself go any farther in.

The most beautiful woman Anna had ever seen stepped forward and smiled at her. Her entire body glowed with a strange amber light, and it only added to her dazzling perfection.

"Welcome home, Anna. We have been expecting you," she said sweetly.

Anna frowned. "Who are you? How do you know my name?"

The women all laughed, which made her face flush with embarrassment.

"I am Hecate, little sister, and this is my coven," Hecate said with a friendly smile.

Anna's eyes nearly popped from her head, "But that's impossible! You don't exist!"

Hecate laughed harder than the other women at this. Tears ran freely down her cheeks in the mirth. "I can assure you, I am very real, Anna. And if you decide to join us, I can teach you secrets and power you only dreamt of."

Ann felt the truth of those words and felt a fire begin to burn inside of her at the idea of having the power to be truly free of her mother's influence. She nodded once. "I think I would like that very much."

And Anna joined Hecate's coven. After so long being lost, not just in the woods but in the life she never controlled, she found herself home.

***

ANNA FELT THE TEARS as they began to run down her cheeks and drip into the bath water as the old feelings rumbled inside her. She had been accepted and nurtured and loved for the first time she could remember since her father had passed away. And it wasn't until she had left the forest, sent out by Hecate herself, that it had all fallen apart. Anna had been in the South of France as the peonies blossomed when she felt the connection to the Goddess of Magic severed, the placid golden light simply vanished from the place it had glowed within her heart, and she found herself alone once again after a decade of connection.

Anna wiped the tears away and stood up. The air hummed around her as each droplet of water separated itself from her flesh and swirled in the air around her. Soon all of the water in the copper tub began to flow into the air, a serpent in liquid form that roared without sound as it spun faster and faster in her bubbling fury of emotions as the runes beneath her skin burned brighter and brighter until the dragon with watery scales evaporated in sputtering hiss of steam that drifted out the window in thick clouds of vapor.

"If it is a trap, there is nothing I can do but spring it," Anna said firmly as her robe wrapped itself around her and the belt cinched tight to her slender waist.

With a wave of her arm the furniture in the room slid to the walls, a flick of her finger, a fine circle of salt was drawn on the center of the floor, and with a final snap, the candles slid into place around the salt. Lightning crackled in the sky outside the open window and the wind howled into the room, yet not a single grain of sand was distributed, nor did a single candle flicker out, if anything the flames burned brighter, becoming sapphire lances that pierced the Tenebrae between the planes. Without a sound, Anna stepped into the circle, and sat cross-legged in the center as small of eruptions of amber electricity arced across her skin.

"By the power of the crossroads, I call forth to the magic that coils itself around the heart of the evening. I beseech the spirits to give me a sign!" Anna shouted as the energy pulsed through her.

The world calmed, the lightning in the skies abated, and the howling winds turned into a gentle breeze that blew around the room, snuffing out each candle in turn. The power dissipated from Anna and her shoulder slumped forward as she sat panting. She slowly raised her head and pushed her mane of blonde hair back behind her ears and exhaled slowly.

Sitting in front of her on the floor was a large frog, easily the size of a kitten, staring directly at her. Anna felt the tears blossom in her eyes once more.

"Where a demon was, a frog now sits, staring lovingly at your exposed ti—"

"Hush," Anna said as she pulled her robe closed, "This is the sign I was waiting for, Archibald. Hecate is out there."

"Forgive me, Anna, if I seem dense, but a frog seems like a faulty pretense."

Anna smiled slightly as the frog hopped closer to her. "Hecate has had many names throughout time, Archie. She has worn many forms. In Egypt, they worshipped her as Heqet, where she had a frog's head and a human body," she explained excitedly. "I have performed the same incantation once a month for the past seven years, and this is the first time I have received an omen."

"If you say so, I'll take your word, but to trust Baba Yaga is still absurd."

Anna gently lifted the frog and set it in a bowl of water. It hopped to the center of the bowl and then sat patiently again, its eyes darted from her to the space Archibald occupied invisibly.

"And what did you find out about the withering eye?" Anna asked as she set a small pot nest to the bowl and swirled her finger in the soil packed within. A small tendril of green pushed itself up through the brown and in a matter of seconds, a white lily blossomed. The sweet pollen filled the room and in mere seconds, a fat fly flew in to investigate. The frog barely moved except for a sudden burst as its tongue grabbed the fly and pulled it into its mouth. Anna smiled contentedly.

"In the pits of hell, I found only dead ends, perhaps you could contact your witchy old friends?"

"I would rather not. Things were strained the last time we spoke. I would rather not give them false hope," Anna said quietly.

"Perhaps the frog is meant as a snack, nutrients to prepare for the crone's attack," Archibald mused.

The frog turned towards Archibald and opened its mouth far wider than should have been possible and let out a croak that shook the entire room and sprayed him with a thick mucus that coated his demonic form and he let out a harsh yell of disgust and surprise. Then the frog turned back to Anna and began to open its mouth again. Anna raised her hands and the rune burst into the air between her and the amphibian. The frog's tongue went through the shield as if it didn't exist and wrapped around Anna's waist and pulled her into its cavernous gaping mouth.

ANNA FOUND HERSELF NOT being propelled into the acidic gullet of the magic frog, but instead floating high in the sky over a grand forest. She stared down in wonder at the seemingly endless blanket of verdant leaves swaying like an ocean in every direction.

"You must retrieve the needle within the withering eye, Dogrose," Hecate's voice came on the breeze. *"But you must not let Baba Yaga lay her hands upon it."*

Anna gasped, "My Goddess! I have searched all over this plane for you and countless others. How can I reach you?"

"I lay trapped, tapped and slowly drained, yet I watch still over my little sisters. The path to me resides in the needle of Clotho nestled within the withering eye."

Anna nodded once. "And where can I find this withering eye?"

Anna shifted locations, a motionless motion that made her nauseous as she snapped back into place. She looked down, still over the sprawling forest, and saw an elliptical expanse of twisted and blackened trees, a blight of foul malignancy she could feel even at her incredible altitude. There, in the midst of the gigantic forest, was a withered eye of simmering evil intent.

"You and your foul-mouthed demon must enter the withering eye and extract the needle. I fear that will be just the beginning, as Baba Yaga will come for you as soon as you have it. Be safe, little sister. My blessing is upon you, even in this tattered state."

ANNA FELT THAT SAME whiplash movement without moving, yet this time she found herself bent over and vomiting on the floor of the room she had just been in. As she stood and wiped the bile from her chin, she saw the frog sitting on Archibald's chest as the demon struggled to move.

The demon ceased his struggles the moment he saw her. *"Fucking shit, if you're not a sight to see, now could you please get this fucking frog off of me?"*

The frog croaked once and vanished in a swirl of lavender notes. Anna raised an eyebrow at the mucus laden demon. "If you shake yourself off like a dog, I can promise you will not enjoy the recompense, Archibald."

"Well, fuck me running if that wasn't a fright, that amphibian bastard put up quite the fight," Archibald said before the mucus quivered, suspended in the air in a confused state, then splattering upon the floor. *"You smell of divinity, cloying and strong, now spill all the secrets, don't string me along,"* he then said from near the window.

Anna stared at the filthy rug with obvious distaste. She raised her hands and touched thumbs and forefingers in front of her left eye and a sigil hummed across her pupil, immediately mushrooms sprang up and quickly soaked up the mystical mucus, growing fat and swollen with a red jelly that oozed down the white stalks from beneath sickly green caps. She busied herself harvesting the fungi and told Archibald everything she had seen.

"Seven years of silence, she sounds bound by a curse, first Baba Yaga, this just keeps getting worse."

Anna shrugged, "Doesn't change a thing, Archie. She tasked me with this. I cannot say no."

"Clothos, the youngest sister of fate, what powers could her needle possibly curate?" Archibald pondered with a foreboding worry.

"That is our second worry. The first is what could possibly be in that section of forest that can keep Baba Yaga out?" Anna asked back.

"So many times, our luck has sucked, but now, my lady, we are good and fucked."

Anna nodded, "We may be indeed. Half the fun is finding a way to un-fuck the whole thing, though."

Archibald gasped, *"Such foul language, I am so proud, soon enough you'll set me loose in a crowd."*

Anna chuckled, "You keep dreaming, Archie. Speaking of which, I need to sleep. We head out at dawn."

THEY LEFT BEFORE THE sun began to lighten the eastern sky, and not a moment too soon, as Anna saw someone had painted the sign of the devil on the door to her rooms.

"It was that woman and her no-good son, mark my words, let me loose and I will gleefully destroy those turds!"

Anna seemed to actually consider it for a long few seconds before shaking her head. "It isn't their fault that they have small minds. Jonas is the one that exposed my being a witch. We need to leave quietly."

They had barely reached the street before the angry mob with prerequisite pitchforks and torches came warily down the street.

Anna pinched the bridge of her nose and let out a long, miserable sigh. She looked at the crowd and tried to smile. "We are leaving town now. There is no reason to dispense your misguided judgment."

"You're a witch, in league with Satan!" a gruff voice called out.

Anna squinted, "Edgar? How is your wife feeling?"

"She is much better, no thanks to your evil powers!" Edgar called back. The crowd grumbled its agreement.

"Actually, that's not even close to true. She was in the throes of a debilitating opium withdrawal. It was my herbs and the help of a nice water spirit that drew the toxins from her system. I am not in league with the devil," she replied.

"Then explain the invisible monster that always threatens people!" a woman yelled.

Anna frowned, "Alright, my power doesn't come from the devil. Archibald is, however, a demon."

A hailstorm of rocks and rotten fruit cake flying down the road. Anna stepped forward and raised her hands above her head. The rocks and fruit slammed into something that shimmered with amber flashes with each strike. "There is no reason to be impolite. I did nothing but help you during my stay," she stated calmly as more fruit splattered against the shield. She looked over her shoulder and smiled. "Show them yourself, Archie. But don't attack."

"Tearing them apart, is half the fun, let's see how fast these piggies run!" Archibald growled loudly.

The barrage of fruit stopped as the unruly mob quieted into a more ruly state of apprehension. Then sheer panic as a seven-foot tall (nine with the curled horns, twelve if you counted the leathery wings of obsidian) red-skinned demon with emerald eyes that crackled with hints of flame just yellowed in a cloud of yellowy brimstone smoke. Archibald hunched low on his black fur covered legs, the knees bending backward as his cloven hooves scorched the cobblestone street, and then sprang to his full seven feet (eight and a half with his head tilted back, thirteen with his wings fully unfurled) and roared so loudly windows cracked all down both sides of the street. The church bells gave out a sickly thud as if in protest at the reverberation of the fearsome sound, even as the waning moonlight glinted off of the rows of razor-sharp teeth of his open maw.

There was a clatter of dropped mob implements and horrified shrieks as the townsfolk stampeded off in the opposite direction.

Archibald turned towards Anna and his form wavered as he shrunk down to under six feet, his skin faded to a pale pink that looked nearly alabaster beneath the fading stars as dawn finally broke in purple bruises above. His fierce features softened and his emerald eyes became a swirl of greens and browns, and a wide smile crinkled his eyes at the screams of horror echoing through the town. "I have to admit, that was fulfilling, almost as much fun as the actual killing," he said softly, lost in her eyes.

Anna smiled at him and ran her hand along his cheek. "The scary demon enjoyed himself. That's nice. But we really should be going before they decide to test their luck with the sun fully raised."

Archibald reached up and gently touched her hand. His eyes said every word his lips could not as he slowly faded from view. *"If you'd let me eat a couple peasants, they'd learn to mind their manners in a lady's presence,"* Archibald said matter-of-factly.

"Maybe next time. An old one. Just as an example," Anna said in a serious tone as she began walking out of town.

"I am well aware that is a jest, but I'm willing to put it to the test," he replied cheerfully.

Anna chuckled, but it sounded hollow as she thought about the blight in the shape of an eye.

<hr>

"CLOTHOS IS THE YOUNGEST sister of Fate, with her needle, she weaves all of life, with something so potent in her control, Baba Yaga would reap chaos and strife."

"And what? I leave Hecate trapped and slowly drained of her very essence. I understand the stakes, Archibald, but perhaps you don't understand how important Hecate is to me," Anna answered flatly.

The Witch of the Wildflowers had summoned a steed made of tangled stems, hundreds of open blooms in a myriad of shades covered beast, and it sped effortlessly down the woodcutter's trail through the forest. A slight displacement that shook the leaves on the branches rattled in the wake of Archibald, who flew alongside her. They traveled in silence. The look on Anna's face, set and determined, told Archibald all he needed to know about her willingness to hear him out. He could read her mood from her simple gestures and the look in her eyes better than the hunters who were raised in this forest knew the trails that crisscrossed through the trees like the back of their hands.

"You think I am being foolish? Racing in. But you know I won't listen," Anna said eventually as the trees seemed to blur into a solid mass around them.

Archibald didn't answer her, which was answer enough.

"You wouldn't understand," she sullenly spat.

"Fucking demons have no souls, between their ears, nothing but holes. Someone has to worry about you, and since there's no one better, I'll have to do."

Anna opened her mouth and snapped it shut again. She winced when she felt the demon fall back behind the blossom steed. They rode in silence throughout the day, and it settled miserably over them like an itchy blanket as they broke for camp. By morning it had darkened and when they headed out again, it was a crevice that ached between them.

TWO DAYS LATER, THEY reached the edge of the twisted region. Anna's flowery steed reared up in fright as she tried to push on into the blackened land. Agitated, she slipped down to the ground and kept down to examine the blight. She plucked a daffodil from the foreleg of the horse and dropped it onto the scorched looking earth where it immediately was drained of color and turned to ash that blew away into the desolation in front of her.

"I see a mortar and three discarded urns, it seems daffodils are not the only thing it burns."

Anna looked into the malicious gnarled trees and saw what Archibald had meant. A giant mortar smoldered beside a half of a human thigh bone sized pestle. Urns in various states of decay lay abandoned all around it. Anna scrunched her nose. "That is peculiar."

"They reek of magic dark and old, of evil power and souls sold. But this rot is something more malign, yet carefully manufactured by design."

"What, exactly, does that mean?" Anna asked.

"Something watches from the trees, a smell of death upon the breeze."

Anna scanned the tree line and a flash of white disappeared in the dark that permeated the unholy grove. "Not much I can do if stepping on this tainted soil will kill me. Could you make out who or what was watching us?"

A little girl's giggles echoed in the distance, sending cold shivers down Anna's spine.

"Oh. Good. A dead child in the creepy forest. I was worried it would be something terrifying."

"Whatever that is, a little girl it is not, but something that seems immune to the rot."

Anna spread her fingers over the corrupt earth. An amber sigil began to glow bright and strong briefly, before flickering and sputtering, then sparking out. She let out a string of colorful curses as she crouched low and raised her hands again before finding herself knocked over by the sudden bucking of her floral steed. Without thought, she put her hands out in front of her to break her fall, then her face went pale as she realized where she was. She scrambled backwards into the verdant grass and stared at her palms, waiting for them to begin to erupt in flame or slowly dissipate. After a few minutes, she stood up and cautiously stepped into the blight.

A dull lavender glow seemed to emanate beneath her feet and she turned back to where Archibald stood with a raised eyebrow. "Did you have my pretty horse knock me into the blight?"

"Well, you think my opinion is for shit. I had a theory and ran with it."

"You had a theory. And what, pray tell, was this great epiphany that you felt worthy of gambling my life upon?" she asked, and it seemed frost came with every word.

"A coincidence that after seven long years, before we set out, the goddess reappears."

"And she blessed me to allow me to enter the withering eye. Blessed us, as the frog vomited all over you. Baba Yaga could not set foot on the wretched land, and somehow, she knew sending me would force Hecate to bless me. I do not appreciate you gambling like that without speaking to me, sound logic or not," Anna said, trying to soften her tone from the arctic chill to something more along the lines of the first winter breeze.

"You can be insufferable when you believe you're in the right, ignoring the obvious signs within your tunneled sight."

"Do you really feel this is the most opportune time to pick a fight?" she said, setting her hands upon her hips.

"Do you really think there isn't something more insidious at hand? There is some link between Baba Yaga and Hecate, I don't yet understand."

"You think they are working together? Then why didn't Hecate just bless Baba Yaga? Or get the needle herself and skip all of this hassle?" Anna asked sarcastically.

"I said I didn't understand, but that doesn't make me wrong. Forgive me for not being obedient and following right along."

"I don't need this right now, of all times. You can connect the dots that don't exist, but I have a goddess to save," Anna muttered and began to walk into the twisted grove. Then she stopped and turned around, "Or Baba Yaga is the one who has Hecate bound. What if she has been draining her?"

"And she relaxed the binding just a little bit, knowing how Hecate could manipulate it."

"And whatever purpose she has for the needle, likely has something to do with Hecate as well," Anna added. "It was all right there in front of me."

"The heavens shake at such a sight; the incompetent demon was actually right."

Anna opened her mouth. The set of her eyes promised something different from an apology, when a small figure in white leapt from the gnarled branches with a squeal of malicious delight. Anna stared up in shock as the ghastly corpse of a small girl flew down at her with a wickedly sharp black butcher blade clutched in tiny pale fingers.

Before it could land on her, Archibald appeared, a rocket of taut red muscle and black leather wings that caught the child by the stomach and flew straight into the obsidian trunk of a neighboring tree.

A sick crunch accompanied the broken branch that splintered as it burst through the girl's chest with a gout of half congealed blood. That wasn't enough to stop the vicious revenant, who plunged the black blade deep into Archibald's shoulders and arms, drawing lines of blood that steamed in the air. Archibald raised his hands to block the foul blade, and the child squirmed down the branch to fall down to the ground silently, swiping her blade down Archibald's legs as she went before scampering into the woods.

Anna rushed forward as Archibald landed heavily on the ground. *"That blade is wicked; the wounds burn and itch. And impaling wasn't enough to stop the little bitch,"* he said through gritted teeth.

Before Anna could respond, the little girl stepped out from behind the large rock, the gaping hole in her chest exposed part of her desiccated heart struggling to pump the thick dark ooze that oozed slowly from the wound. The girl raised her hand and waved once and giggled loudly. Anna stared at her in confusion. It didn't last long though, as the confusion melted into terror as a dozen children peeked out from the trees all around them. The forest erupted in the maniacal giggling and dead eyed stares from all around Anna and Archibald.

"If one of them is that ferocious a malevolency, the only way to fight them is for you, to set me free."

Anna looked around and saw the children making their way towards them, each carrying a long black blade. The rune on Anna's chest started to glow softly in the unnatural darkness, and she placed her forefinger to her lips and kissed it gently before rubbing across the rune, which faded away. "Give them hell, Archie," she whispered.

"Let me handle these despicable little beasts, even the dead shall fear this demon as it feasts."

Archibald's body started ripple, his muscles snapping and reforming in knotted masses, flames roared to life around his hooves, and sigils burnt themselves into the ruddy flesh of his snarling face as he roared his challenge with a great gout of flames that burst into the air and set the gnarled branches on fire above him. En masse, the children launched themselves at Archibald, the crackling flames absorbed by the ebony blades raised high in the air. Anna darted through the trees and spared a brief look back over her shoulder before vanishing into the dark miasma of the withered grove.

Archibald roared as the dead children scrabbled unnaturally up his wings and slashed fast and often as he blew an inferno of blue flame to incinerate those in front of him. He then flew straight up into the air, spraying crimson blood that hissed and sizzled across the tree, before he pulled in a controlled dive with five children hanging off of his wings, right before he crashed into the ground he pulled his wings right and slammed to the soil with a thud that shook the blackened leaves from the trees. The still smoking skeletons of the children that had been caught up in the inferno jumped into the new crater, with their ebony blades in small skeletal hands.

Anna flinched at the roars and almost turned back when she heard the bone shattering impact. "Archie has survived much worse," she muttered under her breath as she ran her hand over her crooked collarbone and remembered the flaring gills of the fishermen off the coast of Dunwich.

Another gout of flames blazed behind her, and she smiled a cold smile. The needle was close. The thrum of power called to her from somewhere ahead, even as the forest seemed to grow more malevolent with every step she took. She quickly ran her fore and middle fingers across her eyes and as quickly as the amber began to shine around them, she let out a yelp of pain and hurriedly covered her face. The entire expanse of woods was blinding with magical power. Whatever curse lay upon the soil was extraordinary. She chided herself at the foolish action and blinked away spots as a wave of nausea swept through her, drawing a sour grimace across her lovely face.

It was a single stick cracking that saved her from having her head cut cleanly off. She yelled as she dove and felt the blade swoosh through the air where she had just been. and stared in dismay as strands of her golden hair drifted in the breeze around her. The little girl with the hole blown clean through her torso stared at her with big black eyes and tried to pull the ebony blade from the warped trunk of what once was a sycamore. The golden glow enveloped Anna, and she quickly thrust both hands in front of her and manipulated her fingers in the air as if playing a game of cat's cradle with string, except the strings formed around the girl and as Anna pulled, they tightened tight enough to the girls' flesh to draw lines of thick dark blood. The girl tried to scream her inchoate rage at the bindings, but the branch earlier had pierced and deflated one of her lungs and the sound came out a wet wheezing gurgle.

"I am sorry, little one. The evil responsible for this shall pay dearly for this affront. Now rest," Anna said, sad yet resolute. She then pulled her hands apart quickly and the strands of light vivisected the squirming girl, who collapsed to the ground in a series of jiggling meat cubes that melted into a viscous black ooze.

The dark magic that coursed through the land seemed to be deterrent enough, the undead children being an anomaly, but Anna felt her pulse quicken as she tried to figure out what it was that had kept the little monsters from simply grabbing the needle and delivering it to Baba Yaga that was now her main concern. She absently stroked her chest where the rune that had bound Archibald had been. The familiar feel of the bond it allowed meant no matter the distance, they were never truly apart. It had been difficult in the vision to judge distance, but the sense of power humming added an eerie vibratory penumbra to the distorted leaves that was a clear indicator she was near the needle.

And just the same as when she had crept out, silent as a thief to escape her Mother's grasp, Anna found herself crouched next to a horrific parody of an old oak, staring into a large open circle. A large, empty circle. Anna stepped out into the clearing and walked towards the middle of the space. Right in the center was the well-worn bare soil where two trails intersected. And nothing else. No traps. No monsters. Just an empty circle.

"No wonder the little bastards couldn't find the needle. It isn't here. Which leads to the question of why they were left behind at all. She wouldn't want to slow me down if I am the only one that could enter," she methodically began to search the area as she muttered to herself. And then she smiled. "Hecate isn't just the Goddess of Magic, but crossroads as well."

Anna went to the bare spot where the two trails met and sat cross-legged in the center and closed her eyes. Her entire body was suffused with amber light as she drew more and more of the power until it radiated from her in blinding waves. Brighter and brighter, she flared until her expression changed from one of calm to one of pain and then she slammed her palms down onto the soil and the light poured through her and into the blighted earth. The earth shuddered and a keening howl came from all around her, so piercing she tasted the blood that ran from her nose across her lips, yet still she channeled her entire might to cleanse the stain in the name of Hecate.

The light began to fade, and then finally winked out and Anna slumped forward, clearly dazed. She blinked her eyes to try to focus them and stared at the twisted trees around her. She was spent and all her efforts had accomplished nothing. Anna felt the same desolation she had felt when Hecate had vanished, but now magnified by Archibald's absence as well, and in the face of her greatest failures Anna began sobbing. And as her tears, mixed with her sweat and blood, dripped onto the cursed ground, the drops pulsed as they splashed with a faint golden glow. Anna did not notice through her inconsolable sorrow. The golden motes flashed, not just from her tears, but randomly all around her. And then green started to push up through black growth, a faint spot here, then a cluster over there, before it soon sprouted from every patch of soil and twisted branch. Anna had calmed herself when she notice the first fresh growth and as she watched thousands upon thousands of bright blooms opened, completely obscuring any trace of the blighted forest in millions of dancing petals.

"Well done, little sister. This will hurt. I'm sorry," Hecate whispered.

Anna looked around for the Goddess, just in time to see a tarnished old needle rise from the ground and hover in front of her. She reached up her hand to grab it, but the needle had other plans and darted straight forward into the pupil of her right eye and vanished within. She raised her hand to her eye in more alarm than pain. She blinked a couple times and felt not even the slightest discomfort. Then her face contorted in sheer agony, and she threw her head back and screamed. The waves of her scream fluttered across the canvas of beautiful blooms detached themselves in the sudden tempest of swirling petals.

Anna fell to her side on the ground and stared uncomprehendingly as the storm of flowers swept away and the withering eye was healed of the curse. A dull clang could be heard from the distance, and with each thud, drew closer to where Anna lay at the crossroads. Soon, a large metal cauldron came crashing down to the ground in the circle next to Anna. The lid of the cauldron shifted slightly and two impossibly long pale arms came out and snatched Anna from the ground and into the pot, where the lid settled with a ringing clang. The cauldron launched itself into the air and began bouncing back the way it had come.

ANNA WOKE UP WITH a groan as the world shifted violently left and then right. She choked down the bile that rose in the back of her throat. It felt the same as being in a ship at anchor in a terrible storm, but mercifully settled down after a few long minutes. Once she was sure it was calm, she opened her eyes and took in her surroundings. The first thing she noted was she was firmly bound to a rough wooden chair that had been nailed to the floor. Thick itchy ropes threatened to cut off the blood flow to her hands and feet, and she struggled briefly but found no give in them. The room itself seemed to be part of a rustic hut, and I front of her sat a large desk with a chair that was held in place by a series of ropes that seemed reminiscent of a spiderweb. In the desk was a large glass jar filled nearly to the top with a sickly looking green tinted liquid, and floating within was a severed human tongue.

"Hello? I believe there has been a mistake. I requested a creepy room without a tongue in a jar," she called out hoarsely. Immediate regret and a grimace of pain flashed across her face. There was no response.

Anna closed her eyes and concentrated, but as quickly as she could summon her power, it was bled from her through the ropes and a sigil began to glow on the floor beneath her. She flinched as pain stabbed through her temples and she let out a deep breath and opened her eyes once more. That's when she heard a strange tapping sound. She cranked her neck, but it seemed to be coming from another room behind her. Her heart began pounding as the sound grew louder and closer, and Anna gave a small start of surprise when a door clicked behind her and swung open with long creaking. The tapping continued again, incessantly and seemingly from behind and above her. Anna leaned her head back, and a gasp escaped her lips as she saw the source of the noise.

Crawling across the ceiling was a hideous woman with long greasy balcony hair that swung down and slapped at Anna's face. The woman wore a tattered old white nightgown that was yellowed with age and stained with dark spots that seemed quite similar to aged blood. The woman gripped the ceiling with pale fingertips and toes that were blackened at the end where they made contact with the wood, which sizzled a little at their touch. Anna saw the entire ceiling was covered in small scratch marks. But the two features that squeezed Anna's heart in an icy grip were the coarse black stitches that sewed the woman's mouth shut and the obviously broken neck that had left her head hanging at a grotesque angle and flipped as the woman suddenly scurried across the ceiling and down the wall before bending backwards over the back of the roped-up chair with a horrific fluidity.

The woman stared at Anna with her head resting awkwardly on her boney shoulder. *"The Witch of the Wildflowers graces my humble hut,"* a serpentine voice hissed.

"It is quite lovely. I'll be honest. The tongue was off-putting at first, but it lends a certain ambiance and brings the entire room together. Do you have a decorator?" Anna asked.

"Do you have the needle?"

Anna smiled. "That's a funny story, actually. Almost as funny as the one about the hoard of undead children that attacked us in the cursed forest. You wouldn't know anything about them, would you Baba Yaga?"

Baba Yaga smiled, her lips stretched, and beads of blackened blood welled up from the incision point of the stitches. *"My lovelies get so bored, they seemed to love playing in the woods. They didn't cause any trouble, did they?"*

"Where is Hecate? The deal was the needle for her location."

Baba Yaga swung up from the chair and onto the desk in one smooth boneless looking move and leaned forward to put her face directly in front of Anna. Baba Yaga's right eye was bright and clear blue, with intelligence and malice in equal measure, while her left eye was a sunken milky mass that reflected the flickers of candlelight. The heavy stench of rot and decay wafted off of her, and Anna swore she saw something skitter briefly between the sewn together lips. *"The needle and then the goddess, tit for tat. Where is it? I can sense its power on you."*

Baba Yaga shifted her shoulders and her head flopped to the opposite side and she stared deeply into Anna's eyes before slipping back off the desk into her chair. The hut began to sway again, and Baba Yaga slid back and forth, the ropes stretched taut in one direction before she slid the other way. Her head lolled back, and all Anna could see was her pale white throat and greasy hair swaying.

"I never had a chance to find it. By the time I had expended enough power to cleanse the curse, I passed out and then woke up tied to this chair in your charming seasick cottage," Anna said after the hut settled back down again.

With one slash of her blackened fingertips, Baba Yaga cut the ropes binding the top of her chair and spun about to face Anna, albeit from an upside-down perspective. *"There is no reason to lie to me, Anna dear. Especially when you consider all the reasons, you have to tell me the truth and give me that which I seek!"*

"My favorite demon taught me how to respond when someone demands something rudely," Anna said with a mischievous sparkle in her brown eyes. "How about you go fuck yourself, you nasty bitch?"

Baba Yaga stared at her and then her hands reached back and began tugging at one of the coarse X's, keeping her mouth shut. Quickly, she unknotted one corner, and the thread slid from the open raw holes with droplets of blood and little slivers of meat, which she dropped to the floor. Anna could only watch in burgeoning horror as the squirming she thought she had seen earlier proved itself all too real and a black insect wiggled out of Baba Yaga's still partially sealed mouth. The insect fell from her lips to the desk and quivered for a moment before finding its footing and shaking the foul drool from itself, then spread open two large wings with emerald sigils that flared from the tender membrane. Another fell to the desk, then another, another, until they seemed to pour out by the dozens.

"If I am honest, it usually doesn't work out very well when Archie says it either," Anna said with trepidation as the nightmare moth army sat staring at her from the desk.

"I have heard so many tales of the Witch of the Wildflowers and her demon companion, but try as I might, I could not find you. Now I see the markings that keep you from sight. Clever girl."

"So, the children were to get Archibald away from me, then you could wait until I was exhausted and swoop in to grab me," Anna said as she watched the head swing back and forth, the great hair sweeping back and forth across the wooden floor.

"Indeed."

Anna nodded. "How did you capture Hecate? Surely such a pedantic plan couldn't have fooled a goddess."

A hissing laugh, the sound of a spider skittering across a skeleton, sent a ripple through the moths, as Baba Yaga began spinning in her chair. *"The gods and goddesses are just as naïve as the cattle in the towns. You give them far more credit than they deserve. You just have to know which thread to pluck."* With that, Baba Yaga reached into the desk and pulled out a rusted hook and began to stitch her mouth shut once more. *"Now, where is the needle, girl?"*

"You seem to be pretty capable with that hook, I don't see what more you could do with whatever needle you seek," Anna said, the feigned disinterest rang false to her own ears, but she still forced a nonchalant crooked grin, and hoped it didn't appear as sickly as she felt. "It is very impressive how you can stitch backwards and upside down. Maybe you missed your calling as a dressmaker."

Baba Yaga lurched out of the chair and climbed the wall behind the desk with that tap tapping scurry until she was directly above Anna. Her pale hands reached down and grabbed Anna by the hair and yanked back so she was forced to stare up through long swaying filthy black hair directly into her blue and milky glare. *"Enough! You don't need that clever tongue to give me what I desire! The needle! It is mine! Your whore of a goddess kept it as plaything, a focus, never using it for its true purpose! But I will, yes, I will because it is my right!"*

Anna bit back a cry of pain and stared through watery brown eyes at the monster above her. She felt rage and hate for this creature who took Hecate from her. Amber flashed in sputters and sparks, only to be absorbed into the purple sigil beneath her. The hissing laugh carved through the air once more and Anna's head was suddenly released as the tapping resumed and the door behind her slammed closed.

The last thing she heard was, *"My precious butterflies will make you more compliant."*

The moment the door shut, the black insects flew off the table and swarmed over Anna, who could do little more than jerk against her restraints as they covered her entire body. She opened her mouth to scream, and they flew past her tongue and down her throat and she felt herself choking on the writhing mass of wings and onyx bodies.

***

"ANNA, DEAR, IT'S TIME for your lessons," a soft voice said.

Anna opened her eyes and blinked at the bright sunlight streaming into the room. No. She blinking at the bright sunlight streaming into her room, her childhood bedroom. Anna looked at the doorway and her mouth fell open as she saw Frieda, the kindest of all the maids in her mother's manor, smiling at her.

"Good morning, sleepyhead, thought you might sleep all day away. Now come on, it's time to get dressed. Breakfast is waiting downstairs. Mustn't keep your father waiting," Frieda said with a smile.

"But my father is dead, Frieda. And I imagine you are at this point as well. It's been nearly twenty years since I last saw you," Anna said in bewilderment.

Frieda laughed, her musical laugh that had a way of making everything seem better. She pinched her own arm and made a grimace, "Lady Anna, I am not sure what sort of dream you had last night, but I can assure you, your father is very much alive and sitting downstairs right now. Perhaps you had too many little cakes at the Mabon celebration."

Anna's heart dropped. She looked around in panic, her heart pounding so loud it seemed to shake her blanket. The day after Mabon was the day her father had been found murdered. The day her life had been turned upside down. The day she saw her mother, truly saw her, for the very first time.

"Give me the needle and I can change the threads of the Tapestry of Fate. You could have the life you were meant to, not shunned for your powers by the rabble," a voice whispered.

Anna clenched her fists beneath the cover and felt something small and metal in her left palm. "It is impossible," she muttered.

"What was that, Lady Anna?" Frieda asked.

Anna got out of her bed and looked at Frieda with a small smile of apology. "It was nothing, Frieda. Just a silly dream I can't seem to shake. I'll be right down for breakfast."

"I shall let your parents know," Frieda said with a curtsey before shutting the door.

Anna opened her closet and stepped inside and looked at the strange golden needle in her palm. It tingled little arcs of energy that felt strangely familiar to her but remained just obscured by a fog in her mind. She knew this wasn't right, that she had experienced this before and could see exactly how it would play out. A part of her screamed in the haze, but she could not unravel the words from the experience. She slipped off her nightgown and reached for a dress when the entire manor shuddered, and she was thrown against the wall. The closet door slammed shut at the impact and when she tried to push it open, she found it was jammed closed. Again, the world quaked and Anna found herself bouncing from one wall to the other as the heaving continued for what felt like an eternity, but in reality, was likely only minutes.

"The needle, girl! Give me it before it is too late."

The closet door opened when she frantically tried it again and she stumbled into her room to see everything just as it had been before the awful shaking. Anna dressed quickly and fled her room downstairs to the dining hall.

"Good morning, Little Sparrow," her father called out with a smile as she entered. "Did you get lost on the way down?"

Anna hurried to him and gave him a crushing hug. He smelled as she remembered, and while she couldn't say exactly what that scent was, she knew it smelled safe and comfortable. "The earthquake tossed me about in my closet. Such a terrible thing!" she cried into his chest.

Her father laughed, a booming laugh that vibrated through her. "An earthquake? Perhaps it only occurred in your room."

Anna stepped back and looked up at him with a confused expression. "You didn't feel it?"

"The only quaking your father felt was from hunger because you chose to make him wait for his breakfast," a calm voice replied. Anna turned to see her mother watching her. A wave of fear swept through her at the sight of the woman that had made her life hell for years, one that still haunted her dreams whose scars Anna still carried. Her mother smiled, not the cold, malicious smile Anna had come to dread, but a warm one that felt alien, and spread her arms for a hug. Anna dutifully walked over and tensed immediately as her mother embraced her. "I was only teasing, Anna, please don't be upset," her mother said as she felt daughter's discomfort.

Anna stepped back and went to her seat at the table without a word. Frieda set a bowl down in front of Anna, oatmeal steamed, and different berries added sharp color. Anna smiled at her and set a napkin across her lap. Without warning, it seemed as if something rammed into the side of the building. The large chandelier swung wildly, spilling gouts of liquid wax onto the table. The tea service went flying off of the table and shattered on the floor. Anna gripped the edge of the table with her right hand and looked at her parents in fright. She had to swallow the scream forming in the pit of her stomach. Her father calmly sat stabbing at the eggs on his plate, even as they slid back and forth with each calamitous shudder. Her mother held her teacup in front of her mouth and Anna watched the hot liquid slosh back and forth.

"Are you alright, Anna?" her father asked as the tumultuous shaking abated. "You look a bit flushed."

"Too many little cakes last night. Don't think I didn't see you sneaking them to her," her mother said with a sharp look at him.

He laughed. Anna had forgotten how easily he had laughed, "a girl needs as many treats as she can abide. They will help her grow big and strong."

Anna wanted to yell or cry, or both, but she found herself incapable. How did they not notice the broken porcelain and rivulets of now solidified wax on the table? She saw wax in her mother's immaculately brushed hair and Anna knew she would not stand for such a thing.

There was something wrong, she wasn't meant to be here, but she didn't know where she should be. It was an itch at the front of her brain that no matter how hard she tried to think on it, it persisted, growing stronger behind her left eye. It didn't feel like a migraine. Somehow, it was worse.

"If you're not going to eat, you may as well head to the study to begin your lessons for the day," her mother said with a raised eyebrow.

Anna ate without enjoyment, the training she had not yet received but had been beaten into her, kicked in automatically.

Her mother smiled, "If that isn't a first, Anna actually listened to me."

"The Little Sparrow is growing up. Soon she shall fly on her own," her father said proudly.

"Please don't go to town today, Father. Stay her with me. We can go riding after my lessons. I found a field of dandelions and we can go make wishes," Anna blurted out after a mouthful.

Her father smiled sadly. "You know I cannot just cancel my day, Anna, no matter how tempting the idea."

Anna felt hot tears spill down her cheeks. "Please, Father."

He rose with concern and walked over to her, and wrapped his arms around her gently. "If you would just give her what she wants, we can make all of those wishes come true, Anna."

"Yes, Anna, give her the needle and everything will be better," her mother added.

Anna pushed back from her father and leapt to her feet. He looked down at her lovingly, the same way her mother was looking at her from across the table. Another loud crash and the entire house shook again, this time sending Anna flying through the air. She did cry out this time as she found herself hurtling towards the large mirror on the wall. Her mother stared at her from the rapidly approaching glass and Anna saw her mother's head sitting at an unnatural angle against her shoulder, with glee on her mismatched eyes of icy blue and shriveled white. Anna prepared herself for the shower of glass her impact would cause, but when she hit the mirror, the entire face turned liquid and quicksilver ran along her outstretched hands and arms, rushing up over her shoulders and neck and Anna felt it coalesce with a freezing cold over entire body.

"I WILL HUFF AND the puff your chicken legged hut down, you rotten witch, and when I finally get inside, it's your turn, you evil fucking bitch!"

Anna turned her head and vomited a sluice of still twitching limbs and wings to the rough floorboards of the hut and managed a tiny smile as she heard Archibald. The hut was already swaying back and forth, Baba Yaga's chair slid back and forth behind the desk with the rhythmic movement. And then the entire hut shuddered awkwardly to one side before slamming back down and resuming its movement. Anna felt the ropes cutting into her as she was jostled savagely yet forced to stay in one spot. Warm blood trickled down her wrist and she found she could squirm it around enough to restore some circulation.

"Anna, if you can hear me, I'm coming for you now, this goddamned shit is resistant, so I am not sure exactly how!"

Anna opened her mouth to answer and the door slamming open behind her held the words in her still burning throat. The tapping grew louder, and she saw Baba Yaga scurry across the floor and onto the desk, where she crouched in a wide-legged stance, seeming to ride the motion of the hut.

"Your pet is quite tenacious, but he will find my warding is more than ample to keep him at bay, even if his commotion was enough to break my spell momentarily. Give me the needle and all of this can end. You will have your father back and I will set you free with no harm."

"And what about Hecate?" Anna croaked.

"Long dead. I drained her years ago and her husk was used to incubate my children."

Anna spat on the floor. "See, that's where I think you're lying. If she were dead, who gave me the blessing to cross the withering eye?"

"Residual divinity I had saved up. I didn't trust it to protect me, so I used you to procure the needle. If you died, it would be no great loss."

Archibald rammed the hut again, and Anna felt her chair wobble slightly beneath her as the hut resettled. She let her head droop down, her hair coming forward to obscure her face as she looked down. The chair leg had splintered where it was nailed into the floor. Not only that, but the sigil seemed to be scratched as well.

Anna nearly smiled before Baba Yaga grabbed her by the hair and jerked her head back up again. *"Give me the needle or I will slowly skin you alive until I find it for myself."*

Anna clenched her fists and nearly gasped as she felt something metal in her left hand. Before Baba Yaga could react, amber energy swirled to life in a blinding burst and Anna yanked her arm free of the rope and hit Baba Yaga with a blast of pure force from the rune on her right palm. Baba Yaga let out a shriek if surprised pain and crashed into the wall behind her desk and slid down to the floor, stunned.

"Archie! Hit it again!" she managed to yell, the words tearing from her raw throat.

Archi roared, and then slammed himself against the hut harder than he had before. Anna let herself move with the force and heard the chair crack apart, and she crashed down to the floor. She saw Baba Yaga begin to stir and Anna frantically tried to call forth more power to free her limbs from the broken pieces of the chair. Anna managed to free her left arm just as Baba Yaga skittered around the desk and threw herself into Anna's chest and drove the wind from her lungs

"I have changed my mind. I'll dig the needle from your corpse," Baba Yaga hissed and raised her hands above her head. A crackling purple arced ominously between her fingers, a lightning storm that promised nothing but death and pain.

Anna coughed, and a trickle of blood ran down her chin. She felt the broken rib piercing her lung as the evil creature straddled her chest and she weakly whispered, "Please. Enough. You win."

Baba Yaga stared at her sideways as her head rested on her shoulder and the electrical crackle faded. *"Mercy? You ask for mercy now?"* Anna mumbled something, but it was lost behind a bubble of blood that formed on her lips and Baba Yaga leaned down. *"Beg me to spare you with your final breath. I want to hear you beg me to let you live. I won't, you know that. And once I have the needle, I'll cut your demon's wings off and mount them over my fireplace. Perhaps I will hang your pretty little head next to them."*

Anna slid the needle up her palm and grasped it between her thumb and forefinger. "I was wrong, which is hard for me to admit," Anna wheezed with a faint grin.

"About what? Thinking you could best me?"

Anna shook her head and coughed again. "No. Not that. I didn't pay enough attention. Hecate told me the truth. What I need the most lies within the withering eye. Not the trees though," she said painfully before thrusting the needle into the milky white eye of the evil witch.

Baba Yaga lurched backwards and screamed so loudly the hut began to break apart from the force of it. Rays of purple energy burst from her pierced eye like lasers that cut through the walls and ceiling as Baba Yaga raged in agony. Anna pushed up onto her elbows and flinched as new pains flooded from the broken rib. But that was nothing compared to Baba Yaga's torment. The old hag's body rippled and contorted. More and more energy leaked from her as her body began to rupture and strain, in turn, destroying more of the hut. Finally, the remains of the roof burst free of the hut and Anna looked up to see Archibald. It was all too much for her, and she slumped down with a faint smile.

FOR WHAT FELT LIKE the fiftieth time, Anna woke up and blearily opened her eyes. She felt no pain as she moved her limbs carefully about. She was on her back staring up at the stars that glittered like a hundred thousand diamonds across the ebony expanse of the night sky.

"And at last, our little sister awakes," a familiar voice intoned. Anna looked over and was overcome with emotion as she saw Hecate standing by a large bonfire. "No, this is not a dream, Anna. You did it. You managed to free me from my prison inside that loathsome old crone."

Anna sat up and found she was completely healed and dressed in all new clothing. "How long have I been unconscious?"

Hecate frowned. "Two months, three days, and fifteen hours."

Anna sighed, "And where is Archibald?' I couldn't have saved you without him." Hecate looked uncertain as to how to answer, and Anna felt her stomach drop. "Is he alright? Where is he?"

Hecate shook her head. "He stayed for a few days, but he was determined to find a cure for you. If I didn't know better, I would say that the demon has feelings for you, Little Sister."

Anna flushed, "And where is he now?"

Hecate sighed. "I don't know. He simply vanished a month ago. No word, no sign." Anna stood up, a bit like a newborn goal, and staggered slightly, but Hecate was there to steady her. "We will find him as soon as you are rested. It will do him no good if you died rushing off to save him."

Anna stepped back and glared at Hecate. "What do you mean, save him? I thought you didn't know where he was."

"He sought to find a genie to wake you. Nothing I did seemed to disturb your slumber, and we feared it was Baba Yaga's death curse that afflicted you. He wouldn't listen to reason. It seems you have rubbed off on him, and stormed off the minute I mentioned the djinn. I had kept track of him for weeks and then suddenly, I could not find him again," Hecate explained.

"You thought Baba Yaga cast a death curse on me? I never even considered that possibility," Anna said numbly as she tried to comprehend the flush of information.

"You cannot beat me at my own game," a voice hissed into Anna's ear. She jumped, started and looked around to see no one near

Hecate looked worried. "What's the matter, Anna? You like you've seen a ghost," Hecate asked.

Anna didn't answer her for a moment and then shrugged as she swallowed her sudden fear. "It is nothing, still not fully with it yet from the nap. Tell me everything about how you were captured and where Archie may be."

Hecate smiled and nodded. "Tonight we feast for Mabon. Tomorrow we search for Archibald. I have so much to tell you, Anna."

Anna nodded, trying not to stare at the long greasy hair hanging from the branches of a sycamore tree behind the bonfire, certain this was just the beginning.

SEVEN

DEATH, AND A DONUT

"ORDER UP! ONE TWENTY, one old-fashioned and eleven glazed!" the man behind the counter announced over the low din of the surprisingly packed donut shop.

Death rose, black robes billowing eerily, the wickedly sharp blade of his scythe catching the wan yellow light of the rising sun. The crowd stopped what they were doing and stared at the grimmest of reapers as he seemed to glide across the black-and-white checkered floor. A cold air permeated him; as if the touch of the grave radiated out.

"Hey, your goddamned robe got in my coffee!" a voice cried out.

The crowd somehow, at one time, managed to remain motionless, gasp, and were now facing the angry bald man in a newsboy cap who, in turn, was staring at the very Spectre of Death, Thanatos, with a defiant glare.

Death, a literal force of nature and unstoppable being, ignored the outburst and continued to the counter, where he set down his ticket. The clerk swallowed audibly in the silent room and picked up the ticket with a shaking hand. Verifying it was indeed number one twenty, he robotically grabbed the white box and two white bags and set it on the counter. "Uh, it's on the house. There are a dozen donuts holes in the bag too. Glazed."

It Is impossible to tell the expression on a bare skull, but if it were possible to infer an expression, the vacant eyes and perpetual rictus smile seemed happy. Death nodded once and picked up the parcels and turned to leave. As the gaunt figure went past the angry man, he casually tapped him with the handle of his scythe. The man's eyes immediately began to liquefy and run down his stubbly cheeks. A soft gurgle came from his throat, followed by a small gout of blue flame. He fell forward, spilling his coffee onto the table to drip onto the checkered floor.

It wasn't until the bells had sounded and the door swung closed again that the room erupted into screaming and chaos.

Everyone else died as scarabs crawled from the rapidly putrefying corpse of the bald man and swarmed throughout the shop, leaving nothing but pristine skeletons in piles. All except for the clerk would live to be one hundred and fourteen. He was never even sick once in his long life, though he would never understand the gift truly as he was driven quite insane by the ordeal.

Death was indifferent to the entire ordeal. A skeletal hand reached into the bag and popped a donut hole into the open jaw. The teeth mashed it into crumbs that fell through the empty ribcage and eventually tumbled onto the sidewalk from beneath the smoky robes. Pigeons darted down and pecked at the morsels of sweetness before stiffening and falling over. Maggots fell from the beak as the tiny tongue lolled out.

Death stopped next to a hot rod hearse parked in a handicapped spot. The car was a nightmare of chrome in angles that gave migraines it contemplated for too long. Death set the box and bag on the roof of the monstrous machine and pulled a set of keys from the voluminous ebony robes. The lights flashed a sinister red as the locks popped and the grim reaper set the scythe on the back seat and the donuts on the rear floorboard.

A police officer stood in front of the hearse with a ticket pad in her hand. "Excuse me, you cannot park in a handicapped spot without a placard or special plates. I am going to have to write you a ticket." Death strode silently to the front of the car and stood patiently as the officer asked without looking up, "I need your license and proof of insurance."

She looked up and her eyes grew to the size of saucers. Death ran a bone finger gently across her cheek and turned towards the car. Where the finger had touched on the officer's cheek was now red and slightly swollen. She reached up and touched it and the skin burst open. The raw edges of the sudden wound seemed to consume the living flesh in a slow wave that ended in gurgling screams from a fleshless face as the hearse door slammed shut.

Death slid the key into the ignition and the engine of hellfire and torment roared to life, causing every candle in a three-block radius to flare deep purple. A deep emerald smoke oozed out of the exhaust pipes, and sparrows fell from the sky as they flew overhead while squirrels convulsed on the grass.

Death turned on the stereo and Hank Williams began singing as a tinny guitar played behind his sad voice. Without looking in the mirrors, the car suddenly burst backwards into traffic, crushing the side of a gray Jeep. A spray of blood suddenly painted the interior of the windshield. The hellbeast vehicle leapt forward into the wrong lane, sending a blue sedan into a parked car. The body of the driver slammed by the steering wheel, now two feet farther back.

Death paid no heed to any of it. Phalanges tapped the steering wheel along with the drums. The donuts had not shifted a bit.

THE PARK WAS QUIET for a warm summer day. A few joggers ran along the manicured trails that wound through the trees and eventually alongside the lake. One, a red-faced man, puffed along, making slow progress but steadily moving forward. A near fatal heart blockage luckily found during an examination gave him a new lease on life. He may not be breaking any records, but he is doing what he could to extend his life. Lionel Richie sang about Sunday mornings, and he wondered if maybe his choice in music was part of the problem.

He stopped and stared at a group of joggers that were running as if their lives depended on it. They looked at him with frantic, wide eyes. He shrugged after a moment, then forced his feet to begin slapping the concrete once more.

"Know it sounds funny, just can't stop the pain,"

He found the rhythm in mellow seventies jam.

"Why in the world would anybody put chains on me? Yeah,"

A calm came over him as he saw the sun over the waters of the lake glistening on the waves.

"I just want to be free, just me, ooooh baby."

And then he found himself stumbling forward. His foot hit something solid, and the ground came rushing up to meet his hands. Both wrists snapped at the impact and he screamed in pain as he rolled onto his back. He squinted through the pain and looked to see what it was that had inexplicably caused him this agony.

It was a dead goose. He looked around, really looked and saw dead geese and ducks all over the ground between the waterline and the jogging path. Confusion warred with the pulsating misery flaring up his arms as he tried to make sense of it. The other runners had run past him, the dead birds littering the ground, the gears turned, but nothing made any of it make any semblance of sense.

Then he saw Death tossing pieces of something from a white paper bag. Donut holes?

It was as if the ducks didn't see the black robes that seemed to shift like the smoke wafting from a fatal wreck. The fight or flight was extinguished in the temptation of sugary dough. His mouth twitched, and he tried to scramble backwards, but his wrists gave out and he let out a yelp of pained surprise that startled the ducks.

The skull of Thanatos snapped to stare directly at him. Again, it is impossible to gauge an exact expression based on a faceless skull, but disapproval seemed to smolder in the empty eye sockets. Death snapped the thumb and middle finger of the skeletal right hand. At first, nothing happened.

The man stared in abject terror, frozen by the hooded skull's unflinching stare. Then the bodies of the dead waterfowl begin to twitch, to convulse, and then to make their way back onto webbed feet. They all turned unblinking dead eyes towards the man and began to awkwardly shamble towards him.

Death sighed, a hollow breath rattling through a birdcage of yellowed ribs, as the screams and sounds of tearing flesh exploded down the trail. The hooded figure stood up, the grass shrank and curled up, first brown, then brittle, then dust, as the reanimated birds fell still one by one beneath the lessening arterial sprays. The now empty white bag carefully crumpled and tossed into a garbage can, Death strode across the carefully manicured lawn and through a small flower garden of desiccated blooms, on his way to the parking lot.

* * *

"JUST LET ME RUN in here for a second. You can sit on the bench and wait for me. I'll look for something sexy," a petite brunette said with a knowing smile.

Her husband sighed, arms already over laden with bags. "Fifteen minutes. The baseball game starts at three and I need to grab cigars."

She kissed him on the cheek and walked into the garish pink store. He turned and carefully maneuvered through the shambling zombies of consumerism with a scowl. He managed to find a bench and let the bags slide down his arms to rest between his legs as he slid the earbuds in to listen to the pregame. He let his mind wander as they talked on base percentages and pitches they would chase, finding calm in the statistics when he saw a white box open in front of him with three rows of glazed donuts. He assumed this was a free sample to try to convince him to buy a dozen, but he was far too crafty for that. He didn't look up, just snatched a donut and muttered his thanks before closing his eyes and falling into the numbers.

It melted on his tongue with sugary goodness, and he smiled, really smiled, for the first time in hours. Too many people, too close and too loud, had pushed him to his limit, but this was exactly the thing to brighten his mood.

A crowd began to gather as he let out his first, and last, strangled gasp. It seemed as if the fluids were just suddenly evaporated from his system, going from normal skin tone to gaunt and then to gray in a matter of seconds. His ear buds fell out and the tinny sound of voices called in the silence as the onlookers stared in horror. Then a crackling sound as a goiter formed on the clearly dead man's throat. It undulated the papery skin as it slowly worked its way to the open mouth. Maggots, thick and writhing, poured across the blackened tongue and onto the faux marble flooring, more and more, and an incomprehensible amount of larvae washed out and against the shoes of the now panicked crowd.

The writhing maggots popped, releasing clouds of green spores that floated along the upper mezzanine and every one that inhaled it broke out in weeping sores and fell screaming to the filthy floor.

Death stood patiently on the escalator, the donut box balanced on one hand and his scythe resting on a boney shoulder, the empty socketed gaze transfixed on one store on the lower floor.

It was Natalie's first day at Build A Bear. She prided herself on her preparedness, always ready for any situation, head on a swivel.

Now, she pumped the button on the floor and forced back tears before saying softly, "Now put the heart to your, ummm, mouth and whisper your love into it, then place it in the body of the owl."

She nearly fainted as the cold of the grave swept along her tan arms. The robe seemed to hunger to touch her but stayed a millimeter off her. She added a little more cotton and gulped, "Is that cuddly enough?"

Death reached down and gave a tentative squeeze on the pudgy tummy of the mischievous barn owl before nodding briskly. Natalie shook as she carried the stuffed bird to the counter, where she avoided looking at the skeleton in wispy black, packing the happy owl into a white box that looked like a little house. "Does the owl have a name? For the birth certificate?"

Death's head cocked at an angle a flesh and blood body could never hope to achieve due to ligaments and the laws of reality. One finger pointed out and neatly tapped the name tag on her vest. The plastic warped slightly.

"Awww." She said, briefly forgetting who it was she was talking with.

She remembered and had to look down at her name tag twice to spell her name correctly as fear drove rational thought from her head as a small spot of cold seemed to radiate from the name tag where the plastic blackened and cracked. She didn't look at the bodies of the two middle-aged women that sniffed a little rudely when Death cut in line. One of the heads stared up from the floor behind the counter by the cash register. Natalie was on autopilot. She put the birth certificate in a small cardboard frame and set it by the little house.

Death offered a donut, but she declined with a forced smile and muttered no thank you. Death shrugged and balanced the boxes and left silently. A group of mall walkers marched in various toddler faced sweatshirts, arms swinging fiercely, eyes down on the shiny white sneakers who walked right into Death.

Later, when she could articulate what she saw fully, she would describe the scene as such.

The five old women marched forward, and it was like one of those car washes, the kind where you sit in the car and the big straps of canvas smack the car as purple and green-colored foam hits the windshield.

Except not. The robe seemed alive as it wrapped itself around the bodies of the walkers; the robes slapped rhythmically against the glass window at the front of the shop. The bears fell off the stands as the sentient fabric pounded harder and harder against the window and then, boom. The robes stopped flailing and a spray of assorted innards sprayed against the glass. She could, with great detail, describe the various viscera as it slid slowly down. She turned in her two weeks' notice immediately.

Death walked on unconcerned, the boxes still both a pristine white even as the rest of the corridor was not so fortunate. Onlookers stood frozen, gore soaked, as Death waited for the doors to slide open before stepping out into the light of the day. Hell had come to the mall, as affirmed by the guttural yells of terror.

• • •

KRISTOFF STOOD STARING AT the glass doors to the grocery store, his service revolver clutched in his sweaty hand. The news had been going on and on about the different scenes of carnage and death throughout the city. It started with a donut shop. As his shift began, he listened to the reports about a mall.

"Goddamn terrorists," he muttered as he tried to will his stubborn feet to move.

He flinched back as a woman slammed headfirst into the glass door. It slowly slid open, and her limp body fell forward. This kept the doors open and the sounds of screaming soon rang out into the parking lot. The terrorists were dressed in long black robes, and the few survivors described them as death itself. Kristoff pulled his belt up over his prodigious belly with a shimmy and a grunt and raised his weapon, using his other hand to settle the slight tremor.

He took his first steps through the open door. Stepping over the unconscious, he stressed the word even though her head seemed to hang at an angle that looked quite unnatural, woman. The body of a cashier hung, torn open as if something huge had crawled out from the empty chest cavity, on the slowly rumbling conveyor, a sick slapping as his innards, now outards, oozed along the black rubber.

Kristoff felt his breakfast, three sausage biscuits, roil in his guts. A drip of sweat fell into his eye, and he blinked furiously at the stinging. He ducked low and tried to survey the scene. Something, something big, had torn down the aisles, leaving shattered jars and torn boxes of food to be scattered all over the half-eaten bodies that lay strewn among the discarded goods. Carts lay on their sides, packages sent all over, filthy wheels hanging limply or strung with strips of flesh and thick mucus.

Kristoff could not think of a single act of terror that left a mess like this behind. He tried to think back to his training and took a deep, calming breath. He had been through scenarios much like this. Admittedly in virtual reality, but he held two distinct speed running records in the remakes of Resident Evil One and Two.

The thought occurred to him that he was indeed playing a game. Or dreaming. Either way, he was in his element. He crept along, past the body on the belt, paying great attention to detail. The way the torn skin hung looked as real as a high-end graphics card could manage.

The noises went from wails to wet chomping sounds as he crept through chemically enhanced sugar-coated bits in bright colors aimed at children's imaginations. A low sound caught his attention, and he froze in place, a sustained hissing followed by a rubbery squeak.

Kristoff choked down a scream as something touched his leg. He spun, sending a wave of pastel marshmallows skittering as he pointed his weapon in front of him and felt his finger grow tight on the trigger.

"Help me–" a faint woman's voice moaned, buried under boxes of oatmeal and toaster pastries.

Kristoff made a noise he hoped passed for calming and grabbed the hand and squeezed it. "Can you make it to the front door? The path is clear."

The hand went limp, and a ragged exhalation came from the bloody mouth of the woman. That is when Kristoff noticed her legs farther down the aisle, a thick pool of blood making the spilled oatmeal swell and take on a pink color. Kristoff sucked in his gut, held back the bile, and crawled forward to the end of the aisle. The hissing and squeaking still coming faintly and itching at the back of his mind.

At the end of the aisle, he peered out and wished he hadn't. The meat section had been ravaged, strips of raw beef and pork, and other cuts he tried not to discern were cast everywhere as if an orgy of feasting had occurred. A butcher was slumped over the deli slicer, his arms thinly sliced in a soupy pile on the other side of the gore encrusted machine that still spun, sending a spray of red to run down the window between him and the counter.

At the far end, at the floral section, Kristoff saw a figure in a long black robe and cursed under his breath. He got to his feet, adrenaline surging through his legs, giving them a teetering effect, like a toddler. He pulled every bit of false bravado he could muster and held his weapon in front of him. He paused slightly as he tried to comprehend what was happening.

A figure that appeared to be the Grim Reaper, nearly identical to the figure immortalized on heavy metal covers and bikers' arms, stood surrounded by blackened flowers that drooped towards the floor, petals drifting like a tepid grey snow, stood filling balloons with helium. A half dozen brightly colored balloons were tied around the handle of a rather intimidating looking scythe. As Kristoff stared, Death pulled the balloon off of the hissing tank and wound the sphincter of the balloon through skeletal fingers, then quickly tied a green ribbon around the balloon knot that was wrapped around the wooden handle.

Kristoff took a steady breath and cocked the hammer back, which was loud in the silent store. "Put the scythe down and turn around with your hands in front of you!"

Death put a balloon on the nozzle, yellow this time, and it inflated quickly.

"No habla Española, Senior Dias la Muerte, so turn your robe wearing ass around, right fucking now!" Kristoff yelled.

Death plucked the balloon off the tank and turned around to face Kristoff, who immediately squeezed the trigger. And the gun barked and lurched up. The bullet flew down the aisle and hit the balloon, right above where Death was holding it. The now free balloon shot up and began to fly erratically through the store. Death managed, again, with a face devoid of skin or eyebrows or even lips, to look annoyed. The robed figure turned and grabbed another yellow balloon and put it on the tank of helium.

"You on drugs, motherfucker?" Kristoff yelled. "I have a fucking weapon! And by the power vested to me by the Union Allied Security Company, I demand you turn yourself in to me until other authorities arrive!"

Death raised a hand and snapped once; it was the sound of a coffin lid locking in the still store. Kristoff opened his mouth to say something but went still when he heard a sound behind him, a wet slithering sort of sound that never ever equals anything good. He turned slowly and for a second got a glimpse of the thing that had torn itself free from the cashier at the front, a skinless slug demon with an impossibly large mouth that opened slowly to show spiraling rows of razor-sharp teeth like the inside of a turtle's mouth somehow more terrifying for the single finger impaled on one of the vicious-looking barbs.

Death left the grocery store, seven balloons bobbing merrily on the handle of the scythe as Kristoff shrieked in agony.

THE HOT ROD HEARSE rumbled, the sound of a thousand souls being smothered by the inevitable hand of eternity, as Death sped down the toll road southbound in the Northbound lane. The stereo crackled a bit, an old song obviously recorded off of vinyl began to play, a sort of ethereal hollowness to the guitar. Robert Johnson began to sing about the crossroads as Death looked to the left at the darkening sky.

Horns blared and cars swerved lanes, careening off the concrete barriers and each other as the chrome hell chariot raced along the tollway. A large blue semi with a long white trailer jerked, smashing the car on its left directly on the driver's side, the impact caused it bounced over the right side into an empty yellow school bus that crumpled before teetering over on top of a red sports car trying to zip past on the shoulder.

There was no place for it to go as the hearse hit it head on. From the side, had anyone been alive to see it, the cab of the truck seemed to swallow the hearse. In slow motion, the driver found his bottom half on the windshield of the hearse that came tearing through, while his still conscious upper half was propelled through a hailstorm of shattering glass from the truck's windows. A ripple ran down the side of the trailer, solid matter forced into a seemingly mercurial state until the hearse burst out of the back of the trailer in a stream of ice cream and intestines as the laws of physics caught up to the metal which exploded, the shrapnel cutting through vehicles and concrete alike.

The windshield wipers did little but smear the chocolate and feces with a marshmallow bile swirl across the glass. Death didn't even get to see as the car barreled through a jack knifed eight-wheeler with a windmill blade strapped to the back. The halves of the trailer swung pendulously and destroyed the barriers on either side, crushing vehicles on the Southbound side and frontage road. Death turned up the radio to drown out the screeching metal and explosions before wrenching the wheel left and heading into the night, eschewing roads for the fields filled with errant cattle.

DEATH WATCHED AS THE last rays of Helios fell behind the horizon before stepping out of the vehicle to stand beneath the field of twinkling stars. Carefully, the blade of the scythe carved a crescent moon into the soil. The outline crackled with a purple light that flared brightly, and in the skies above, the stars winked out, one by one, until only darkness swirled above.

What is it, Thanatos? A voice, sinuous and smooth, spoke from the dark.

Death held out a paper plate, the old-fashioned sitting in the center with a lone candle swaying in the breeze.

This foolishness again? The voice sighed, a note of disbelief ringing coolly.

Death stood implacable, staring into the night.

Fine.

The inky blackness seemed to detach itself from the sky and coalesced, moving the same as the robes that clad the gaunt horseman to form a figure of perfection that stepped down from the heavens to stand in front of the reaper. Her beauty made everything else lesser simply by her proximity, yet it was balanced by a coldness that spoke more of warnings of danger than poetic odes.

Nyx, one of the first beings, the personification of darkness, stood with her hand on her hip and a note of inconvenience set on her perfect face.

We have existed since long before Kronos himself stepped forth from Chaos before time existed. Why do you insist on this charade every year?

Death held the donut in front of Nyx silently. She made a sour expression before leaning forward and blowing out the tiny flame. Death plucked out the candle and reached into his robe, pulling out a blanket and spreading it carefully on the ground.

Nyx sighed and sat down and carefully inspected the donut.

This looks horrifying.

Death just pointed, and Nyx broke off a piece of the golden dough. She sniffed it hesitantly before popping it into her mouth. Her eyes widened, and she smiled, albeit against her will.

Oh my. This is truly ambrosia.

Death went back to the hearse and returned with the seven balloons and a white cardboard house and sat down next to her.

Nyx arched her eyebrow at the colorful balloons.

More theatrics, Thanatos?

Death released the balloons, one a time, red then orange then yellow. Green, blue, and two different shades of purple slowly drifted into the night.

Nyx stared at them in confusion for a moment.

This is lost on me.

Death placed both hands together above his head and slowly spread his arms down until they were parallel to the ground.

A rainbow?

Death nodded and looked away from her. Nyx gasped softly and watched the balloons, a rainbow in the darkness, an impossibility made real. The stars reflected off the years that formed in her black eyes as she followed them higher and higher. Her cold hand slid over to rest on top of the skeletal one sitting on the blanket. They sat silently until all that remained of Nyx's rainbow was the memory of it floating into eternity.

Death passed the final box over to Nyx, who looked at it with an odd expression. She popped open the top and pulled out her owl and tried to hide her bewilderment. She pulled out the piece of paper and looked it over.

Natalie?

Death shrugged.

Nyx looked at the owl for a long while before finally pulling it into her chest and squeezing it.

I believe that I love it.

Then she leaned in and brushed her lips against the cheekbone of the skull.

Thank you.

Nyx rested her head on the shoulder of Death, her owl squeezed close to her chest and sighed happily.

And Death, even though there was no real way of telling the expression on an expressionless skull, seemed content, if not downright happy as they quietly sat together on a blanket, under the stars, together.

EIGHT

WAITING ROOM

"Number one twenty, one, two zero, we are looking for numbers one twenty and one eleven," the bored voice called over the intercom system.

I looked down at the slip of paper in my hand, eleven-eighteen. Fuck. The waiting room was filled with people, all looking at their own pieces of paper in disappointment. I glanced at the woman next to me and saw her paper with one twenty in a small print resting on her thigh as she snored contentedly in the uncomfortable plastic chair.

I briefly considered switching pieces with her, but instead tapped her shoulder gently, needing to dodge an elbow as she let out a startled yelp and laid the darkest glare on me I had ever witnessed.

"They just called your number," I said, apologetically.

She didn't make a sound, except for a low grunt of exertion as she stood up and headed to the counter.

"You could have switched numbers with her," an older man in the row behind me said.

I shrugged. "Didn't feel right, you know?"

He eyeballed me intently and then smiled. "I do. Still. Nowadays, most people would have just switched numbers and had at it. I'm Ralph. Nice to meet you."

"Edgar, same," I said back, torn between not needing a new friend and knowing it could be hours until my number was called.

Ralph had no such misgivings and quickly scurried to the open chair next to me with a devilish grin. "What are you here for?" he asked as he sat down.

"I need to get—" I paused.

Why was I here? For the life of me, I couldn't quite recall.

Ralph laughed. "Maybe you're here to get your memory checked."

I laughed, but my mind raced. I looked around in a panic. I didn't even know where I was. I could feel my pulse begin to quicken as I looked around the bland beige room filled with restless people. A big display by the counter showed one, two one in red numbers that flashed every couple seconds.

"Why are you here?" I asked Ralph absently as I wracked my brain.

Ralph looked at me with concern. "You alright Edgar? You went pale as a sheet."

"I don't know why I am here. Or where here is," I said, confusion heavy in my tone.

Edgar nodded, as if this was perfectly normal. "You are sitting in the Waiting Room. I imagine you have an appointment. Nothing to worry yourself sick over."

An appointment. That made sense. I've been so busy with work, running from airport to hotel to meeting, rinse and repeat for the last year and a half. When was the last time I just sat down and relaxed?

A year back, most likely, before Debra left.

I tried to smile at Ralph, but I could feel it come off sadly. The look on his face said he saw right through it, but he was a gentleman and didn't say a word.

I loved Debra, deeply and madly, in a way I had never loved anyone before. And then I got the dream job that would turn everything into a nightmare of motion. It's funny when you get exactly what you want in life and everything just falls apart, anyway. I had the perfect girl, and we made it through some very lean times together and came out stronger for it. We both worked two jobs to squirrel away enough to buy a house. We were living a fantasy life. Then the call came in. The hundred thousand dollars of debt for a piece of paper finally paid off.

We knew this new opportunity brought its own set of challenges, but when you have been through the fires of hell, what is there left to fear?

Complacency. The silent killer of suddenly having the means to get whatever we wanted while losing sight of the things that really mattered. I was gone longer and longer and the time I spent at home was less about us incrementally until one weekend there just wasn't an us any longer. We had become friends. And Debra wanted more than a live-in friend with occasional sex.

I threw myself into the job. Drank at the hotel bar when I would have called her to bitch about inane things. Slowly, over time, I began to see all the things I had done wrong. Too late to change them, but I got to relive them at the bottom of every bottle, let them fall onto my tongue from every upturned shot glass.

I should have called her. Apologized. Told my boss that I needed less time on the road and more at home with Debra.

I didn't. I couldn't say why, not really. Pride, maybe. Fear. Stupidity. You pick. Maybe a mixture of each. Until one day I blinked, and it had been a year, and I was on my way to the airport in the back of a cab answering an email and wishing I could just tell her one more time how much I always loved her, despite letting every minor inconvenience lay between us.

"That sounds rough," Ralph said.

I just stared at him, not understanding at first. "Did I say all of that out loud?"

Ralph sputtered and then barked out a braying laugh. "Unless I am one of them X-Men with telekinetic whatchamacallits, I would say so."

"Telepathic, telekinetic means you can move things with your mind. Telepathic is reading thoughts," I corrected absently.

Ralph stared at me intensely with one hand to his forehead and the other pointing at me. The pointing hand quivered as he spoke. "You're thinking of the number forty-two."

I laughed at the ridiculousness of it. "I am now that you said it. That much is true," I answered.

Ralph lowered his hands and smiled. "If you had the chance, would you call her? Tell her everything you just told me?"

I shook my head uncertainly. "I don't know. It has been a year. I probably missed my window by this time."

Ralph shrugged. "Stranger things have happened."

We both grew silent. One four eight flashed above.

"You married Ralph?" I asked to break the quiet that felt too heavy.

Ralph didn't answer for a long bit. "I am what you might call a confirmed bachelor," he said finally. "Love and I were never acquainted; I didn't have much interest in it, and it seemed to feel the same about me."

I felt a warring pity and jealousy well up within me. What did Shakespeare say? It's better to have loved and lost, then to never have loved at all? The unparalleled heights were indescribable, but the fall from grace was equally profoundly life changing.

I wondered what Ralph thought love was. Did he only know shadows like one of those people in Plato's allegory? Was it like being colorblind with a box of crayons in various shades of gray, only picking based on name and an inaccurate idea of what blue was?

"Had a ton of sex though, imagine that probably balances things out in its own way," Ralph mused, breaking my thoughts.

I couldn't help but laugh. "I guess it sort of works to smooth things out," I agreed.

"My advice? The advice you most definitely did not ask for, supplied free of charge by someone with zero experience in these things? If you get the chance, you should call her," he added.

Even though I knew he was right, that there was no harm or ill intent behind his words, they angered me a little. Possibly because of the truth in them, or because it bristled me to have a stranger tell me what I should do. I have never been one to do as I was told, which led to a fair share of problems, but was also what made me so damned good at my job.

"What do you do for work, Edgar?" Ralph asked, oblivious to my change in mood.

"Data security consultant for law firms and corporations," I answered flatly.

"That sounds like words you just made up," he replied.

I looked at him in surprise. He was an older fellow, wrinkled and hunched a bit, but not so old that he shouldn't have at least some knowledge of computers and protocols. "I promise you it is not," I said curtly.

"Oh, I didn't mean anything by that. There is plenty I don't know nothing about. Never took to technology all that well, keeps moving forward and changing and I am okay at my own speed," he said with a self-deprecating grin. "I still remember when a portable phone meant it had a super long cord that was a mess of knots."

I couldn't help myself and chuckled, feeling the upset bleed right out of me. I looked at Ralph, who was staring up at the flashing red digits, and asked, "What do you do for a living?"

Ralph looked at me curiously. "That is an odd way of looking at a job, isn't it? Doing it for a living? I try my hardest to live for a living. Work is just a penance to keep from having too much of a good time."

I hadn't thought of it like that. The idea of working ourselves to death to try to find the means to live suddenly struck me as an ass backwards approach to life.

Ralph saw the realization dawn on me, and he nodded. "It seems to me that we have put such a focus on hard work and dedication, we forget why we go to work in the first place. It is what happens when billionaires buy the newspapers and take control of the narrative. It is noble to give your all to the job." He leaned close and looked me in the eye. "You know why we get weekends off?"

I nodded. "They started the five-day work week to give the workers time to spend the money they made. Work in the car factory all week so you can then purchase a car, return the money, plus interest, to the company."

Ralph slapped his knee and let out another one of those braying laughs. "And the suckers did exactly that! Brilliant play by that Nazi sympathizer, Ford. I imagine it won't be long before some company decides to reintroduce the old mine owner company store's gimmick. You're not a slave if it is voluntary, right? What do they call them, indentured servants?"

I didn't answer, couldn't form words. I felt as if I had been punched in the stomach as the truth of his words hit me. How many times did I call my boss and hear the sounds of water in the background? Or his dogs barking when someone rang his doorbell? I was in whatever town for the week, putting in fourteen hours' days, and he was at home, or on vacation, living an actual life while mine had fallen apart.

"Work shouldn't be your life, but a means to living your best life. The higher ups try to make it seem like an honest way, putting the company before yourself, but what is the end result?" Ralph asked me, watching my face.

"The company makes more money and I get two days off to spend the pennies I make off of every hundred dollars they get," I muttered.

"And you consider yourself fortunate to have that?" he asked casually. "Seems to me that you lost more than you ever earned money wise."

I thought about Debra and what we had when we didn't have anything at all except each other. I just shook my head as the number ticked up to two zero seven.

Ralph looked at me seriously. "Why are you here?"

That sheer panic struck again when I tried to remember why I was here. The room was too big to be a waiting room, too many people say in row after row of hard plastic chairs, looking at tiny scraps of paper anxiously, darting eyes that showed the same confusion I was drowning in. If I tried too hard to focus, a stabbing pain began to develop behind my left eye. If I continued, it went to my right as well. I stopped looking around the room and quickly bent down with my head between my knees as my stomach roiled.

The carpet caught my eye, the same bland beige that dominated the room. The strands seemed to sway slightly, probably the intense headache pulsing, but the more I stared, the more frantic the movement.

I leaned closer to inspect, but was startled by Ralph's hand on my shoulder. "You okay, Edgar?"

I looked at him and shook my head once. "I don't know why I am here."

He nodded sagely. "What is the last thing you remember?"

I opened my mouth to answer and then closed it again. I could not recall driving here from the hotel. Or was it home? I couldn't remember anything except for—, "I was on a plane."

Ralph smiled, "You didn't take a plane here, though. I doubt the parking lot is big enough to land it."

"No, of course not," I said, trying to remember. "I was in OKC at the capital, testing the new system we had installed. It went well, besides a dirty needle and a cup of piss in the stairwell. The plane boarded on time, a short flight from OKC to Dallas. I was not happy because I was supposed to go home, but they had an emergency at CBRE and needed me on-site."

Ralph listened but didn't say anything as I struggled to piece things together.

"I had a few to drink at the airport while I waited. Called it celebratory as I got bumped to first class due to the insane amount of miles I have accumulated. I guess I had too many and fell asleep on the flight." I looked at Ralph, knowing the answer but asking anyway, "Is this CBRE in Dallas?"

"I have been to Dallas a few times, and buddy, this ain't Dallas. I don't know what that alphabet soup is either," Ralph said, throwing his hands up.

Two three nine flashed above us and I looked at my ticket again, eleven-eighteen still.

"And now you sit in this waiting room, but what are you waiting for?" he pushed.

"I am a patient boy. I wait. I wait, I wait, I wait. My time, water down the drain," I sang to myself, distracting myself from the pain that ebbed throughout my head. "Everybody moving, everybody moving moving moving moving, please don't leave me to remain."

"Tell me about the flight," he prodded.

Lightning flashed across the wings as the stewardess poured a can of coke and passed me two bottles of whiskey. She was cute, and the plane was half full, headed back to DFW for routine maintenance, so she sat down, and we started talking. I wasn't listening. Her skirt had pulled up and all I could see was her inner thigh.

Thunder boomed and the entire plane rocked. I was startled, and she laughed a little. One of those wild storms that whips itself up over the Arbuckle Mountains to attack the dusty plains, she said, resting her hand on my knee.

"What color were her eyes?" Ralph asked softly.

When her hand touched my knee, I looked up in surprise. My first thought as I stared into her bright blue eyes was of Debra's soulful brown gaze. She stared at me, and I knew she wanted me to kiss her. Her lips were parted slightly, and I saw the tip of her tongue.

"And what happened?" Ralph asked, leaning forward.

I gave him a curious look. "Can you hear my thoughts?"

This should have freaked me out, I know it, but it didn't. The stadium sized waiting room, the carpet that swayed on its own, the giant red digits flashing, and an old man that could read my thoughts all seemed perfectly normal to someone who was suddenly somewhere he had no recollection of going, waiting for something he had no clue what it could possibly be.

"Edgar, what happened next?" Ralph asked, undisturbed by my question or my thoughts.

I leaned back. The only lips I wanted to kiss belonged to Debra. She was upset, but not for long.

"Why not?"

My eyes widened as I remembered.

The plane ripped apart. One moment, the stewardess was angry. Then she was gone. The entire side of the plane was gone. I was only still there because of the seatbelt.

I remember falling.

"And what did you ask for as you fell?"

If I had one more chance, I would beg Debra to take me back. I would quit the job and go back to working two. I knew I was going to die, and all I wanted was one more minute with her.

I looked at Ralph, then around the room. "Am I dead?"

He smiled. "Not completely."

"Can I go back?" I begged.

Ralph sat back and looked up at the red numbers. Eleven-seventeen. "Would you squander a second chance?"

I laughed. "Who would answer that truthfully?

Ralph looked me dead in the eyes. "You would."

I sighed and shrugged. "I don't know. Best intentions and all that. For a while? Of course. Forever?"

The voice called out, "Number eleven-eighteen."

I stood. And Ralph was gone.

NINE

LOST IN EPHEMERA

THE VERMILLION SUN ROSE over the western horizon of Flouron, painting the sky in crimson trails that refracted playfully off of the crystalline structures of the small planet's capitol city, and main hub for scientific endeavors, Leonine XII, in a dazzling display of dancing hues, a sight once considered one of the ten most breathtaking in this far-flung quadrant of the galaxy.

Bel Et, Flouron's brightest mind, and leader of the scientific community, saw none of the splendor though, his clear blue eyes were focused on the information glyphs spilling down the display in front of him. He swiped his hand in the air in front of him and the data dissipated as he rapidly tapped the keys of his holographic keyboard, only to sigh in frustration as the same sigils populated the screen. "I told them this was coming, but the fools all ignored me," he muttered, frantically trying new equations to the same futile results.

"Bel, my love, come sit with us for a moment," his wife called from the kitchen.

Bel swallowed his frustration and anxiety as well as he could and joined his beautiful wife and their newborn son for a morning repast of sloggons and whipped thistle berries.

"Any progress, darling?" Kira asked as she bounced little Karl on her knee, where he smiled a gum-filled smile and giggled as streams of thistle berry ran down his chin.

Bel was careful to hide his building fear and simply shook his head before sipping mindlessly at his frothy cup of kaffe. "All the simulations yield the same results, though none of my peers will even entertain that they may be correct."

Karl cooked and reached out with his pudgy little arms towards Bel, who happily grabbed him.

"Perhaps the situation is not as fire as you suspect, my love. If so. Surely, at least your father would acknowledge your findings," Kira said with a tired smile.

Bel nodded slightly. "Perhaps you're right."

A small tremor ran through the home, causing Karl to giggle as Bel lifted him up from the sudden deluge of kaffe running across the table.

Kira stared in fright at Bel. This was one of the signs he had been expecting for weeks now, the first tremors of the eventual quakes that would reduce Flouron to nothing more than debris in space.

"Eddie! Eddie! Where are you?" a shrill voice called out, shattering the silence.

"I'm in the back closet," Eddie answered meekly. He carefully closed the comic in his hands and slipped it into the plastic bag.

The closet door swung open. "I've been calling you for the last thirty minutes. Have you been reading those fucking comic books again? I thought you were packing them up to sell?"

Eddie nodded and reluctantly slid the now bagged book back into the flat box, making sure it went into the right position. "I am, just tidying them up. There is a collector coming this weekend to look at the entire collection."

The entire walk-in closet was filled with flat boxes, mint condition action figures in unopened packages, and signed artwork from the nearly seventy-year run of Eddie's favorite comic book, Fantastic Man. A lifelong collection that had been his pride and joy until he met Jen. Now it has become something she made him feel ashamed of.

Jen snorted at him from the doorway, "You think you can sucker some poor loser into buying all of this trash?"

"One man's trash. Is another man's treasure, my dear," Eddie said, barely flinching at her harsh words. "Fantastic Man is one of the most popular characters in all of comics."

Jen frowned down at him and sucked her teeth slowly, "It is fitting you keep your precious collection in the closet. Just like the majority of the stupid comic fans. What a waste of time."

Eddie didn't say anything. He knew nothing he said would convince her otherwise. He had tried, in the beginning, to share his love of Fantastic Man with her, to no avail. If anything, it only made her hate it more. And now, as their wedding date grew closer and closer, she had demanded before she would move in with him, with her husband, he had to get rid of the collection. She wanted to use the closet for clothing, not dolls and poor artwork.

Jen sighed, "I am going out to lunch with my mother. See if you can manage to do something more than sit in this closet of shame and read all day while playing with your dolls."

Eddie smiled sheepishly at her as she slammed the door. He barely managed to catch the Diamond Edition, 1997 Re-Birth of a Legend Edition before it slammed onto the ground. "Oh Shit! Are you okay?" Eddie asked the action figure as his hands shook. This was one of his favorite pieces, from the edgy reboot period, if it had hit floor and been dislodged from position in the slightest, the value would have plummeted. As it stood now, the pristine, formed plastic was worth triple what he had spent on Jen's engagement ring.

"I am sorry, Karl Et, son of Bel Et, and last son of Flouron. She doesn't understand. It isn't her fault, you know. She was raised in a house with no encouragement for art or imagination. She couldn't begin to understand the subtle nuances of your long story," Eddie said sadly to Fantastic Man, who stared at him with his famous cocksure grin and arched eyebrow. He had to admit that the stark nineties look of the redesign with shoulder pads and pouches everywhere, compared to the classic look of spandex and red underwear the character was most remembered for was probably not the best changes, but it was what he had first read and held a special place in his heart.

Eddie reverently placed the figure on the floor next to him and opened the flat box back up, and began digging through the issues, carefully sealed to maintain their value. A smile came over Eddie's face suddenly as he pulled out a personal favorite and held it up for the figure's blank blue stare to take in. "Issue 228, the first appearance of your true love, Ace Reporter, Veronica Valentine." Eddie slid the issue out carefully and flipped through the pages, keeping the comic in view of the sealed figure. "They didn't try to make her some kind of damsel in distress, always something I appreciated, especially for such an old issue. No, they found a suitable equal for you, which made the relationship feel real."

Eddie's phone buzzed in his pocket and startled him for a second as he tried to re-bag the comic and pull the phone out at the same time. It was the doorbell camera app, he noted, puzzled. He highlighted the camera and tilted it down and saw one of his favorite things in the entire world sitting on the porch, a brown package with a sticker shaped like the diamond crest on Fantastic Man's uniform, a bold, stylized F in deep crimson emblazoned in the center next to Eddie's name on the label.

Eddie looked at Fantastic Man. "I didn't place any orders, especially not with how hard Jen has been riding me about getting all the collection out of here. Wait right here. I'll be back in a minute."

Eddie was true to his word, and a minute later sat on the floor with breathless excitement as he carefully slit the tape on the side of the box and lowered the flaps to expose a wooden box inside, which he slid out carefully. He let out a low whistle as he examined the dark wood, ran his fingers over the intricate etching of the same diamond and stylized F, before he popped the small brass latch and opened it up to show a carefully placed black velvet pillow. Eddie ran his hand over the full gray metal that lined the inside of the box, feeling the complex line work in the soft feeling metal. A curious expression crossed his face, and he ran his thumbnail along it gently and saw a slight crease form. "Is this lined with lead?" he muttered softly to himself. His hand drifted across the velvet, and he felt something solid and carefully spread the velvet open to expose a lavender crystal shard, and his eyes widened.

Eddie lifted the crystal out and held it up to the light, enamored with the way the light played through the unpolished gem. He held it out for the Fantastic Man figure to look at. "Holy shit, would you look at this? It is a perfect recreation of the rarest type of Flouronite from the comics, Purple Flouronite!"

Eddie set the crystal next to the action figure and slid one of the many boxes out of the stack onto the floor next to him. He flipped through the bags and, with a triumphant smile, pulled out the issue he has been looking for, *Fantastic Man Secret Files, Issue 2*, and gently turned the pages until he found the section he had wanted.

"Purple Flouronite is considered the rarest form of Flouronite, and also has the strangest effects on the Last Son of Flouron. Unlike the more common variant, Sapphire Flouronite, which is one of the few materials known to not only injure Karl Et, but with prolonged exposure could possibly kill him, the Purple Flouronite had the ability to change Fantastic Man's powers fundamentally, and in certain cases, removed them entirely," Eddie read excitedly. "How fucking cool is that? I have seen plenty replica Flouronite shards online, but never one this nice, and not purple as far as I can remember. There hasn't been a story that revolved around this variant since the early 70s, if I remember correctly."

Eddie grabbed his phone and did a quick search and pulled down two more boxes and extracted the issues which centered around the mysterious rare Flouronite.

EDDIE WAS IN THE kitchen when he heard the front door open and smiled when he heard Jen gasp as she saw the candles on the dining room table. "The wine should have had enough time to breathe, dinner will be done in about seven minutes," he called to her as he stirred the vegetables.

"What is the special occasion?" Jen asked as she poured a glass of red and let the delicious aroma wash over her.

The oven timer chimed, and Eddie quickly pulled out the ham and carried it to the table so it could rest. He looked at her and smiled, "You have been so sweet to me. It seemed the least I could do was make my favorite lady's favorite meal."

Jen frowned at him as she slipped her wine. "And how, exactly, was I sweet? By going out for the day and giving you time alone?"

Eddie laughed, "Of course not, my love. I got the present you ordered me today."

Jen eyed him warily. "I didn't order you a present."

Eddie laughed again, albeit a little less assured, "Of course you didn't. Give me a moment, the rolls are nearly down, and I need to brush them with butter once more."

Jen drained her glass and refilled it as she listened to Eddie humming in the kitchen. He soon returned and set the Brussel sprouts and honey glazed carrots on the table next to the ham. One more trip and the rolls steamed happily as well as he sat down and poured himself a glass and topped hers off as well.

Jen stared at him as he carved the ham, "What is this present I supposedly got you?"

Eddie looked at her with an arched eyebrow. "Supposedly? If it wasn't from you, I don't know who would have gotten it for me."

Jen let out a warning sign, "What is the present?"

Eddie looked at her, genuinely confused. "Wait, are you being serious? I left it upstairs when I came down to cook."

Jen stood up and drained her glass quickly. "Show me this mystery present that made you so happy you cooked my favorite meal."

Eddie felt off balance, but nodded and led the way. Jen didn't say a word as she followed him up the stairs and to the closet door, but her agitation thrummed in the air around him with a palpable sense of danger like an angry hornet. Eddie opened the door and walked over to the ornate wooden box and held it up to her as he slid it open and showed the shard of purple Flouronite.

Jen clucked her tongue, "And what in the fuck is that supposed to be? Some kind of healing crystal that will cause you to finally grow the fuck up?"

Eddie's jaw dropped. "It is a replica of the rarest Flouronite from the comics." He knew immediately that was not the answer she wanted as her eyes tightened into angry points that seemed to burn through him.

"For a minute, maybe even two, when I got home, I was actually excited. You know why? Because you genuinely seemed to be acting like a fucking adult. The house was straightened up, dinner was going, and none of the childish bullshit was anywhere to be seen. I thought maybe that hint of maturity you have shown so rarely was going to blossom. But it wasn't, was it? You spent the day playing with your goddamned toys because, for some stupid fucking reason, you thought I suddenly supported this immature bullshit. And the worst part? I'm not even disappointed with you. No, I'm disappointed with myself for thinking you could change," she spat.

Eddie flinched at her words as if physically struck. "I don't know what to say," he muttered sadly.

Jen laughed, a harsh and humorless sound like ice cubes grinding. "Don't say anything, Eddie. This was long coming, and as loathe as I am to admit it, my mother was right. I just needed this pathetic little show to see it. This relationship was never going anywhere, and all I have done was embarrass myself by continuing the charade. For every step of progress that I think we have made, it is erased by your singular immaturity."

Eddie felt hot tears spill down his cheeks as he tried to find words to express this bitter hurt he felt flare through his whole being. He never managed to get a word out though as a sapphire blast suddenly filled the closet, and as he watched, Jen's head simply melted in the blue light to ooze down her now twitching body in rivulets of gore.

"What a fucking cunt!" a new voice yelled. A familiar voice.

Eddie couldn't comprehend what was happening as Jen's body slumped down in the doorway. He looked over for the source of the voice and the pristine plastic around the diamond variant action figure had melted and was bubbling on the top of the flat white box. As he stared in disbelief, Fantastic Man, or at least the *one*-seventh scale figure of him, stepped out of the mess and stared up at him with that same confident grin.

Eddie looked at the small plastic figure smiling at him and then at the smoldering ruin where the head of the woman he loved had just been. The front of his khaki shorts darkened, and Eddie fell to the beige carpeted floor in a heap.

Fantastic Man watched him for a moment and shrugged, "You're welcome, True Believer."

EDDIE OPENED HIS EYES and stared up at the ceiling of the closet in confusion for a moment.

"Welcome back. I was beginning to wonder if you were ever going to wake up."

Eddie sat up and looked around at the mess that had taken over the normally pristine closet. Comics lay all over the place, along with discarded bags and boards. Then his eyes widened, "Oh my god, Jen! is she okay?"

"That depends on your definition of okay. She seemed like a total bitch from what I saw, so you could say at least now she is at peace," Fantastic Man said as he leapt off a shelf and landed on Eddie's chest.

Eddie stared at the action figure in horror. "You killed Jen!"

Fantastic Man nodded. "Yes, a tragic accident. But frankly, that is not the most pressing issue we have to face." Eddie tried to speak but only a pathetic mewling made its way out of his throat. Fantastic Man awkwardly patted him on the cheek with his small plastic hand. "It would seem my arch nemesis, Wes Whistler, has trapped me in this plastic body in some sort of alternate universe. Our first priority needs to be finding a way to get me back to my version of Earth."

Eddie shook his head. "There is no alternate universe. Wes Whistler doesn't exist. He is a fictional character in the comic books. This is a nightmare. I hit my head and none of this is happening."

Fantastic Man sighed, "This isn't my first rodeo in the infinite iterations of the universe, True Believer. I understand it is confusing for you, a regular person suddenly and inexplicably caught up in something beyond your reckoning, but you need to listen to me. The fate of multiple worlds depends on getting me back to my Earth."

Eddie pushed himself up to his feet. "No. That's impossible. You aren't real. You are a comic book character created in the nineteen forties. I don't know how, or even if, you've come to life, but there is no getting you back to your planet. This isn't happening. I fell and hit my head and am in a coma. Jen will find me. None of this is real."

Fantastic Man flew up and hovered in front of Eddie and hit him with a jarring slap. "I don't have fucking time for this. What do you want from me? An apology? Fine. I woke up trapped in plastic and that woman was screaming at you and I accidentally melted her skull with my Sapphire Vision. I'm sorry. But there is no unfucking that now. All we can do is move on rationally."

Eddie stared at the seven-inch flying man and held his cheek for a second before turning and opening the closet door and running into the bedroom. He made it nearly five steps before his foot caught Jen's leg and he tripped and landed on top of her corpse, that had been covered with a thin bed sheet. He panicked and began flailing and the sheet slid down, and he found himself staring into the ragged and burnt stump of her neck. The screams that had been welling in the back of his throat tore free and filled the silent room.

Fantastic Man flew into the room and watched as lights came on at the neighbor's houses. "You need to calm down and stop scream-ing," he said to Eddie calmly. Eddie continued screaming though and Fantastic Man flew in and slapped Eddie once more, knocking him off

Jen's body. Fantastic Man swooped down and covered her body again and hovered in front of Eddie, who was rubbing his jaw with a crazed look in his eyes. "I see you are having a tough time processing all of this, which is understandable. But I am going to need you to breathe and find a way to keep yourself calm. The last thing you want is for the police to show up. The faster we figure out how to reverse whatever Whistler did to me, the sooner this unfortunate incident gets behind us both."

Eddie stared at him in disbelief. "I can't believe what a fucking asshole you are. You killed my fiancé and then demand I help you? Go fuck yourself. How about that, you murderous, plastic fuck?"

"You might want to rethink your tone, Eddie. If you were too much of a bitch to speak that way to the dead whore on the floor, do you think it is wise to talk to a fucking superhero that way?" Fantastic Man taunted as he darted through the room.

Eddie sat down on the bed and tried not to stare at the headless body of Jen. "This is a nightmare. None of it is real. It can't be. I'll wake up and get rid of all the shit in the closet," he muttered softly. "Fucking Flouronite. It's all a bad dream. Impossible."

"What was that, Eddie?" Eddie didn't answer, he just sat staring off into space mumbling to himself. Fantastic Man flew over and grabbed Eddie by the collar and pulled him forward. "I said, what did you just say about Flouronite, Eddie?"

Eddie blinked at him. "You were there when the package was left. Ornate wooden box. No return address. Purple Flouronite."

Fantastic Man let out a whistle, "Purple Flouronite? Do you know how unpredictable that can be? Of course you do, Eddie. I saw your collection. You're obsessed with me and my adventures." In a blur, the small figure raced from the room and back again and dumped the wooden box on the bed. "We figure out who sent this, and we can unravel this entire shit show. It has to be Whistler. Or that imp from the fifth dimension. This reeks of his foul magic."

Eddie shrugged. "There is no magic here, just nightmares."

Fantastic Man let out a hoarse laugh, "For such a fan boy, you make a terrible fucking sidekick, Eddie. The quicker we get this shit figured out, the quicker you go back to your pathetic life reading comic books in the closet."

Eddie looked at him warily, "And Jen? What about her?"

"Omelets and broken eggs. But if it is the imp, he can bring her back. Or possibly find a better version of her that is actually supportive of you and your hobbies. Hell, he can bring you to my world and you can live out the fantasy of your funny books," Fantastic Man answered with a smile.

"None of it is real. There is no Whistler or magic imps. You're not real, just a fucking toy, and I am delusional. Fuck off back to whatever corner of hell you have come from. I'll wake up and all of this will be a bad dream," Eddie said flatly.

"We have a term for people like you where I come from, Eddie. You know what it is?" Fantastic Man said as he leapt into the air and hovered in front of the bed. "You are a loser. A pathetic little sack of shit that does nothing to make the world around him a better place. Your precious Jen was right about that much, despite what a repugnant cunt she seemed to be. I should have flash fried your skull into jelly when I did her, saved this desolate world from having you stain it with your spineless nothingness."

Eddie watched the action figure floating in front of him with trepidation that began to turn into a simmering rage. As the pinprick plastic eyes began to glow with sapphire light, Eddie grabbed Fantastic Man from the air and turned him around in time for the blue beam to slice through the wall and window facing the street. In a panic, Eddie grabbed the wooden box and slammed the frantically struggling figure inside, and clicked the brass latch shut. The box began bucking and jerking as he clutched it tight to his chest. "Lead-lined, you psychopathic fucking toy, not only able to shield the effects of the Flouronite, but your Sapphire Vision as well!" Eddie taunted with a hard shake of the box.

Sirens rang out in the distance and Eddie looked out at the ruined wall and saw the flashing red and blue lights growing rapidly closer. The wooden box nearly jerked itself out of his hands as he stared outside at the emergency response vehicles racing down the street. Two police cars hopped over the curb and slid to a stop on the front lawn below and Eddie looked around at the demolished wall and Jen's body beneath the sheet on the floor and felt his stomach drop. He kept a tight grip on the box and made his way down the stairs as the pounding began on the front door, which burst open as he reached the ground level.

"Hands up!" the first officer shouted as she stormed in with her weapon trained on Eddie.

Eddie lifted his hands while keeping the box held firmly. "I live here!"

Two more police officers entered through the splintered door with weapons raised, and the three stood staring at Eddie with the box suspended over his head. The initial responder stared at him in confusion. "Set the box down, sir, slowly. I'm going to need to see some identification."

Eddie stared at her. "I don't think I should set this down, ma'am. It is too dangerous. You wouldn't understand, but he has already killed once. If he escapes, I am worried he will kill again."

"Sir, I will ask one more time for you to comply with my direct order. Set the box down, slowly," she replied warily as her finger tightened noticeably on the trigger of her gun.

Eddie nodded nervously and with exaggerated slowness, set the box on the floor next to the bottom step. His eyes darted back and forth from the three police officers and the now motionless wooden box. Before he could raise his hands again, the two male officers rushed forward and grabbed Eddie roughly and slammed him against the stairs as one of them yanked his wallet from his khakis and the other pinned him down.

"Edward Elliot, according to his license, he is the resident," the officer, not driving a knee into his back, said and Eddie gasped as the pressure on his spine released and he was pulled back to his feet.

"Mister Elliot, you said there was a killer on the premises," the female officer stated. "Is he still here?"

Eddie nodded and glanced down at the box, and tears began to spill down his cheeks. "He killed Jen, my fiancé."

"Where is he?" she asked quietly.

Eddie pointed at the wooden box. All three officers exchanged bewildered looks as they looked at the box. "Don't open it. The lead is the only thing keeping his beams in check," Eddie pleaded through his sobs.

The female officer sighed and went over and picked up the wooden box and shook it gently before turning to Eddie. "You believe there is a killer in this small box?"

Eddie nodded. "Please don't open it."

"Because the tiny person that lives within will escape and kill again?" she asked with a smirk.

"I know how it sounds, but you have to believe me. If he gets out, I don't know what he is capable of. You have to listen to me," Eddie begged.

She nodded once and reached her hand toward the brass latch, and Eddie leapt toward her. The other two officers quickly restrained him, and Eddie struggled against them as she clicked it open. The officers leaned forward to see what kind of monster lay within and all three chuckled as she pulled out the action figure and held it up to Eddie. "This is the killer. A Fantastic Man doll?" she asked him incredulously.

Eddie nodded, defeated. The male officers laughed even louder, and Eddie felt his face flush a deep crimson for a moment. Then the color drained as Fantastic Man winked at him. In a blur, the action figure flew out of the now shocked officer's hand and directly through the skull of the cop on Eddie's left side. With another blast of air, the cop on his right made a strange mewling noise as a hole erupted in the center of his skull. Fantastic Man then hovered in front of the female officer with gore dripping from his fully articulated plastic form and a blast of sapphire liquefied her left eyeball before blasting out of the back of her head and into one of the cars on the front lawn, which promptly exploded.

Eddie watched in horror as the tiny figure flew out the door and screaming began as the emergency responders found themselves being taken out by something they couldn't seem to track and bursts of blue energy. He felt the warmth spread in his already sodden crotch as the carnage mounted outside and he knew, eventually, Fantastic Man would return for him. A slow, mad laugh tore itself from his throat as the screams grew louder and he began to rock back and forth in the growing pool of blood from the three dead officers. "Never meet your heroes!" he cackled as the last of his sanity splintered.

TEN

DEATH OF CREATIVITY

LAURIE DESCHAMPS SAT AT her polished oak desk and idly traced the fingers of her left hand across the keys of her trusty typewriter. The shelves behind her were lined with her world-wide best-selling series of mystery novels and the walls of her office were covered by plaques and pronouncements covering her storied career. Her right hand, papery flesh with bright blue veins lurking like eels, held her phone to her ear.

Laurie shook her head, the large golden bangle of an earring slapped against the glass screen, and her lips pursed, "I don't care about the money, Sid, I have enough now that my ungrateful family is fighting over as if I were already dead. I am retired. Death no longer follows my travels, and that is a relief."

"There won't be a murder, Laurie. They want to pay you two million dollars to visit their new resort. You don't have to do anything but fly to the Mediterranean, pretend to look for some clues, and solve a mystery that never existed," Sid said slowly for the fifteenth time.

Laurie frowned, a mass of wrinkles no amount of foundation could hope to conceal erupted like a spider web across her face, "But you said there would be a death."

"A terminally sick man, one who has stated his dream is to be a part of one of your adventures, has agreed to be the victim."

"I won't kill him, I told you. I am retired."

"You don't have to kill anyone, Laurie. You didn't kill anyone for any of your other books. I don't understand why you continue to bring this up. You are the author who solved the murders."

Laurie turned and looked at the hardcovers. All thirty-two plus international editions seemed to stare back. She shook her head once more and chose to ignore way she had been spoken down to as if she was no longer in control of her own faculties, "I am not interested in what amounts to little more than a sham, it is beneath me. The answer is no."

Sid sighed, *"But Laurie—"*

"Goddamnit Sid, the fucking answer is no!" Laurie yelled and jabbed her gnarled finger against the screen to hang up.

She ran her hand along the spines of her books and smiled. Sid would never truly understand what it took to be an author. She didn't have that spark in her; the creativity needed. And neither did Laurie any longer. But still she reached her hand down and opened the center drawer of her desk and pulled out an old beat-up fountain pen with a deceptively sharp silver nib that seemed less to shine than to absorb the light around it.

The ornate clock at the opposite end of the office began to clang and chime, and the little yellow tit came out on its stand and cuckooed loudly, which startled Laurie enough that she almost dropped the pen she held reverentially in her hand, then snorted at how easily frightened she had become all of a sudden. Her stomach growled loudly, and she decided a pot of tea and an entire sleeve of cookies was not a bad way to spend her afternoon. She slipped the pen into the pocket of her shirt and grimaced as her knees popped when she stood up. A long sigh snuck out as she made her way to the kitchen.

She had just set the kettle in the sink when her phone rang. It was Wanda, another writer friend who had chosen the slow dying of retirement. Laurie let out a yelp as she answered, "Wanda! I forgot it was Tuesday! I just had the most dreadful call with Sid, and everything slipped from my mind."

"A sign of senility, I am sure. Get your wrinkled old ass to the restaurant. I'll tell the waiter you are being fashionably late as a cover. You remember where the restaurant is? Should I send a driver to pick you up?"

Laurie snorted, "Listen here you old bitch, I'm as sharp as a whoopie cushion and twice as hilarious. I'll be there in fifteen minutes. Get some of those—"

"Scotch eggs. Yes grandma. I'm going to settle for Scotch."

Laurie left the kettle in the sink and grabbed her keys with a smile on her face. She felt cooped up all the time. This was good for her. Better than some cockamamie—

"—NEW RESORT IN SOME country that didn't exist in my heyday wants to," Laurie lowered her voice and leaned closer to Wanda, "kill some terminally ill man and have me 'solve' the murder."

Wanda let out a cackle, "Anything to make a buck!"

People looked over at the two older ladies, laughing loudly and talking animatedly to one another. They lived in a small, affluent little town far enough away from the cities that they had become urban legends throughout town. Laurie was called the world's greatest detective and mystery writer, and Wanda was considered the original queen of smut. The friendship was not as strange to the ladies as to the populace, but carefully manipulated images often clashed with the true character of a person. Never had that been proven so true as in the modern age of always connected yet seemingly always apart. There were no secrets that remained buried, not like in the old days.

The problem with lunches with Wanda was Wanda wasn't kidding about the Scotch. Laurie had mostly stopped drinking, eschewing the sad washed-up writer wasting alone in a perpetual haze of alcohol induced ephemera, and choosing the solitary existence her unfortunate cat allergy prevented from fully blooming into. But today felt different, everything seemed to taste better. Laurie devoured almost all the Scotch Eggs herself and considered ordering another to go. And the Alfredo was creamy perfection, a savory cloud on her tongue, not to forget the correctly cooked chicken breast with fresh herbs that tickled her tongue.

"Are you stoned?" Wanda asked. "I don't care. I do. I'm offended you didn't offer, if so."

Laurie shook her head. "Not in about five years. The last time was on Bukowski's birthday with Edgar. Edgar died a few weeks after, and I never had the urge again. Although I think that time has passed. Tomorrow I am calling Doc Butler and getting one of those cards."

Wanda laughed and set a small plastic device on the table. Laurie looked at it in confusion and Wanda grabbed it and put it to her mouth and pressed a button. A moment later, she exhaled a slight cloud of vapor that smelled like blueberries. She put it on the table again. "How old and out of touch have you gotten? It's legal here. I bought this on the way from a gas station. It's called Sour Pimp Cheetah Cock. I liked the name."

"What is it? I don't think a cheetah cock sounds all that much like something I want in my mouth," Laurie asked with a frown. "Though there was that weekend in Vegas with that blue-eyed fellow. He qualified as both, I would imagine."

Wanda's eyes widened and she let out a fresh round of cackles as Laurie made a surprised face for a moment and then let out a raspy cough and grabbed for her water.

"Kicks like a mule, too. Keep that one, I've got two in my purse and a few all over my house," Wanda said as Laurie looked at the contraption. "I remember getting grass in a grocery bag, back outside of San Francisco in the sixties. Now I can get it at the gas station. We somehow moved forward in places that surprise me, yet remain woefully neglectful in others that stare us right in the face."

"The little things that seemed so important no longer exist. We have become dinosaurs, Wanda. The very thing we swore to never be," Laurie said as the haze suffused her brain.

"That's where you're wrong, Laurie. I told everyone that would listen that one day I would be rich, famous, and getting high with my friends. So far, I'm exactly where I wanted to be. You're just upset they want to murder a man to drum up vacation business. You bet your wrinkled snatch, if they asked me to show up to some sex lodge as the guest of honor to lead an orgy, I'm saying yes and making sure my will is up to date ahead of time," Wanda replied as she signaled for a fresh Scotch.

"That is possibly the most horrific thing anyone has ever mentioned to me in my entire life. Make it two," Laurie said in disgust.

Wanda looked at her with a lecherous grin, "Honey, they can dunk me in a barrel of lube and feed those stallions whatever pills necessary to take this old bitch off on one last fantastic voyage."

The waiter stood in a state of horrified shock with two glasses of scotch.

Laurie and Wanda both laughed uproariously.

By the time she realized it, Laurie found herself high as a kite and a little more than tipsy in the backseat of Wanda's car. Wanda did not drive; she had never learned and saw no point in it. She was fabulously wealthy and managed to cycle through young, handsome chauffers at a near scandalous rate. All by design, of course, same as using younger photos on the books, the illusion was important to keep the readers entertained. Wanda was no better than Laurie. She sat surrounded by her books, stoned and lost in yesterday. But she was always a good time, and the ladies tipped well enough that their antics were ignored. Most of the time.

With the promise of the same time next week, Laurie wafted out of the car. She grabbed her keys and found the little doodad, a vape, Wanda had said, and took a puff. "I doubt the veracity of cheetah cock tasting anything like blueberries," she muttered as she exhaled the fine mist and unlocked her door.

After she hung her keys on the hook, and placed her jacket in the closet, Laurie stood with a half-smile and a plan to eat the order of scotch eggs sitting on the counter when she heard a slight rumble from the kitchen. She paused, a heightened sense of paranoia swept over her, and then she relaxed. Then the shrill call of the kettle come to boil screamed out, and she threw the Styrofoam container to the floor in a start.

She scrambled to pick up the food, moving slowly with the combination of age and drugs as she tried to remember if she had turned off the kettle. She was positive she had left it in the sink.

These moments frightened her. Senior moments. Time lapses. She hadn't had them herself, but she had heard friends talk of them. It was never a good sign after that.

Laurie set the food back down and made her way to the kitchen as the kettle whistle sang and when she turned the corner and was about to flip on the light, she saw the second strangest thing of the evening. It was dark in the room except for the ring of fire on the stove beneath the kettle. And that flame burned with the most beautiful lavender glow. Laurie stood for a few seconds watching the pretty lights flicker before flipping the switch.

That's when she saw the first strangest thing of the evening. Standing in the kitchen was a large gaunt form in black robes that coalesced like smoke all around the skeletal personage that stood staring at her with empty sockets and yellowed teeth. Laurie nodded her head, shocked yet not surprised. She had expected this day for nearly the entirety of her life. Since the age of sixteen, she knew one day she would have to face Death, himself.

"You here about the pen? Or do we have other business?" Laurie asked. "Be a dear and grab the package of cookies from the cupboard. I have scotch eggs in there, but they took a spill."

Death stood silently as Laurie grabbed two cups and saucers and placed them on the tea tray. He cocked his head slightly as she exhaled a rather hefty cloud from the device she had clutched in her hand. Death turned and opened the cupboard and grabbed the package of cookies. And then, even though it is impossible to tell with a blank skull, he seemed to grow happy and grabbed another package and held it out to Laurie.

Laurie shrugged, "Sure. Animal crackers are always a good idea. The good tea is in the glass canister. I'll set the table."

AND SO, LAURIE SAT having a late tea with the grim spectre of death, Thanatos. Neither of them acknowledged the faint tremble in her hand as she poured the water into the delicate bone china cups. Death sat, bare phalanges entwined, silently watching Laurie.

"You don't seem like a big talker. I should be scared, more scared than I am at any rate. But I've been expecting you forever. I often have wondered if you knew who I was, where I was. But I imagine you know who everyone everywhere is. No one escapes you. When you didn't come, I thought perhaps the pen hid me in some way. But now that I am older, I understand you a little better, I think. You're patient. You knew we'd meet again one day. What is time to death, really?" Laurie said.

Thanatos nodded. He picked up the silver ball filled with tea leaves and seemed to marvel at the intricate designs etched along the surface before putting it into his cup.

"A thoughtful gift from a dearly departed friend. We would often sit hunched over our typewriters for hours on end, only breaking for tea and chatting. When I got my first big contract, she gave me this set, and we promised to use them every Sunday," Laurie said sadly as she held her infuser to the light. She reverently let it slide into the cup. "My career went one way, and hers never managed to take off, though. It got so hectic being famous, I lost sight of who I was before. The dark side of fame, where the rich whine in opulence."

Laurie pulled the pen from her pocket, surprised at having forgotten she had it, and set it on the table. Death looked at it but made no move.

Laurie smiled at it. "We have a moment while the tea steeps, and if you'll indulge an old woman, I can tell you what happened after I stole your pen."

Death nodded and settled back in his seat with the box of animal crackers held to his chest. Laurie took another hit of cheetah cock and offered it to Death, who shook his head.

"I was sixteen and had snuck out of the house—"

I REMEMBER WALKING HOME and deciding to cut across the field. The far end was usually free of the bull and would save me fifteen minutes walking along the road where any one of my father's friends would see me and offer a ride, then tell him all about it at the barbershop on Saturday. The stars were bright; it struck me as odd, and as I crossed that field, they swelled brighter and brighter. I wondered if I had been slipped some kind of drug at the party as the entire nighttime sky swirled into the form of the most beautiful woman I had ever seen. I knew I should run away, get home and go into bed, but I had to see if she was real.

That was when I first caught a glimpse of you, and a squirt of pee trickled down my thighs as I beheld your great robe like smoke and your bare skull. I was sixteen. Immortal still. But not any longer. No, sir. And yet you stood with your skeletal arms wrapped tenderly around this personification of the night sky. It was much later I found the name of your love, Nyx. I never considered that two primordial beings wouldn't notice a gnat like me buzzing around, and I had seen that moment of being lost in one another. I crouched behind a monstrous beast of metal machinery I could only guess was yours. The aesthetic fit neatly, but I was still half terrified and half curious. Until something caught my eye, a twinge in the darkness that pulled my eye. There I saw the pen sitting carelessly on the bench seat of your vehicle.

I don't know what possessed me to grab it, but I felt compelled to have it. Without thought, I reached into the window and in a flash, it was in my pocket. Clutched tight in my hand. And for a second the world froze, and I swore you looked right at me. I was sure I was going to die, and I shut my eyes and willed myself to be as silent as a rabbit when the hawks circle. When I opened them again, I was still alive. Not one to question fate, I crept away and hoped to never see the faint skeleton or the beautiful woman again.

THE TEA WAS PROPERLY steeped, and Death tapped the table twice as Laurie offered the sugar cubes. A delicate plink-plink filled the silence, as ripples ran along the pale brown surface, the waves of time passing before her eyes condensed into that perfect cup of tea.

Laurie realized at this moment she was quite stoned. She wanted an egg, but that was impolite with a guest.

Death waved off cream and then tore into the small red and yellow train car box with happy cartoon animals leaning out. She wondered if his finger bones were slick, but he effortlessly tore the bag open.

She dropped three scandalous sugar cubes into her own cup. She was trying, and absolutely failing, not to stare as Death lifted the dainty cup to his open jaw. There was no sipping noise, no intake of air at all. He simply turned the cup until it clanked against his skull and tea sloshed into his empty body and, Laurie assumed, all over the chair and carpet beneath. She wondered what she thought would happen.

The tea would disappear? He was clearly a skeleton, yes, an animated one in a majestic cloak, but a skeleton, nonetheless.

She didn't even bother hiding her stare as he poured the animal crackers out onto the table. Crumbs danced across the mahogany. She took another long drag off the thingy and marveled at how ripe the blueberries tasted. Death separated the animals. First broken and unbroken into piles, and then by animal. Laurie burnt her mouth sipping the tea but quelled the profanity on her tongue with a sharp intake of breath. She didn't want to miss this. He wanted nothing to do with the broken crackers and dropped them into the train car. His silence added a certain gravitas as he pondered which animal would be best. Laurie found herself holding her breath, then remembered it was the hit she had just taken.

Death selected a monkey and held it up before his vacant eye socket and then popped it into his mouth. He mauled it into a fine dust that rained down his bony body, bits sticking to droplets of tea that had not fallen all the way through. He looked at Laurie, somehow conveying, expecting her to continue without a single tic.

She sipped her tea, now a more manageable temperature, to wet her lips. "It wasn't long after that evening that I discovered the magic of the pen. I hadn't used it yet, but I carried it everywhere with me," she began.

MY HEAD WAS IN the clouds as I walked down the crowded hallway of high school. Robert Ursa, the handsome boy I had a crush on, even when he was just a chubby boy the other boys called Blobert, smiled at me and said hello. I felt like a princess roaming the halls until Rebecca Utley bumped into me. My books went flying and skittered across the floor. I hurried to grab my books when I saw my pen roll to a stop at Rebecca's saddle shoes. I watched her reach down and felt a sudden stab of anger at her daring to touch *my* pen. And then she jerked her hand back with a sharp cry. I saw the red bead of blood on her fingertip as I grabbed the pen. We both apologized and giggled, the incident forgotten except for a pinprick and a moment's chaos.

Or so I thought.

That evening, I sat with my journal by the open window, moon-eyed and dreaming of Robert as I rolled the pen between my fingers. Then I saw that speck of blood on the tarnished nib. I scratched the pen across the paper and the world dissolved around me as the crimson flowed across the page. I didn't understand what was happening as I watched the world through now unfamiliar eyes, where I was just a passenger as we crept through a dark hallway. Briefly we passed a mirror, and I looked over and let out a silent gasp as I saw Rebecca Utley creep past. I tried to speak, to ask what was happening, but Rebecca seemed unaware of my presence and my words were swallowed in the silence. We went down the stairs, careful to avoid the third from the bottom. It creaked. I don't know how I knew that, but I did. Then we were sliding the door shut, both flinching at the loud clock that sounded like a gunshot in the stillness of night.

She, we, crept down the street, keeping to the shadows until we were a few blocks away. Then, once the coast was clear, Rebecca undid her long jacket. I gasped in the silence. She was dressed in a tight black dress that was shockingly high above the knee. It was then I realized I wasn't stuck at a fixed spot at her shoulder as I had been hovering at, because in my surprise I fell back behind her by several feet. With only a thought, I was back at her side, and then I drifted in front of her. She had makeup on! I was no angel, as shown upon my late-night thievery, but this seemed on a wholly different level.

I wondered where she was going. Was this a dream? I let myself be pulled back to her shoulder as she walked, a thousand questions in my head. Which were instantly obliterated.

As was Rebecca.

We had both seen the car driving toward us in the distance. The two yellow beams had been steadily growing closer for the last few minutes. The rev of the engine didn't seem all that out of place until the two beams bounced as the car went up over the curb and then slammed into Rebecca with a wet thud. Her body tumbled brokenly through the air. I thought of a china doll being tossed, yet instead of the porcelain shattering, there was a loud wet splintering sound. She slammed into the windshield, which cracked like the ice on the river when the boys would hurl heavy stones off the bridge. And then I watched, dislodged in the initial impact, as what was once Rebecca, bounced off the roof and to the road.

The car bounced as it went back onto the street and drove off into the darkness.

And then I was back in my room, my heart pounding as I replayed her death. I was young and impetuous, but I was never stupid. I knew I had witnessed her death even if the how was beyond my mere mortal reckoning. The next day, I nearly collapsed in tears as Rebecca came walking down the hall. We had never been close friends of friends, and she seemed quite shocked when I threw my arms around her in relief. I pulled her into the girl's room and tried to warn her from sneaking out in that black dress. She feigned ignorance and stomped away.

She was found two days later, the victim of an apparent hit and run. The pictures in the paper showed her broken in the park, a pale blue dress stained with blood clung in torn patches. There was no outplaying death.

I grew obsessed. Over the next few months, I carefully pricked everyone I could. Not everyone showed me their death, though. I was puzzled by the random nature of it. I even worked up the courage to try it on myself, but to no avail.

The times it did work rattled my brain. I can still see them, long after the names have faded. I began studying death, you, reading every book and poem I could find. But you were considered an abstract, a cold reality, but still no more than a myth. I kept my macabre habit up through high school and into college.

That's when inspiration hit me.

I had always been good at English and writing, and now there were magazines that published new authors and actually paid them. I began writing out the death scenes and trying to add to them, flesh them out enough to be stories. It worked. Soon I spent all of my time writing and slowly failed out of school. My parents were horrified until I explained to them that the hot new writer in the magazines, J. Schommer, was their daughter. I had to use a pen name at the beginning to even be considered for printing.

It wasn't until I began writing mysteries that I could use my own name.

DEATH LOUDLY PULVERIZED A lion as Laurie sipped her tea. It was pleasant, in an unsettling way. Death casually wiped his hands on his robe and stood up. Laurie's eyes widened in fear as he bent down and grabbed the pen. In an instant, the pen was no longer there, and Death stood majestically holding his weathered scythe. He slashed the dully gleaming blade once through the air, and black squiggles seemed to follow the blade as it tore the fabric of reality itself. Laurie watched as her tablecloth was sliced perfectly in half and the far end fluttered to the floor to land in a lace infested pile. She marveled at how there wasn't the faintest scratch on the table itself even as she was disappointed about losing her favorite tablecloth.

Death set his scythe on the table, where it reverted back into a fountain pen and sat back down. He reached forward and grabbed another lion, and paused to stare at her. Again, somehow that plain skull managed to convey to her to continue. With a last look at her ruined tablecloth, Laurie sipped her tea.

"I was onto something with this, your pen," she paused and cleared her throat, "rather, your scythe as it is, could be used in conjunction with my talents to get me out of debt. And I had an idea where to start."

I HAD RUN OUT of casual acquaintances to poke and slowly I figured out what made it work. I could only see the death of someone who was murdered. My circle of friends was not the most exciting bunch, and the small town I was living in wasn't exactly the murder capital of America. Then it hit me in a flash. The magazines I had been sending stories into had become a springboard for becoming a writer in Hollywood. While that sounded absolutely atrocious to me, it was a different class of person and that class seemed to always be into something nefarious behind the scenes. Or at least we're tangentially in contact with those that were. I decided to go visit some of my friends and hobnob with the elite.

It was a different era then, one of glamour and hidden lives. All the stars were doing drugs and sleeping around. I was an anomaly for the times, an independent woman that wrote and drank, yet wasn't a lesbian. It didn't take long before I was buying a new dress and going to my first party with my writer friends. It took even less time to become disillusioned about the whole scene. The writers all sat together, chips on their shoulders, grumbling about pay. The pretty people, or the ones in power, stood in small circles. All of them were vapid fools. But one guy had caught my eye, an olive-skinned man in a nice suit with nervous eyes that seemed to always be looking in the corners of the room for danger.

My anonymous anomaly status helped to carry me from group to group until I finally made my way to the bar and the man of mystery. Everyone seemed to defer to his judgment, kowtow to his whims, and I decided to skip the game. I set my purse on the bar next to him, and accidentally let the pen roll over to rest against his glass. It took him a moment, but when he noticed it, he cocked an eyebrow at me. I demurely nodded and, like a gentleman, he handed the pen to me. Not before it nicked his finger, though. We made small talk as I sat clutching my handbag.

My intuition paid off.

I watched excitedly from my perch over his right shoulder as he sat at a table with a group of gentlemen that carried his same air of confident power. Cuban cigars burned in crystal ashtrays as beautiful half-dressed women carried silver trays overladen with drinks. I listened for a minute as they described the ladies and the many assorted things they would never do to them before detaching and checking out the club. Hollywood stars sat looking distinguished as they guzzled drink after drink in various darkened booths. I wafted past, catching snippets of conversations and gossip that set my cheeks to burning. This was the secret to finding big success. The glamorous people and their filthy lives was a license to print money. It had to be.

I felt myself snapped back to his shoulder; it took a second to stop the vertigo which the rubber banding caused and when the world stopped spinning, I saw the face of an angel standing in front of the booth. I recognized him from posters outside the theatre, but I had never seen any of his movies. The men around the table sat staring at him dispassionately, as if he were a fly circling the picnic basket. The man in whom I was death hopping, the term I gave these little excursions, was named Rocky, and he looked at the handsome young actor with the same expression a lion gives a gazelle, flat and emotionless, with a hint of danger that shined clearly through.

They argued back and forth about money, a bad loan and late payments, and the actor held up his arm to show off a fresh cast, which brought a round of laughter from the table. I had never experienced such a tense situation where no one showed an ounce of concern. The actor got angrier and began to shout. A mistake. Rocky looked at the men at the table and simply nodded his head once. The men rose as one unit and picked the now terrified and furious man up under his arms and carried him to the door. I tried to follow, but I couldn't leave the club itself. That was another rule I had discovered; I could only go so far from the victim.

The atmosphere relaxed back into a quiet debauchery when the men arrived back at the table, slightly disheveled and with specks of red on their knuckles. Throughout the evening, different starlets or overly polished gentlemen came by the table and spoke briefly, it felt to me like what I imagined a meeting with the pope would be like, solemn thank you's and ring-kissing yet not in the grandeur of the Vatican, but the back of a room layered with velvet.

The evening ended with the group walking and laughing under the washed-out sky to their vehicles. Everyone was relaxed, the booze and assorted pills and powders settling into a heavy fugue of smiles and talk of breakfast. They all seemed so nonchalant as they climbed into the black cars, and I was buzzing around, looking for the violence I knew was on its way.

I saw him first, standing in the mouth of an alley, torn shirt streaked with blood and his cast soaked from the puddles from the earlier storm. He smiled at the men as they finally caught sight of him and waved his good hand.

Then the world around me exploded, literally, or at least the car I was hovering in did. I watched a chunk of the dashboard obliterate Rocky's manly square chin in a flash of red mist that was immediately boiled in the air and turned to dust before being expulsed into the humid air by the crackling flames in a greasy haze.

I saw the actor smile once and then fade into the darkness right before I came to in my hotel room. I quickly grabbed the newspaper and checked the weather. The forecast predicted rain in the coming week. I picked my brain and tried to recall every face I had seen in that club and made a list of names. Over the next few days, I stayed in my hotel room and my fingers danced across the typewriter as I wrote a new story, a mystery in the seedy side of Tinsel Town. When I finally stepped out for cigarettes and fresh air, I saw the rain clouds had already settled gloomily over the city. After pulling some strings with my friends, I managed to weasel my way into the velvet club as the rain fell and the dirt on the building ran into streaks of mud that smeared across the asphalt.

The actor, James, came in and was beaten badly, as I had seen before. As the night ended, I made my way to the alley and stood in the shadows. The rattle as the car exploded shook the dumpsters and sent the alley cats racing in a fluffed tail panic. And when James turned to leave the scene of his crime, he saw me standing with a grin.

This was the beginning of my true career, and a friendship with James that would propel my books from niche mystery to global phenomenon. I had him by the balls and he knew it, and when I explained I only wanted to be part of his layer of society, he didn't seem to believe me. We both knew he had no choice. I changed the names up, but when my publisher got my manuscript detailing the murder of the year so far, he and the readers knew who all the players were except for James, my new secret weapon.

The true elite, the ones that rule from the shadows, the money men and their lackeys who secretly pull the strings, were now no longer secret, but a part of this new sphere I found myself in. If I had thought the actors and mafiosos were vile, I hadn't seen a thing yet. And neither had my readers. It wasn't long before I had years of as yet uncommitted murders filling my notebooks. I began to get traction in the true crime circles as well as the mystery group. But I needed an edge over my competition. Something that set my stories apart from the rest. I read all the greats, but Agatha Christie had developed the perfect formula. People were consumed by the rich and the lives they led, it just took a binding agent, a regular person thrust into this magical world to tether it enough anyone could imagine they were part of the cream that had risen. It didn't take long to realize that cream was curdled though. To be fair, I did have a different glimpse than that I portrayed in my first books. I needed a heroine to solve these murders.

And why shouldn't it be me?

DEATH PAUSED AND STARED at her with his empty sockets, a monkey held lightly in between two phalanges. Laurie knew this expression, even though all sense said she shouldn't since the skull staring at her was incapable of expressing anything.

"I understand the ego it required to put myself in the center of my tales. It isn't as if I named the character after myself."

Death just stared.

"Fine. Laurel is not that big of a change, and it was just assumed that she was me and I was her. It didn't change anything. There were murders and I solved them. The name I use for the character meant nothing."

Death set the monkey down and grabbed the pen, then scribbled on the half of the tablecloth that was pinned in place by the vase and tea service in block letters, *Murder She Wrote?*

Laurie's face blushed a bright red. "Angela Lansbury can go fuck herself!"

Death shook his head once and set the pen down and picked the monkey back up and pretended to examine it.

"Murder She Wrote was supposed to be a series based on my books! They didn't want to pay the licensing fees and created that vapid cunt Jessica Fletcher based on me. I hope she burns in hell, and they use nothing but broomsticks and doorknobs to torture her. That old whore set my career back decades with her homespun lectures and pedantic crime solving. It was Scooby Doo without the good writing."

Death munched the monkey and then slid his cup over the offending words. Laurie choked down her anger and accepted the mea culpa with a strained sigh.

After a moment of calming herself, Laurie continued, "I used my career as an excuse to travel abroad as I chased these visions of death I had collected. I filled volumes of notebooks with these endings, but I purchased a special custom journal shaped like a skull I used for the perfect murders."

THE FIRST, AND THE one that truly catapulted me from a minor writer into the stratosphere, took place in Cairo. I had not developed my reputation at this point, so I was practically incognito at the palatial hotel with a breathtaking view of the pyramids that managed to frame the great edifices and not the slums that lingered just around them. I explored the Valley of the Kings and made sure to leave enough of the reality of Egypt out to make it mysterious and magical, much like the hotel view. I could afford to, the previous six months had been spent studying the victim, Patrick, and his murderer, Leonard. I knew everything about them; the tensions boiling over; the novel was done except for the finale.

I spent the three days leading up to the murder in bed with a lusty Frenchman. It was heavenly; he spoke a little English, and I spoke no French. It was a sore walk to the docks to *stumble* upon the body, but worth it. It was disappointing how easily things fell into place from there. I had found the body and insinuated myself into the story, and after a few days of shadowy conversations in the view of Leonard, he broke within minutes of my grand explanation. I embellished it quite a bit in the book for dramatic effect.

The story spread and the book hit mere months later. No one expected such a rich story in so short of a time. They didn't know I cobbled together a better ending, switched some names, and had it to the editor two weeks after I returned to the States.

The next trip was to Maui, hell, I know. I was snorkeling with dolphins as Bernadette was stabbing her husband, Edgar, thirty times in the chest and head. It was during a whale watching excursion that I spotted his body floating on the waves. What was left of it, at least. It was mostly a torso and a gleaming bald head. Bernadette was a tougher nut to crack, bless her heart, even if she and her husband were atrocious people. I had to do some real gymnastics linguistically to make her even slightly endearing to the reader.

Girl power, or whatever.

By the time this one came out, I was taking calls from directors and starlets that felt they understood me and just needed my stamp of approval.

I could go on about the wondrous places I had seen, but they are already written out. What was just as exciting was when I had really gotten a reputation. Scotland Yard had an open binder on me. Every major intelligence did. It became a spectacle when I arrived at the airport as they wondered where my knack for being close to murder drummed up interest. It became irrelevant if I found the corpse or not. Inevitably, the police just came to me. High-profile cases meant more revenue for the police, not to mention being written up in glowing terms and made to seem as if they were not bumbling fools who missed the obvious evidence, but actually astute detectives.

Laurie looked at Death. "Do you think Angela Fucking Lansbury ever called to chat? No, because she was an inconsiderate old whore."

Death eyed the cookies in front of Laurie but decided discretion truly was a form of valor. Instead, he grabbed a camel and glared at it before biting off its head.

I could go on about the wondrous places I had seen, but they are already written out. What was just as exciting was when I had really gotten a reputation. Scotland Yard had an open binder on me. Every major intelligence did. It became a spectacle when I arrived at the airport as they wondered where my knack for being close to murder drummed up interest. It became irrelevant if I found the corpse or not. Inevitably, the police just came to me. High-profile cases meant more revenue for the police, not to mention being written up in glowing terms and made to seem as if they were not bumbling fools who missed the obvious evidence, but actually astute detectives.

I hadn't even written in years, not really. I had safety deposit boxes filled with manuscripts that were finished except for the endings. I still tried to give them each a personal touch, but that was less writing and more maintenance. It's funny how getting exactly what you always wanted still leaves you, I don't know, lacking; I suppose. I had seen sunrises that would inspire the greatest poets for lifetimes, and they had grown mundane.

I became a shut-in, the eccentric woman that courted death. I remember going to the store and a little girl, maybe nine, saw me and her face went pale, and she ran from me. Later, I passed her and her mother and heard them talking about me as if I was a serial killer. I was a curiosity and a curse, and that made for a lonely life.

I had become an actress when I went on vacation and a shadow when I was at home.

I left the pen in my desk drawer and shut the door to my office behind me. I became obsessed with notebooks. Even though it hadn't worked with Rebecca all those years past, I had still tried to divert your path again and again, to no avail. No matter what I attempted, I failed.

Mysterious car trouble, unexplainable issues and roadblocks that prevented me from acting, and maybe one or two details were slightly different, but the end result never changed. No matter how successful one became, dead was dead. So, I went on my macabre and mundane trips and slept, walked through crime after crime, stuck in a loop until the day I retrieved the last manuscript from the bank.

I was retired. Rich. I could do anything I wanted, and all I did was read the notebooks and remember. I was only alive when I relived death. I was powerless. So very tiny in a sea of infinitesimal dust motes.

"Now I sit here with Death himself, and I can't help but wonder, did I waste my entire life?" Laurie asked, surprised by the tears that welled up in her eyes.

Death sat motionless for what felt like an eternity. Then, he reached into his robe and pulled out an old tattered paperback copy of her first book, *In The Shadow of the Sphinx,* and set it on the table. He set the pen on top of it and pushed them both to Laurie.

Laurie sat dumbfounded.

Death stared at her, and she nodded, understanding he was wondering why she was waiting, almost instinctually.

"I can't believe you actually read one of my books. A few times by the condition of this, I can get you a new copy from upstairs," Laurie said too fast, overwhelmed by the answer Death had given.

Death shook his head, and after looking at the inscription, slid it back into his robe.

Laurie looked at him with a sad understanding. "This doesn't end with you granting me immortality or a second chance, does it?"

Death shook his head.

Laurie nodded. "It was nice to finally get to talk to you. But there is one important thing I haven't done." Laurie stood up and curtseyed as low as her old knees let her, and with tears in her eyes looked at Death, "Thank you for letting me have this life, even if I squandered most of it."

In one motion, Death stood, and the pen flickered into a scythe and a brief rustle of wind traveled through the room, disturbing the curtains. Laurie stood staring at Death in surprise and then a thin line of red blossomed around her throat. Her hands rushed to clench the wound, but too late as her head slid off her neck and hit the table with a thud. For a moment she stood there, headless, as Death watched. Then a great geyser of blood shot from the stump where her head once was and sprayed high into the air, leaving a work that would have made Pollock envious on the wall and ceiling.

Death turned and opened the front door, careful to turn the brass lock as he pulled up his hood and then shut the door behind him with a soft click. Death stood on the front porch of Laurie's home for a few minutes before turning around and kicking in the door, walking back in and grabbing the package of cookies off of the table.

As he walked down the street, the night sky swirled, and all the stars coalesced into the heavenly form of Nyx. She slid right into his side and his arm wrapped around her waist in a way that was positively predestined for perfection. He offered her a cookie, and she turned her nose up. He shrugged and popped the chocolate chip cookie into his mouth and crumbs tumbled down through his bones and trailed down the road behind him.

Nyx looked up at his skull and smiled. "One last unsolvable mystery for the famous mystery author?"

Death didn't look at her, but his embarrassment was palpable despite his inability to convey emotion.

Nyx laughed and nuzzled in closer. "Just another reason to love you."

Death said nothing, as was his way, but tingles ran through Nyx all the same as he squeezed her tighter.

AFTERWORD

YET AGAIN, THAT WAS a lot. I don't read my stories; I figure if I wrote them, I get it. I'm always thinking of the next story as I write the current one. It's my insanity.

When it came time for this collection, I sat and went through each story for the first time. Typically, I finish, type the end and send it to wherever it is going and forget about it until someone mentions it and I slightly panic as I try to recall which one they mean.

But I always remember the time I wrote it.

Here are the stories behind the stories. A peek behind the madness. And proof it truly takes a village to keep a fool going.

Golden Lazarus.

I was working with a friend, helping her go through submissions, giving whatever assistance I could. She asked if I had an idea for an anthology. I did. Virtues and Sins. We gathered a group of fourteen writers to give their take on an assigned sin or virtue. I got gluttony.

I struggled with finding an idea. I asked Natalie, my favorite poet, for help. She came back a few hours later with a bible verse about gluttonous feasting on snakes, spiders, and toads. I loved it. I just needed something to wrap around it.

Growing up, my father loved wrestling. Every Sunday, he put it on before football. I remembered watching the larger-than-life character try to kill one another. This one couldn't have happened without either of them.

Bitter Petals.

The sins and virtues anthology was doomed. It never came out. But two weeks before it was supposed to, we were short one story. Chastity. I had no ideas but volunteered to write the story.

I told Candace I had no ideas and needed ten thousand words as soon as possible. She suggested I do a period piece. I have always been obsessed with flowers, and when I started looking for ideas, settled on the South of France, where there were fields of lavender, my favorite color.

I wrote the entire story with the idea the father was the killer. And then, right at the end, I realized he was never the killer at all. Took me by surprise. The guidelines for the anthology were a minimum ten thousand words. I hastily added the epilogue to hit the word count. I thought it was a nice bow on top.

Shallow Be Thy Name.

RJ asked me to submit a story for his anthology, Old Scratch, which was themed around Satan. I hate titles. So, I told RJ to give me a title. He sent me Shallow Be Thy Name.

I based it in the actual oldest gentleman's club in Illinois, The Lamplighter, which does in fact sit on a hill overlooking Ottawa Illinois. If you've read my previous works, both Cuckoo and I Saw It From the Upstairs Window take place here as well.

I am an absurdist with a large nihilistic streak. Lucifer and I agree in this one.

Red Moon Over Red River Station.

This started off as a sub for a Texas themed anthology, but I got busy and when RJ asked for a summer themed story, I just transitioned it for that.

The idea came from a late-night talk with Natalie about random thing. I had already decided on Red River Station as the setting, having recently visited it on a long drive down the Chisholm Trail. I wanted the ghost town to be alive, but wasn't sure how. She offered up a blood-red moon. Originally, I thought the rays of the red light would show the trapped for what they were.

Instead, I did a take on coming of age. And got to kill Patrick yet again in a story. I've lost track of how many times I have killed him. And I am not done yet.

Insatiable.

Of everything I have written. I am least happy with my Splatter Western, Hunger on the Chisholm Trail. It is a solid story, with some things done decently, but it was clearly a new writer who had yet to find his voice. People asked for more Karl Beck. I tried. But it wasn't there.

I decided to write an epilogue of sorts, anyway. I was asked to submit to a wendigo themed anthology because I was fresh off Hunger, and had just beat what would become a wave of wendigo tales to market. I went different, more along the lines of the writer I was becoming. I stand by this one, because for better or worse, it is me not trying to be anything else.

It was rejected due to too many male pronouns. Most of the cast is male. I still don't know how to process that.

Within A Withering Eye.

Another Roles title. This time for Season of the Witch. All I knew going in was that Baba Yaga was the villain, and I wanted to try a rhyming demon. I get asked for a sequel often. I was very against the idea of sequels for a long time. But since revisiting Blobert and Death, my stance has softened. A little.

There is a demon to rescue. And what was up with Anna and Baba Yaga? Weird.

Death, and A Donut.

Candace asked me to do an anthology/labor of love of hers, Baker's Dozen. I asked for a title. She gave me Death and a Donut. I added the comma. It seemed right.

I was fresh off Cuckoo, and I wanted to play. I did not suspect I would enjoy Thanatos as much as I did. I approached this one with a rare confidence; I knew the story I was telling. I knew where it went. Could I pull madness and random chaos into an effective tale without giving anything to the reader? Mere mortals aren't privy to the inner workings of the hollow skull of Death.

I knew it was a love story. I love the final scene.

Waiting Room.

In Notches, there is a story called Choices, about a suicide who ends up in purgatory. I have been obsessed with that waiting room ever since.

Lost in Ephemera.

RJ will just randomly send me titles. He sent this one the same day KJK asked me to be part of his Sapphire Horror anthology.

I love comic books. And I have my own closet of shame. I wanted to play around with comic tropes. There are more stories in this universe. One day. Maybe.

Death of Creativity.

Before I went back to Blobert, RJ told me he wanted a story for an anthology themed around Death. I really wanted to write my version again. And I had an idea in the back of my head about how the great detectives seemed to always be around death and murder. As if they were the actual killer. So, I called Angela Lansbury a whore from a show I barely remember from my childhood.

This time, the challenge was to make Death an emphatic character when he was incapable of any range. And I knew he was a fan of Laurie and would want to give her a fitting send off. An unsolvable murder. I like the idea that Death is sentimental. Has love. He still operates on a level we cannot comprehend, but maybe we rubbed off on him a little.

About M Ennenbach

M Ennenbach

M Ennenbach is a poet and writer from Texas. *"dreamwhispers"*, an evocative collection of short fiction and his novel *"CUCKOO"* are available from Uncomfortably Dark Horror. A half dozen poetry collections are available on Amazon. Follow him at https://mennenbac h.com for daily poetry.

ALSO BY M ENNENBACH

Fiction

Cerebus Rising- A poet, a master of horror, and a master of suspense join forces as Cerberus. With three prompts—Cabin Fever, Letters, and Chaos—the three-headed beast dishes out nine novelettes. Cerberus Rises with their unique styles to take you on a journey through nine different levels of Hell. (includes stories by Patrick C. Harrison, III and Chris Miller).

Hunger on the Chisholm Trail-The first cattle drive of the season leaves Texas for Abilene, Kansas along the Chisholm Trail, but unforeseen terrors lay hidden in the natural beauty of the land. In the heart of Indian Territory lies the sleepy town of Duncan, a friendly respite from the dusty land. But something lurks in the untamed West-a powerful creature that hunts to satiate its horrifying hunger. The land will run red with blood, and only Karl Beck has a chance against this ancient evil. (Part of the Splatter Western Series from Death's Head Press).

Notches: A Collection-A Collection of dark, twisted and some humorous stories, including an epic dark poem from the tormented mind of M. Ennenbach. Each story will give you a window into the darkness of the soul. Fueled by raw, powerful emotions. They will chew you up and spit you out, leaving you quivering on the floor in a gruesome mess, begging for more. Are you brave enough to traverse the dark path laid before you, or will you become another notch on the wall?

Poetry Collections

(un)tethered-(un)tethered by rationality, adrift on waves of bipolar dissonance, a collection of pining odes to wildflowers and succulent agonies in the grip of divine madness as told by a fool drowning in words.

(UN)POETIC-Unscaled highs, perilous lows; this is a journey filled with both. A free form dance in the form of poetry; tended with loving care that drips sorrow. Darkness tinged with hope, forged in the fires of life. Of the sea, of the stars, of the night air as the sun breaks on the horizon. A desperate love in the guise of loving desperation. (un)poetic is anything but. No rules. Just pure expression poured on the page with shaking hands and envisioned through tear-filled eyes. This is different, this is new. Raw. This is poetry, here and now.

(un)fettered-to soar free of inhibition. a collection of poetry that skims the surface of fathomless emotion, leaving waves across the placid sea. m ennenbach plumbs these ripples in search of connection.

sometimes the only answer is to tear down everything and examine it in its basest form. (un)fettered.

(un) requited-unwanted. unfulfilled. unworthy. in the moment you offer every bit of yourself, mind, body, and soul, only to find you were not enough. broken-hearted and alone. (un)requited.

Available on Amazon

**editors note: the lack of capitalization and punctuation exists on this page because of the author's preference in his descriptions. They are listed here exactly as they appear on his books.*

www.ingramcontent.com/pod-product-compliance
Lightning Source LLC
Chambersburg PA
CBHW022120310726
48972CB00007B/2123